THE DARK PLACE

D1417267

Winner of the Martin Healy Short Story Award, the Brian Moore Award for Short Stories, the *Cork Literary Review* Writer's Competition and the Aisling Award for Art and Culture, Sam Millar is the author of four previous novels, *Dark Souls*, *The Redemption Factory*, *The Darkness of Bones* and *Bloodstorm*. His writing has been praised for its "fluency and courage of language" by Jennifer Johnson, and he has been hailed by best-selling American author Anne-Marie Duquette as "a powerful writer". He is also the author of a bestselling memoir, *On the Brinks*.

www.millarcrime.com

Also by Sam Millar

Fiction

The Darkness of Bones

Dark Souls

The Redemption Factory

Bloodstorm

Memoir

On the Brinks

SAM MILLAR

THE DARK PLACE

A KARL KANE NOVEL

BRANDON

A Brandon Original Paperback

First published in 2009 by Brandon
an imprint of Mount Eagle Publications
Dingle, Co. Kerry, Ireland, and
Unit 3, Olympia Trading Estate, Coburg Road, London N22 6TZ, England

www.brandonbooks.com

ISBN 9780863224034

2 4 6 8 10 9 7 5 3 1

Mount Eagle Publications/Sliabh an Fhiolair Teoranta receives support from
the Arts Council/An Chomhairle Ealaíon.

Cover design: Design Suite, Tralee
Typesetting by Red Barn Publishing, Skeagh, Skibbereen

I dedicate this book to my great friend from the University of LK,
Gerry (Blute) McDonnell and his wife, Christine,
for their kind thoughts and deeds over the dark years of my life.

May your gods watch over you everlastingly.

Prologue

"He was a ferocious man. He had been ill-made in the making. He had not been born right, and he had not been helped any by the moulding he had received at the hands of society. The hands of society are harsh, and this man was a striking sample of its handiwork."
Jack London, *White Fang*

"You smell so beautiful when you've washed," said the woman, watching him towelling the watered beads from his body.

He smiled shyly, loving the way she studied him, her eyes moving slowly over the map of his naked body, making it tingle.

Moving beside him, she began sprinkling talcum powder generously over his skin, kneading it into the pores.

"You like this, don't you?" she whispered.

"Yes . . ." he managed to say, his voice a croak of anticipation.

He didn't just like it; he loved it. Loved the empowering magic her probing fingers brought to his body; loved the smell and texture of talc on his skin, the way it made him feel brand new. Sometimes, when he had been very obedient and good, she used baby oil on his penis, making it glisten like a Greek warrior's weapon preparing for battle.

Finished with the talc, she made him turn his back to her, his face directed towards the slightly opened window with his ghostly reflection staring back at him.

Leaves were moving eerily on one of the many large oak trees stationed outside the house. A bird nestling between the branches was strangely silent, its voyeuristic eyes watching his every movement, seemingly fascinated. It was a raven, and it kept moving its beak in and out, as if secretly communicating.

Somewhere directly behind, he could hear the fabric of her dress rustling, his mind's eye seeing her slip seductively out of it, panties and bra following obediently.

Gently she pressed against him, the roughness of her thick pubic hair feeling like a Brillo pad on his smooth buttocks, and began gyrating her body inwards, her hands clasped on his hips as if he were some flesh and bone bicycle to be ridden. He could feel the coolness of her pale breasts sponging into his back.

A small breeze suddenly entered the room and touched his nakedness. Like a dark whisper, tickling the pubic hairs rooted there. He could feel his penis slowly rising as the smell of freshly cut grass filled the room, mixing with the loving smell of the talc and her perfume, the one she used for special occasions. He could smell her other smell, also; the salty iron smell of menstruation.

"You're beautiful. So exquisitely beautiful," she whispered, the words on his neck making his skin tingle.

He continued watching his ghostly reflection in the open window; watched her distorted face stationed near his right shoulder. Slowly, her hands began sliding from his hips, down to his penis.

They both let out a sigh simultaneously – a dark percussion so soft it was barely audible.

"Nice?" she asked, pulling gently but firmly on the swelling penis.

"I . . . I can't hold it in," he said, his voice lost somewhere in the large bedroom.

"You can and you *will*," she hissed, the tone of her voice suddenly changing while wedging fingers and thumb on the now fully erect penis, blocking its inevitable release. "Control is *everything* . . . it always brings its rewards . . . control is god. Repeat that."

"Control . . . control is god."

"Good. Now, listen very carefully," she instructed, her voice slightly hesitant. "I need to tell you something. Something very important. We can no longer . . . do these things . . . the things we love. It has become . . . too dangerous. Do you understand?"

Her words stole his breath.

"But . . . you . . . you promised. Promised that you would always love me . . . always."

"And I will. *Always*. But not like this. Not any more. Do you understand?" she asked, squeezing tighter on his penis. The pain was excruciating. It was beautiful, filling his eyes with dark red shadows.

"No . . . I don't understand. You . . . you promised . . ."

"You *will* understand, eventually. It's the way of things. For now, you will control all feelings concerning me. *Do. You. Understand?*" The last three words sounded threatening.

He could feel tears beginning to form in his eyes and immediately despised their weakness.

"Please," he pleaded.

"Please please please! Always the please," she admonished, shaking her head with disgust.

"I'm sorry."

"*Shhhhhhh. It's okay. It's okay,*" she whispered, kissing his neck, his back, guiding her lips down his spine. He could feel the lips mingling with the talc, her voice resting between his buttocks. "Just enjoy the moment . . . then we'll get ready before the Thompsons and other guests arrive. I'm going to make this special . . ."

She reached for the oil . . .

The afternoon was beautiful, hardly a blemish in the normally moody Belfast sky. Perfect shooting weather. The gathering hunting party – chiefly though not exclusively male – was flawlessly kitted-out like a miniature army preparing for battle. Some of the participants were commenting excursively and confusedly, the good wine slowly erasing all common sense in their heads. For such a potentially dangerous situation, it was almost comically vaudeville. Bird dogs – pebbled leather noses crayoned black – began barking, excited by the potential to have blood and flesh clamped between their eager mouths.

"Good hunting!" shouted the master of the hunt, and immediately the group cheered, spreading out, following the pattern of the zigzagging dogs that were awaiting their opportunity for first blood to come flying from hidden niches in the ground.

Wild heather was everywhere, mixing with the swamp of leaves and ferns. With little contrast, it was easy to get lost or disorientated.

Less than fifteen minutes later, the dogs began growling softly, almost secretively. The ground-breeding birds were near.

"Robert? Are you okay?" asked Frankie Gilmore, the gamekeeper's son. "You look a bit dazed."

"What? . . . Oh . . . yes. I'm always okay, Gilmore. Now mind your own business!"

But he wasn't okay. *She* was ignoring him, refusing to glance in his direction, her bawdy laugh contagiously making the men – and even some of the women in the hunting party – laugh along with her. She was good at that. Manipulating. Was she talking about him? Telling them how pathetic he was, crying like a child in the bedroom? Was that the big laugh?

Suddenly, his head began throbbing. Her laughter was drilling into his skull, her grinning mouth producing a donkey's guttural bray. *Haw haw. Haw haw. Haw fucking haw . . .*

He studied her face, one more time, before gently squeezing down on the shotgun's trigger. The single blast abruptly cracked the sky open, its sound absorbed by the vastness. He watched the ejected orange shell parachute to the ground in slow motion, a split second after spreading tiny pomegranate seeds of black metal outwards like a swarm of flies.

The sound from the shotgun was immediate and demanding. She stopped laughing. They all did. It was over in a split second; a split second that was the culmination of a decision made in cold, calculating blood.

She turned to look at him, her face puzzled. Her mouth opened, but nothing came. Her hand went to the back of her head, probing. She stared at her fingers covered in thick blood, before suddenly collapsing into a tiny stream of murky water and warm dog shit.

Everyone began rushing towards her. Everyone except him.

A disturbing exhilaration of fear and wonder in equal measures suddenly flowed over him while watching her body twitching elliptically in the filthy muck. Almost immediately, her eyes began dimming. Eye sockets shadowed. The verdict was in. The penalty in his hands had spoken. Retribution demanded and received. The swift, fierce satisfaction he felt was almost sexual in its intensity.

She was gone.

It was truly beautiful.

PART ONE

THE COMING OF EVIL

CHAPTER ONE

"Deep into that darkness peering, long I stood there
wondering, fearing . . ."
Edgar Allan Poe, *The Raven*

Inside the tomb-like structure, dead light stabbed on to the red concrete floor from high, barred windows, bouncing off chipped tiles around the toilet and sink. Shadows formed on the heavy doors' thick locks and peeling paint.

The young girl, naked and terrified, walked stealthily on blistering feet and toes wet with blood. Running her hands gingerly along the leprous wall, she began feeling her way in the darkness.

Immediately, the structure began crumbled at her touch.

Shit! Flaky metal paint speared her fingertips, wounding and stinging. Blood began flowing freely. Quickly, she smeared the walls with the blood, sponging her fingertips with dust and cobwebs. It hurt like hell, but she uttered not a sound.

Beyond each section of wall, an alcove disrupted the steady flow. Metal doors of some sort. If only she had better vision. The darkness was thick with stench and dread. It tasted alive.

S-s-so c-c-cold, she thought, through chattering teeth. Shivering uncontrollably now, the combination of fear and cold began attacking. She bit down hard on her teeth, hoping to prevent their terrible castanet noise exposing her presence to him.

Plodding slowly onwards, she felt horribly distended. Thighs too big. An unfamiliar weight of body preventing any sort of speed. She hardly recognised this alien structure of fat on her body. All the aberrant heaviness was crushing her ankles, making her breathing laboured.

They can't take much more of this pressure. Soon they'll collapse, taking me with them. This fat, this terrible disgusting fat, is suffocating me. She suddenly felt ugly, as if her organs were disfigured and disproportioned, lacking any symmetry.

Stopping only for a second, she listened for noise. Her heart was beating furiously inside her skull, blocking out all sounds. She wanted to suffocate it. She needed to listen. *Where is he? Is he watching me, right at this moment, his night-vision goggles tight against his ugly, smirking face?*

Above the beating of her heart, she could hear water dripping on to the semi-flooded concrete ground. *Where is it coming from? Is it the same incessant drip that has tormented me for weeks? Shouldn't I be walking away from it, not towards it?*

The guiding wall was becoming more difficult, like a maze confusing every step.

Without warning, she slipped, landing on jagged bricks. The searing pain forced a wince and a silent moan. Her skin was shredded, stinging like hell. Blood began spilling out, but somehow the leakage made her feel alive.

Taking a deep breath, she slowly exhaled, repeating the process three more times. Felt slightly dizzy but moved cautiously on, the soles of her feet thwacking off the watery ground, echoing in pulses off the wall.

Oh my God! In the distance, a light, a small rectangle of opaque glass. *A window of some sort? Oh God, please . . .*

She began following the light, its rectangle shape growing steadily larger.

Don't take your eye off it. The light began stinging her eyes. *Don't you dare blink! Don't you dare . . .*

There! In there!

Swiftly, she entered a room of some sort with permanent light squeezing in from the outside. A rusted bedspring and frame housed in the room's bare corner. *Creepy shit,* she thought, shivering uncontrollably. Old discarded newspapers carpeting the floor. Bits of magazines attached to the walls. Nude and semi-nude girls, posing provocatively. They seemed to be sneering at her.

Her stomach began tightening.

Above her, a large, wire-glassed window grilled with bars. Neck-breakingly high. Slightly open. She could hear the sound of distant traffic coming from it. Voices. Laughter. Welcoming night sounds of which she once was a part in the happy days of freedom. When? Weeks? Months? Time had become one elastic dark band, stretching beyond her understanding.

She wanted to scream for help, but terror and street-smart instinct stilled her voice. Help may not be what comes along . . .

Think! Stress and panic began building, burning her chest. *The bed frame!*

Stealthily, she began easing it over towards the window, trying desperately to prevent its soft screeching on the bare floor.

Standing on top, the bed brought her tantalisingly close to the iron bars. *Another few inches . . . you can do it . . .*

Struggling to stand on tiptoes, her fingers finally touched, stretching before intertwining with the bars. Desperately, she tried pulling herself up. Too weak. Too much weight.

Fuck that! You're strong. Not weak. Pull! Pull that fat arse up; don't allow it to win, weighing you down. Pullllllllllllllllllllll!

With sheer determination, she managed to pull her face up to the bars at a section of damaged wired glass. Peering out, she could see thickets of greenery. Overgrown weeds? Grass? Other than that, there was little sign of life.

"Martina?"

The man's voice startled her. He was on his stomach, gazing in at her through the window, only the filthy wired glass separating them. The night vision goggles on his grinning face made him look like a giant grasshopper hidden between the overgrowths.

"You're a very naughty girl, Martina. I told you not to try and escape from my kingdom."

"Please . . ." A croak. Her voice? Was that her voice? "Let me go. I'll . . . I'll do whatever you ask."

"You've *already* done what I asked, Martina. Remember? I'll be with you in a jiff. Don't lose that pose. Here I *co-ome*. Ready or *no-ot* . . ." sang the man, pushing himself up from the ground before disappearing.

Chapter Two

"Down these mean streets a man must go who is not himself mean . . . a common man and yet an unusual man. He talks as the man of his age talks, that is, with rude wit, a lively sense of the grotesque . . ."
Raymond Chandler, *The Simple Art of Murder*

Karl Kane sometimes goes on a hunch – a feeling in his piss – and today, sitting in his favourite chair in his office/apartment in Belfast's Hill Street, was no exception. Private Dickey running in the three o'clock race. The horse favoured firm ground. Last time it ran, it came fifth. An improvement from a previous race, staggering in eighth like a drunk on a Saturday night.

Not to be deterred by cold statistics, Karl pencilled the eight-to-one long shot in with the rest of his certainties, all with the ease of casualness that Saturday afternoons bring.

"I've a good feeling about you," said Karl, wiping his forehead for the umpteenth time in a desperate attempt to shift the lazy sweat camping on his face and semi-naked torso. Despite two cold showers in less than an hour, the insufferable heat was saturating his body with uncomfortable sticky dampness, wilting a nicotine patch on his upper arm.

Standing, he walked to an open window, trying to widen it further. The air travelling through felt gummy on his skin. A chugging ceiling fan directly above his head did little to moderate the stifling air. "Bastarding heat," he mumbled, scratching vigorously on the legend of his underwear: **Caution: Contains Nuts.**

Checking the newspaper again, his thoughts were suddenly interrupted by a voice screaming his name.

"Karl!" exclaimed a young woman, popping her head in through the doorway, applying lipstick to her mouth while talking – a feat that always amazed Karl, no matter how many times he witnessed it. Extremely attractive and lissom, Naomi Kirkpatrick was dark-skinned with large hazel eyes, and wild black hair cascading in every direction. Despite the northern cadence in her voice, there remained a slight trace of the south.

Twelve years Karl's junior, Naomi had met Karl three years earlier during a fist-fight between Karl and a writer at the John Hewitt pub in Belfast. On the verge of being arrested, the spirit-filled Karl was quickly spirited into the night by an amused Naomi. Two days later – offered a job as secretary to the debt-ridden Karl – Naomi reluctantly accepted, with the strict understanding that there was to be no hanky-panky. Recently over a messy, financially draining divorce, Karl fully agreed. The last thing he wanted at that particular moment in his battered life was another relationship with a woman. Within one week of the agreement, they had become lovers.

"Huh?" mumbled Karl.

"What are you doing staring out the window, newspaper in your hand? You haven't even dressed!" There was accusation in Naomi's tone.

"Can't we just have lunch here, save all the hassle, Naomi? We can head out later for a drink at Nick's Warehouse. Don't forget, we've still got unfinished bottles of Hennessy and Bacardi in the fridge, screaming to be emptied."

"No, we can't stay here," answered Naomi, quickly snatching the newspaper out of Karl's hands. "Five days a week in this place is enough punishment for anyone to endure. Now, get your clothes on. I'll be finished in a minute. And make sure that you bring your wallet with you this time. I'm not ending up paying the bill *again*. And remember: this is pure vegetarian. No meat, under any circumstances."

"No meat?" Karl made a face. "You've become very militant since becoming a vegetarian, all of six weeks ago."

"Stop being sarcastic. You know that I don't like the taste of meat any more."

"I could answer that with a witty riposte . . ."

"I was always a vegetarian; didn't realise it until I saw that horrible documentary about the abattoir in the city. It isn't right, eating living creatures."

"In case you haven't noticed, Naomi, they're usually *dead* by the time they reach the cold plate."

"Don't start, Karl."

"Answer me this: if God didn't want people to eat animals, then why the hell did He make them out of meat, and to taste so damn good roasted?"

Naomi's face was reddening by the second. "I'm really not in the mood for this. Just hurry and get ready before we miss our place in –"

The doorbell to the office, down below, sounded.

"I don't believe I just heard what I just heard," said Karl. "Can't people read nowadays? Big sign on the door saying closed all day Saturday and Sunday, and if that –" The bell rang again, irritatingly longer. "Finger must be stuck. I've a good mind to go down there, and –"

"You're going nowhere in your underwear, except to get dressed," stated Naomi. "If you go down, you'll end up falling for a sob story. Could be the postman with a delivery."

"Probably my latest manuscript rejected by the publishers," said Karl, a wry smile appearing on his face. "More than likely it's Jehovah's Witnesses, though. Tell them we're Scientologists and that Tom and Katie are dropping by for tea and plenty of crumpet, later on. Do bailiffs work on a Saturday? Bet the bastards do."

While Naomi journeyed downstairs, Karl began dressing, finally shoehorning into a pair of nice Samuel Windsor leather loafers, all the while scanning the discarded newspaper, trying to pick more potential winners. Just as he eyed one, an irritating ache echoed from his arse.

"For fuck sake . . . don't you start." Quickly opening a drawer, he removed a cap from a tube of haemorrhoid cream labelled Roid Rage.

Dropping his pants, he quickly applied the cream to the offending area, sighing with relief as the cream's coldness calmed the heat between his buttocks.

"Karl!" Naomi's voice sounded from downstairs.

"For fuck sake . . ." he hissed, almost dropping the tube.

"Karl! I need you down here."

"Give me a bloody minute!" shouted Karl, quickly pulling up his pants before dumping the tube back in the drawer.

"Karl? Can you come down, right *now?*"

Slipping into his jacket, mumbling, Karl quickly descended the stairs, tripping in his haste.

"Almost broke my bloody neck, Naomi. I told you I was. . ."

"Karl," said Naomi, rather sheepishly, "this is Geraldine Ferris. She's come all the way up from Dublin."

Geraldine Ferris, to Karl, looked about thirteen years of age. Pretty but unhealthily concentration-camp thin, with a face full of festering freckles and hair the colour of scrapyard rust. Large doe-like eyes complimented the rest of her face.

"Yes," said Karl, slightly puzzled. "What can we do for you . . . Geraldine?"

"I'm searching for my younger sister, Mister Kane. The ones in charge of the hostel, where she normally stays, claim she ran away, almost a month ago. She *didn't* run away. I get vibes from her. She'd have told me first. I know they're all lying. You've got to believe –"

"Easy. Easy. Come up for air, Geraldine," smiled Karl. "Try and calm down a wee bit."

"I'm sorry."

"To be honest, we don't usually operate on a Saturday, Geraldine, and normally we don't cover alleged runaways. You've spoken to the police?"

"Yes," replied Geraldine, nodding half-heartedly.

"What did they say?"

Geraldine's mouth suddenly tightened. The bones of her face looked like they would rip through the skin. "Lies."

"Whatever they told Geraldine, Karl, it obviously hasn't alleviated her anxiety," cut in Naomi. "Isn't that right, Geraldine?"

Geraldine nodded.

"Why don't we let Geraldine answer, Naomi?" said Karl, barely containing his irritation. "Geraldine?"

Geraldine swallowed hard before answering.

"They . . . they said she has a reputation for running away, and they can't waste valuable resources on runaways. Said she's probably down in Dublin."

"Has she? A reputation for running away?" asked Karl.

"Sometimes," conceded Geraldine, glancing at Naomi for some support. "But there's no one in Dublin any more for her to run away to, except me."

"You know what cops are like, Karl," interrupted Naomi. "They don't have time for teenagers or their problems. They want newspaper-grabbers."

"Thank you for that, Oprah. That was very enlightening," said Karl, before turning his attention back to Geraldine. "If you don't mind me asking, Geraldine, why aren't your parents here enquiring about your sister instead of you? You must be no older than what? Fourteen or fifteen?"

"I'll be seventeen next month – one year older than my sister – if you need to know," stated Geraldine, irritably. "My da's in Mountjoy Prison. He's doing a stretch of twenty years."

"Twenty years?" said Karl, feeling his arse tingle in a bad way. His haemorrhoids were beginning to act up, again. "And your mother?"

"My ma is dead, Mister Kane. She was a heroin addict – just like me."

"I'm sorry to hear –"

"My first memory of a needle was my mother injecting herself while I watched. Often, she would break the needle off and let me play with the syringe when she was finished. I remember everyone telling her that heroin would kill her. They were wrong. A man killed her. My father."

Naomi stood closer to Geraldine, gently touching her elbow.

"You've come to the right place for help, Geraldine. If anyone can help find your sister, Karl can. That's why he's Belfast's greatest private investigator. Isn't that right, Karl?"

Karl's eyebrows almost fell from his face. "Let's not be too hasty,

Naomi – or condescending." He gave her a what-the-hell-are-you-play-ing-at look.

"You sit down, over there, Geraldine," encouraged Naomi, indicat-ing a group of chairs. "Karl was about to order some food for us. Weren't you, Karl?"

"What? Oh . . . of course," responded Karl, slipping off his jacket while easing out of his Samuel Windsors.

"How did you hear about Karl, Geraldine?" asked Naomi.

"This," replied Geraldine, handing Naomi one of Karl's business cards. "There were loads of them stuck in all the phone boxes in Royal Avenue. When I first saw them, I thought they were those other type of cards. You know, the ones with the phone lines to naked women?"

Naomi glared at Karl. "Don't tell me you're sticking your business cards any old where?"

"A brass neck sometimes leads to a silver lining," replied Karl, look-ing slightly uncomfortable. "Besides, if I hadn't placed them there, Geral-dine wouldn't be standing here now, seeking my help. Well? Would she?"

"You always have an answer."

"Do you have any recent photos of your sister, Geraldine?" asked Karl, ignoring Naomi's sarcasm.

"I've one," replied Geraldine, searching her tiny handbag before pro-ducing a photo. "This was taken last year. It's a bit creased, but it was the best I could find of her."

A skeletal girl with a denim jacket too big stared out at Karl. Point-ed hipbones jutted out over the waistline of her jeans. Her face was seri-ous, as if all the fun in her life had been sucked out, her fingers seemingly playing nervously with the tines of a comb. But it was the left eye that Karl found himself focusing on.

"She was stabbed in the eye with a pen, when she was ten," said Geraldine, as if reading Karl's mind. "She lost the eye, and they replaced it with a glass . . . with an artificial one. She hates it and has a terrible complex about it, thinking everyone's staring at her. She doesn't believe she is beautiful. But she is. That's why people stare at her."

"I hate to have to ask this, Geraldine, but does your sister take drugs?" asked Karl.

"She . . ." Geraldine seemed to be pondering the question. "Yes, but she's been clean for almost six months – both of us have. Why? Does this mean you won't search for her?"

"At the minute, we're up to our necks in work, Geraldine. I don't honestly know if I could take more caseloads. It wouldn't be fair to either you or your sister. And even if –"

"None of our ongoing cases involve a missing person, Karl," cut in Naomi.

"Really? I didn't know that," replied Karl, sarcastically, giving Naomi a withering look.

"I've got some money saved up. You won't be working for free, Mister Kane. Tell me how much you charge and I'll get it – one way or another."

Before Karl could reply, Naomi began smiling, saying, "I'd be willing to work on it, Karl, for free. I do have a few weeks' *holidays* coming up, if I remember correctly."

"Holidays?" replied Karl, gritting his teeth. "Every day is a holiday for you here, Naomi. There's a law against blackmail. You know that?"

"Everything I *know* about the law, I've learned from you, you lovely man. Should I pack my holiday suitcase, or not?"

"Okay, blackmailer. You win. But don't start moaning about being paid."

"I've already told you, Mister Kane," said Geraldine. "Somehow, I'll get the fee you charge."

"We can discuss fees later, Geraldine. For now, I need you to relax a wee bit. Worrying solves nothing; only exaggerates the problem. Okay?"

Geraldine slowly nodded.

"Chinese or pizza, Geraldine?" asked Naomi.

"I'm really not that hungry . . ."

"Yes, I can see you're a picture of health," interjected Karl, searching the top drawer of his desk before finding a menu. "Here. Find something in this. Either you tell Naomi what you want or I'll have to guess it. You really don't want me to guess."

For the first time since entering the office, Geraldine smiled slightly, taking the menu before scanning its table of contents.

Naomi smiled all luvvy-duvvy at Karl. He quickly returned the smile with a wait-until-I-get-you-alone withering look, mouthing, *"And you have the cheek of accusing me of falling for a sob story?"*

Studying the photo more closely, Karl asked: "Your sister's name, Geraldine? I don't think you told us it."

"I'm sorry. It's Martina, Mister Kane. Martina . . ."

Chapter Three

*"I think the greatest rogues are they who talk
most of their honesty."*
Anthony Trollope, *The Three Clerks*

Karl parked his car – a Ford Cortina GT – inside the hostel's car park, before walking to the front door of the Victorian building on Victoria Street.

A CCTV camera began swivelling its metal neck as he pressed the buzzer cemented against the hostel's crumbling wall. Seconds slipped away, but no answer from inside the building. He buzzed again, longer this time.

"I heard you the first time, *sir.* You really only need to press the button once," said a bored voice from the intercom. "I'm security. How can I be of help?"

"I have an appointment with a Mrs Beverly Thompson, programme leader. Spoke to her on the phone about an hour ago."

"It's *Miss* Thompson," corrected the guard. "Your name, *sir?*"

"Kane. Karl Kane," replied Karl, detecting immediately the resentment in the *sir.*

"One moment, *sir . . .*"

Seconds turned to minutes. Karl was about to buzz again, when a loud click sounded, followed immediately by the front door sliding open.

Smell of over-cooked food immediately attacked Karl's nostrils as he entered the small foyer of the hostel. White noise was everywhere, reminding him of schools and hospitals.

"The car park is for staff only, *sir*," said the guard, housed securely inside an office shielded by wire-reinforced glass. "You really shouldn't be parking that car there, at the front of the building – especially on a Monday morning."

"Car? That's not just any car. Do you know where that came from?"

No response from the guard.

"Okay, I'll tell you, then. *The Sweeney.* Remember that classic TV show? That's the actual car they used *in* the show."

"I need to see some sort of identification, *sir*," requested the unimpressed guard.

"Certainly," replied Karl, pushing a business card through a slot no bigger than a Mars Bar. "They don't make shows like *The Sweeney* any more. Nothing but so-called talent shows to show people with no talent."

"I don't watch TV, *sir*."

This is more like a prison than a bloody hostel, thought Karl, weighing the security guard up. The man was all glut and cheap cologne, and resembled Peter Lorre with a mouthful of teeth caramelised by too much nicotine and coffee.

Seemingly unimpressed at Karl's business card, Peter Lorre asked for a photo ID.

Producing his driving licence, Karl slipped it through the Mars Bar, a wry smile appearing on his face. "If I were paranoid, I'd say you were trying to prevent me coming in."

"Simply doing my job, *sir*. Keeping the residents safe," said Peter Lorre, glancing at the licence and then at Karl's face. "Okay, *sir*. Take the lift over there. Get off at the fourth floor. Miss Thompson's office is directly to your right, the moment you step out of the lift. She's expecting you."

"Thanks," said Karl, quickly pocketing the driving licence while heading for the lift.

The door to Beverly Thompson's office was opening as Karl stepped from the lift. A large, rotund woman with a face that could stop a raging grizzly bear in its tracks indicated with a wave of her meaty hand for Karl to enter.

"A private investigator? My," smiled Beverly Thompson, indicating for Karl to sit in the chair opposite, "how exciting is *that?*"

"Not very," replied Karl, making himself comfortable. "It's not like you see in the movies, if that's what you mean. More bills than thrills."

"A bit like *Rockford,* then?"

"Well, *Rockford* was always in debt and trouble, so I guess you could say there is a similarity."

"I loved James Gardner. Ruggedly handsome. You're not unlike him, Mister Kane."

"Yes, I get that a lot," smiled Karl, quickly warming to Beverly's bullshitting. "Though I'm more of a *Columbo* fan, myself."

"I could never warm to him. Always annoyed me with that *one more thing* thing that he always did. Would you like tea or coffee?"

"Coffee, please, if it's no bother."

"Why would it be a bother?" asked Beverly, smiling, picking up the phone. "Alison? A pot of coffee, please, and some shortbread. Thank you, dear."

The heady smell of flowers was overripe in Beverly Thompson's office. Everything seemed covered in scent. Karl could feel a sneeze coming on.

"Now, Mister Kane," said Beverly, returning the phone to the cradle, "you were asking on the phone about one of our ex-residents, Miss Martina Ferris."

Karl nodded. "Her sister got in contact with me two days ago, saying that she's worried about her. She hasn't seen her in almost a month."

"To be honest with you, Karl – I may call you Karl?"

"By all means . . . Beverly."

"To be honest, Karl, we're not permitted to disclose information about any of our clients – even ex-clients. Comes under confidentiality."

"I'm fully aware of that, Beverly, and I very much appreciate you giving me your time. I need to know if she had any problems, while she was here. Hopefully to give her sister peace of mind."

"Strictly off the record?"

"Strictly."

"Well . . . Martina wasn't an easy girl to accommodate. At times she was violent towards staff and other residents. Despite this, we did our utmost to ensure safe and habitable surroundings for her. You know she ran away from here, quite a few times?"

"No," lied Karl. "Really?"

"Oh, yes; but of course her sister wouldn't have told you *that* piece of information," replied Beverly, rather stiffly. "Despite all that, we welcomed her back with open arms, each time she requested a return. Can't be too bad of a place if she cried to come back. Can it, now?"

"I hear what you're saying."

A young woman knocked on the door, interrupting the conversation.

"Ah, Alison," said Beverly, smiling. "Would you be a dear, and pour for us?"

Setting the tray down, Alison began pouring a stream of coffee into a large blue mug for Karl.

"Sugar and milk, sir?" asked Alison.

"Black, Alison. Thank you," said Karl, reaching for the mug before sipping it slightly with a nod of approval. "This is great coffee. Must get the name of it before I leave."

"Glad you like it," said Beverly. "I've been drinking it for years. Imported. Slightly expensive, but really worth it."

Karl took another sip, longer this time. "I was wondering if I could have a look in Martina's room, to see if there are any clues to her state of mind before she left."

"Oh, the room was vacated weeks ago. It's been repainted," replied Beverly. "Actually, we have a new resident in that room, now."

"What about Martina's possessions? What happened to them?"

"That will be all for now, Alison," said Beverly, once her delicate-looking cup had been filled.

Alison nodded, quickly leaving the room.

"Martina didn't have many possessions, Karl," continued Beverly. "One black bin liner, if I recall correctly. We held it for as long as we could, but when no one came to collect it, we had to dump it. Her so-called caring sister couldn't even be bothered to come by and collect it. We don't have a lot of room, Karl, and can't keep things in storage indefinitely. I'm sure you understand?"

Karl nodded, before taking another large sip of the fine coffee.

The next forty-five minutes were spent on small talk. Beverly, Karl soon realised, was as much of an expert on being evasive as he was on being intrusive.

"Well, I guess I'll have to hit the road," said a defeated Karl, standing, but not before finishing the coffee.

"I'm sorry it's been a wasted journey for you," smiled Beverly, standing also, extending her hand.

"I don't think any journey is ever wasted – provided you finish it," said Karl, returning the smile while shaking the outstretched hand. "Good day, Beverly. It was nice meeting you. And thanks for the lovely coffee."

Outside the office, Karl pressed for the lift. Listened to the gears growling in the housing. A few seconds later, the lift door opened, revealing Alison.

"Thank you for the lovely coffee, Alison. It was –"

Alison thrust something into his hand before rushing onwards towards Beverly's office, never looking back.

Karl could see Beverly Thompson staring at him from her office window, wearing a painted smile. Alison quickly entered and began collecting the tray and its contents.

Stepping into the lift, Karl waited until the door closed before glancing at the item in his hand. A note. Badly scrawled handwriting. He balled it quickly in his fist, seconds before the door opened, revealing Peter Lorre.

"Miss Thompson says you are to stay here, *sir*, in the lobby. She's coming right down. Needs to see you urgently."

Stepping out, Karl listened to the lift ascending.

Shit! Beverly must've spotted Alison's clumsy sleight of hand! Karl tightened his grip on the note. Wondered how to dispense of it, unseen by Peter Lorre.

The lift began descending. Peter Lorre refused to take his eyes off Karl.

Do the old cough trick. Hurry! Swallow it!

As he was about to bring his hand up to his mouth, Beverly Thompson suddenly stepped out of the lift and handed him a small package.

"Rio," she said, smiling.

"Pardon?"

"Rio coffee. I had a spare package of it in one of my cupboards. Enjoy."

Before he could thank her, she was gone, back into the lift, humming like a busy bee.

Outside, Karl allowed a breeze to cool his hot face. The package of coffee felt heavy in his right hand. The note in his left hand felt a lot heavier.

Chapter Four

". . . there was about him a suggestion of lurking ferocity, as though the Wild still lingered in him and the wolf in him merely slept."
Jack London, *White Fang*

"Cleanliness is next to godliness. Always remember that, Martina," he sang, setting her down on the slick black tiles, before adjusting the showerhead so that the water sprayed over her filthy and bloodied body.

Martina sat terrified with knees huddled against her chest until he gently pried her legs apart to soap that most private area.

Finishing ten minutes later, he turned the water off. There was nothing but quietness, interrupted only by her heavy breathing.

"Good. Almost new again," he said, smiling, scooping her effortlessly off the floor. "You really wouldn't recognise yourself. All that weight you've put on instead of that horrible skinny frame you existed in. And spotless! My! Remember when you first came here, infested with fleas and lice? And that horrible stench of unwashed flesh and raggedy clothes? Now look at you. Practically reborn!" he exclaimed, burying his head in her wet hair, sniffing like a curious dog. "You smell so beautiful when you've washed. Yes you do do do!"

Martina tried speaking. Her mouth began leaking sounds, but the words dropping from it were like dull coins, as if she couldn't remember how to form language.

Gently, he placed her on top of a steel table. It was freezing. It chilled her immediately. She began shivering. Leather straps tightened themselves around her, like tentacles.

"Soon have you nice and warm. But first, there are a few more hurdles we must get over."

From a large plastic container, he scooped up a handful of items and sprinkled them about her body.

Leeches.

She tried to scream, but nothing came.

"Don't be alarmed," said his voice hovering over her, his fingers dropping more leeches on to her body. "These are your friends, helping to eat all the bad flesh. Leeches get dreadful press. People associate them with death, not knowing they can be life savers, if guided correctly." He continued placing the leeches strategically across her body. "That was very silly of you, trying to escape, a few days ago. Don't you know there are only bad things out there, waiting?"

"Please . . ." Her teeth began rattling with the cold. "Jjjjust . . . just lllet mmmme go . . . I . . . I . . . wwwwon't say a word . . . I . . . I ppppromise . . ."

"Don't try to talk. You're safe now, my dear. Everything is going to be fine. You must let our little friends do their work."

Cupping her neck gently in his arm, he tilted her head slightly, easing a small amount of strange-looking liquid into her bruised mouth. The liquid punched its way to her stomach, staying down only for a few moments before erupting from her busted lips.

"Easy . . . easy . . ." he encouraged. "Don't try to rush."

He tried again, more successful this time.

"Good. Much better," he encouraged. "Now relax and let the medicine do its job."

Suddenly, her stomach was in turmoil. A sensation of growing pressure started in her gut, stabbing down into her bowels, seething like a geyser.

"I . . . I ccccan't hold . . . hhhhold it in . . ."

"You can and you will!" he hissed, the tone of his voice suddenly changing. "Control is *everything* . . . it always brings its rewards . . . control is god. Repeat that."

"Control . . . cccccontrol is . . . ggggg . . . god . . ."

"Good! Now, again."

Before she could repeat the words, her bowels let go, funnelling everything on to the steel table.

"Filthy creature!" he shouted, pushing away from the table, a look of revulsion on his face. "Now look what you've done! Can't you even control your own shit!"

A mixture of shame and relief bit into her as the stench of shit and piss grew.

"I . . . ccccouldn't help myself. Don't . . . don't bbbbbbe angry with mmmmme . . . Please . . ." Tears ran freely down her petrified face.

"Please! Please! Please! Always the *please*. Now I've got to wash you all over again," he said, shaking his head with disgust. "This time, I won't be so gentle."

Opening a small medicine cabinet, he produced a long silicone tube. Her eyes widened with terror.

"Please . . . nnnnot that . . . please . . . I . . . I'll take mmmmy medicine . . . ppplease . . ."

"*Shhhh.* You must remain quiet and still. It's only dangerous when you talk. Now, open wide."

She thought of resisting, but remembering the last time she was foolish enough to try, quickly relented.

"That's better," he praised. "Nice and wide. Good girl."

She felt the greased tube slide down her throat, worming into her stomach. She wanted to vomit, but the tube's placement made it impossible.

He began pouring the brown liquid into a funnel attached to the tube's other end.

Almost immediately, her stomach began swelling. She could feel the liquid rattling inside. She believed her stomach was about to explode.

Oh God . . . oh God . . . let him kill me . . . get it over with . . .

Ah, much better," he proclaimed, touching her stomach gently. "Much much better, indeed. You've almost reached the golden weight. Soon. Very soon, indeed. Then it'll all be over, I promise."

CHAPTER FIVE

"Let them be brought to the house of 'She-who-must-be-obeyed'.
Bring forth the men, and let that which they have with them
be brought forth also."
H. Rider Haggard, *She*

Karl revisited the note handed to him this morning by Alison. The young girl's handwriting was difficult to decipher, but with Naomi's help and patience, they eventually managed to decode it. Martina, apparently, had been living with a group of homeless people over at Custom House Square, not too far from the hostel. Alison had managed to speak with Martina on a couple of occasions, bringing her some smuggled-out food from the hostel's kitchen. Ominously, contact stopped when Martina no longer showed at the prearranged meeting place.

"I'll be back in about an hour," said Karl, pocketing the note.

"Where're you going?" asked Naomi.

"To the going place."

"Don't be flippant."

"Don't flipping ask, then," said Karl, gathering keys and wallet from atop the kitchen counter. "I'm cranky enough in this bastarding heat wave without you cranking me up further."

"You're not serious about going out in the heat?"

"How about if I wear a clown costume, look less serious?"

"Didn't you hear the weather report? The weatherman issued a warning, telling people not to go out unless absolutely necessary," retorted Naomi, folding her arms impatiently.

"The weatherman. What would he know about weather? Besides, it *is* absolutely necessary. Anyway, it's only over to Custom House and the surrounding area. Probably my dog of a mind chasing after a cat of an idea."

"Please be careful."

"Am I ever anything other?" he replied, smiling, before kissing her on the lips. "Did I tell you Peter Mullan is doing a book signing at Eason's, Donegal Place, this Wednesday?"

"Who's Peter Mullan?"

"Who's Peter Mullan, she asks. That proves you never listen to me. Peter Mullan has had about six bestsellers, to date. Three of them have been made into movies."

"That's great. But I don't remember you ever reading any of his books."

"Er . . . well, they're not exactly my sort of book, to be honest."

"Why the big interest if you haven't even read any of his stuff?"

"Because Peter and yours truly went to the same school when we were kids. I'm going to ask him to have a look at my manuscript, see if he'll do a blurb for it. That could go a long way to getting the manuscript accepted by potential publishers."

"That's great, Karl!" exclaimed Naomi, giving him a full kiss on the lips. "I have a feeling this will be your year for publication. Honestly, I do. You're going to prove all those silly rejection slips wrong."

"I love the way your eyes light up when you fib, but I love you anyway. See you in a couple of hours."

"Oh! In case I forget, there's a do on at Billy Holiday's for Ivana's birthday, Friday night. We'll have to get her something."

"I'm not really in the mood for any party."

"I promised her that we'd be there. She's expecting us. We can't let her down. How much money do you have? I'm going to buy her something nice."

"Won't a bottle of cheap wine from Tesco and a card from Oxfam suffice?"

Smiling, Naomi held out a hand, chanting, "Give, give, give, give, give."

"Okay, okay. No need to rip the arse out of it," said Karl, reluctantly producing his wallet before removing two twenties.

"I'll need a bit more than that. I saw a lovely necklace in Lunn's. It cost two hundred."

"Two . . . ? Are you out of your head, Naomi? It's Ivana's birthday, not Elizabeth bloody Taylor's."

"Stop your moaning. She's my best friend. She was the one who looked after me and gave me shelter when I first came to Belfast, way before you came on the scene. Just give me another two twenties and I'll put the rest to it."

"Bloody rent due at the end of the month," muttered Karl, surrendering the money, before quickly exiting the room.

Stepping into Hill Street and the afternoon heat, he immediately felt as if a plastic bag was hugging his face. Hot. Suffocating. Above, the sun was floating on a ghostly haze. He considered the air. It tasted like exhaust vapours. Everywhere he looked, people were sucking on the toxic traffic fumes like stranded fish.

People said this muggy, claustrophobic weather made Belfastians strange. Sometimes it made them do *strange* things. Karl's retort to that sweet idiom was that the people of Belfast didn't need excuses to do strange things.

Only supposed to be mad dogs and Englishmen who venture out in this type of madness, thought Karl, wiping his brow with a damp handkerchief as he strolled by the palatial Merchant Hotel in Waring Street. *You're neither, so what the hell are you doing, joining them, you big eejit, getting your loaf toasted by the baking sun?*

Despite it being a mere five-minute walk from where he lived, the oppressive heat was making him exhausted and even crankier than he had been in the apartment. To exacerbate matters further, his sinuses were killing him, making his eyes feel sandpapery each time he blinked out sweat. Thankfully, despite the heat, his haemorrhoids weren't arsing about.

Quickly cutting across Victoria Street and into Custom House Square, he spotted a parcel of homeless people shadowed outside an old derelict church, not too far from the impressive Italian Renaissance-style Custom House building. The homeless all looked skinny, lined up against the church walls like pencils in some cheap stationery shop before suddenly disappearing inside out of sight.

"What an existence," muttered Karl.

The abysmal conditions of the homeless in his hometown never failed to shock Karl. He had always believed that their growth had been cultivated by an obscene dichotomy where, a few streets away on the Waterfront, the affluent helped to fill the coffers of corrupt, greasy politicians and city councillors, backing their plans to make the homeless invisible with the help of thugs in and out of uniform.

To Karl, the old church seemed to be swelling in the heat, casting shadows further down the street. Long gone were its begging tongues and burning candles, but somehow it still infused his atheistically inclined imagination with agonising angels, their alabaster faces all majestically attuned to a vivid tapestry of concrete heaven.

"Hello? Anyone in?" he asked loudly, tentatively poking his head in through the large, ornate door of the church. "Hello? Anyone –"

"Get yer big fucking head out of our house!" screamed an intimidating voice, making Karl step backwards quickly.

A bear of a man appeared from the mouth of the door, his massive face covered by a forest of unruly beard, eyes flat as flint. What skin could be seen was jaundice yellow – matching his sporadic teeth. A bruise as big as an infant's fist lamp-posted his forehead. The man was wearing history clothes – someone else's history – with a wine bottle protruding from his pants like a pickpocket's arm.

"I . . . I was wondering if I could ask a few questions?" asked Karl. "It's about a young girl who's been missing –"

"Want to dirty my skin with bruises, punk?" asked the homeless man, motoring unsteadily towards Karl. "Ye better kill me – cuz I'm coming for ye! See? *See?* Whaddya hear, whaddya *sssayyyyy?*" Like lightning, the man produced something long and shiny from his coat pocket.

"Let's not do anything silly, or hasty, friend," urged Karl, tracking the man's eyes, simultaneously watching for any sudden movement from his hand.

The man growled a howl not unlike a wounded animal. He appeared to be preparing to leap with the weapon in his hand. Karl readied himself.

"Leave that man alone, John-Jack," said the voice of another homeless man, suddenly emerging from the doorway of the building. "What's this stranger done to offend you?" The man had dozens of tiny metal hoops implanted in his ears and some in his nose. His grey hair was a long, ropey ponytail.

"He's poking his big nose in, uninvited to our home, that's what he's done. Probably trying to steal our grub, Michael," stated John-Jack, tightening his grip on the item in his hand. "How would he like any of us poking our heads into his kitchen without permission?"

Karl flashed his palms up, saying, "You're one hundred per cent correct, John-Jack. My apologies for that. To be honest, I couldn't see any other way of alerting someone to my presence."

"Okay, John-Jack? See? The man apologised. Now, go back in and finish your dinner."

Slowly, John-Jack eased back towards the entrance, but not before sticking out his tongue at Karl. The tongue was carpeted in baked bean sauce and sores.

"He's harmless," explained Michael, as John-Jack disappeared out of view. "Just a bit paranoid. One of the risk factors of being homeless."

"I wouldn't call brandishing a knife harmless."

"Knife? Oh . . . you mean this?" replied Michael, producing the offending item: a piece of sagging rubber wrapped in tinfoil.

Karl felt quite foolish.

"It looked so real . . ."

"Fear can make many things look real. Don't feel bad. One of the benefits of being homeless is that people *expect* you to be half crazy. It's a myth that helps us create illusions, such as rubber strips transformed into deadly metal knifes. That way, people leave us alone." Michael laughed, a touch nervously, before offering his hand to Karl. "Michael Graham."

"Karl Kane," replied Karl, shaking Michael's hand while studying the man's features. Older-looking than his years, Michael's face sagged, as if the dogs of poverty and depression had stolen every bone from it. His nose was knotted, like a boxer's. To Karl, Michael's entire face was a map of hardship.

"What can I do for you, Karl? If you don't mind me saying, you don't look like you're ready to join our nomadic family." The eyes in the ruined face sparkled.

"I'm a private investigator," stated Karl, extracting a business card from his wallet before handing it to Michael. "I'm looking for a young girl, missing for almost two weeks." Karl produced the photo of Martina Ferris. "Ever see her about this place?"

From his shirt pocket, Michael produced a pair of thick eyeglasses before scrutinising the photo.

"My eyesight isn't the best. This looks quite grainy."

"Granted, it's not the best of pictures, but it's all I have at the moment."

Michael looked at the photo again. "She looks vaguely familiar. Do you have any money on you?"

"Very little with me. You're not going to run off and get a drink?" said Karl, regretting the last sentence as soon as it emerged.

"Ah, another myth. All homeless are drunks and thieves. Actually, I'm a boring teetotaller and one of the leftover petals from the flower people."

"I didn't mean the way it sounded."

"I'm well used to it by now," responded Michael, a forced smile appearing on his face.

"How much do you want?" Karl tagged a ten spot from his wallet.

"It's not for me," smiled Michael. "Probably about twenty quid."

"Twenty . . ." Against nagging doubts, Karl replaced the ten spot with one of the few twenties left in his possession, reluctantly handing it to Michael, along with the photo of Martina.

"You wait here, Karl. I'm going to talk to someone very special. Give me about five minutes."

While waiting, Karl sucked in the history of the adjacent Custom

House, picturing the Victorian novelist, Anthony Trollope, sitting at his desk in the local post office section of the grand building in the nineteenth century, labouring away until finally getting his big break as a writer. *Bet you had your fair share of rejection slips, Tony, old lad. Though not in the same tonnage as yours truly, of course.*

Five minutes turned to ten, and the oven-like heat had transformed into a microwave. Sweat began trickling down Karl's back, pooling between the cracks in his arse. He felt like he had pissed himself. Hated the thought that he might have been taken for a fool. Considered entering the dimly lit building, go searching for boring teetotaller Michael weighed down with his twenty spot.

"Sorry, it took a bit longer than I expected," exclaimed Michael, re-emerging suddenly from a side door. "Cathy enjoys her sleep. Behind her back, they call her Cathy the Cat because of her nocturnal ways. She's our *de facto* leader." Michael's smile broadened mischievously. "Follow me. Watch your footing. It's a bit treacherous in places."

"How on earth do you survive?" asked Karl, stepping over discarded boxes of rotten fruit.

"Being homeless, you mean? It's the freest you'll ever feel. You can walk through this town at midnight and not worry about getting mugged, because you have nothing worth stealing," smiled Michael.

The vast interior of the building was an organised shambles, with makeshift tents scattered chaotically like oily puddles. Pews – the few that had escaped being burnt as firewood on cold nights – were pyramided like marooned canoes against a far wall. Adorning the many other walls, a coterie of carved angels and classical deities remained remarkably unscathed, looking down upon the huddled masses. The outstretched arms of forsaken saints, though, had met a more mortifying end, being used to dry tattered clothing as well as holding a small army of TV antennas that somehow managed to pick up signals for the contingent of discarded black and white television sets flickering eerily in the charcoal light. A large crucifix with a tortured Christ dangled precariously above, looking down upon a badly chipped Madonna, most of her face gone.

To Karl, the entire scene resembled something out of *Apocalypse Now*, and as Michael furthered him to a one-time sacristy now converted into a rickety semblance of a bedroom, Karl hoped that Cathy the Cat wasn't going to turn out to be a shaven-headed Colonel Walter E. Kurtz.

"Cathy?" whispered Michael, tapping meekly at the door. "Cathy . . . ?"

"I heard you the first time," hissed the scissoring voice. There was a sound of movement coming from inside the room before permission was finally granted to enter.

Cathy the Cat was sprawling out upon a badly stained mattress, her skinny frame propped up by a family of orphaned cushions. A sunburst of red hair fanned on the cushions. Her eyes were green and luminous as absinthe. Star of David earrings were tooled tightly into the lobes of her ears. She was wearing an anarchist tank top depicting a cracked, inverted champagne glass with the words **Fuck The System** stencilled in black, goal-posted strategically between two very erect nipples. Faded tattoos – most of which appeared to be self-made, prison-types – branched from her arms. Only one of the tattoos appeared to be professionally done. It was creepily ornamented: a pubescent angel with a syringe being inserted into its wings, transforming them into sharpened blades of dripping blood. **Hell's True Angel** stated the legend directly beneath the angel's feet.

Despite Cathy's slenderness, Karl thought that her arms looked muscularly chiselled for giving headlocks, and that he would certainly hate it to be *his* head in the wrestling match.

The room smelled wet and rusty. A faint lofting stench of urine and reeking chemicals that smelled like rotten eggs mixed with paint thinner.

"Hello," said Karl, his hand outstretched towards Cathy. "My name is –"

"I already *know* your name, and your supposed business here. What *exactly* is it you want?" asked Cathy, ignoring Karl's hand. Tilting an egg-timer, she began watching its contents flow softly, filling the empty glass belly underneath. "I would say you have less than two minutes."

"I was told you might be able to help me with my enquiries. Michael explained that you –"

"Michael can tolerate hunger, but silence has always been a mean torture for him. He can't keep that bucket mouth of his shut. Isn't that right, Michael?"

Without replying, Michael slinked sheepishly away, leaving Karl and Cathy alone.

While Cathy watched Michael's shadow disappear, Karl studied patches of baldness on Cathy's head.

"From numerous bottles being smashed against it," said Cathy, almost blasé, catching Karl. "The numerous dead wounds have left tracts where my hair will never grow again. Pretty, isn't it?"

"I didn't mean to stare." Yet, despite the ugliness of the scars, it was obvious to Karl that Cathy had once been extremely attractive.

"Here. Take your photo back," said Cathy, standing slowly up, allowing her hair to fall over the balcony of her shoulders. "I don't like your look or smell. You have the sneaky stench of a cop about you."

"Cops travel in a totally different direction from me. *Persona non grata* is the phrase they normally use when describing me."

Cathy studied Karl for a few seconds. "What's her name, the girl in the photo?"

"Martina. Martina Ferris."

Cathy yawned like a sluggish cat. "She said her name was Angela Reilly. Came here a few weeks ago, wanting to 'fit in'. She didn't strike me as the type that could 'fit in' anywhere, let alone in *this* world."

"You refused to let her stay?"

"This is my kingdom."

"I notice there are no other women here."

"That's best for the family. The men get confused. They still retain their testosterone, despite how they look. Their minds are inclined to wander into darkness, allowing their cocks to become stiff dowsing rods."

"I see." Karl gave a quick cough. "You don't feel threatened by all the men in here?"

For a moment's flash, Cathy's green eyes did a strange movement of tiny flickering. Her face tightened, and then just as quickly relaxed. Suddenly, she stood toe-to-toe with Karl, her face close to his, her mouth seductively open. Her breath smelt of stale medicine. He noticed for the first time the family of metal studs embedded in her tongue. They made him think of silver mushrooms.

"Do I look the type of person easily threatened?"

"Not the type at all, Cathy. It was a silly question. You have to forgive me. I'm notorious for asking silly questions."

"Good. Understanding goes a long way," replied Cathy, glancing at the egg-timer. "I think you've overstayed your welcome, *Karl.*"

"What about Martina? Is there anything you can tell me? She could be in danger."

"You're very persistent for not being a cop – *allegedly.* What's in this for you?" Cathy placed a sharp fingernail on Karl's cheek. Traced his jawbone. "Did you pimp her out? Has your fat golden goose fled its cage, left you with rotten eggs on your face?"

"Nothing like that. Just trying to make sure she's safe."

Cathy's fingernail travelled to Karl's mouth, tracing the little flesh indents on his lips.

"She said something about heading down to Dublin, find a friend who's in a hospital of some sort," said Cathy. "Now, go. Visiting is over."

CHAPTER SIX

"And when, on the still cold nights, he pointed his nose at a star
and howled long and wolflike, it was his ancestors, dead and
dust, pointing nose at star and howling down through the
centuries and through him."
Jack London, *The Call of the Wild*

"Not too far now, Max," said the man, patting the dog's head before continuing the journey towards Black Mountain via the pathway known as Mountain Lonely. A few minutes later, he cut across Hatchet Field – so-called because of being shaped like an old hatchet – and let the dog off its leash despite a warning sign advising against such action.

"Go on, Max! Good dog!"

The dog went bulleting ahead, barking with excitement.

Less than thirty minutes later, the man finally rested atop Black Mountain, taking in the spectacular views over Belfast with a pair of Pentacon Cobra wide-angle binoculars.

"Beautiful!" he exclaimed, rotating slowly, catching sight of Donegal in the far distance, before capturing Scotland, the coasts of England and the Isle of Man, all in one panoramic scoop. "Where in the world would you get see such sights on a Wednesday morning, eh, Max?"

Max commenced barking at his master's voice before drinking

quickly from a skinny stream veining inwards from the hillside. Seconds later, the dog was away in hot pursuit of a motley crew of flea-infested rabbits out enjoying some early morning sex.

"Max! C'mon, boy. Don't go too far ahead."

Abruptly, the dog stopped dead in its tracks, standing stiffly before growling at a small mound of puckered earth where one of the rabbits made good its escape. The hairs on the dog's back suddenly began spiking eerily.

"Max! C'mon the hell with you, now!"

The dog, normally obedient, ignored him.

"*Max!* Get back here!"

Max was getting old *and* deaf, thought the man, justifying the dog's unusual behaviour.

As he approached, Max began howling and sniffing at the ground, throwing its body back with a jerk, as if its nose touched something hot.

"Max? I don't have time for this nonsense with rabbits."

Max began barking uncontrollably, digging furiously.

"Max! Will you cut that out! Look at the state of your –"

Suddenly, hordes of filthy flies – wings lit green with small splashes of light through the slats – buzzed angrily at the man, hitting his face forcefully, some entering his mouth and windpipe.

"Bastards!" he shouted, almost choking on the black sludge. The flies tasted like excrement and raw meat. He felt like vomiting, but stubbornly held it. "Filthy bastards!"

Max's barking became louder.

"Max! Get the hell away from –"

The sun came into play, just at the right moment, landing rays on the washed-out piece of whiteness slightly hidden in the darkened soil.

"What on earth?"

Covering his mouth with a hand, the man nudged the ground with his boot, overturning the soil. The earth was spongy and easily succumbed to the push of the boot. There was a muted metallic odour to the overturned dirt that made him think of decaying onions.

At first, he thought the whiteness a piece of broken plate or an upturned cup from a campsite. Only when his boot investigated the soil further was all revealed.

"Oh dear lord . . ."

The face was barely visible behind a mask of leaves and soil. The gaping skull had been bleached so thoroughly its lines held dark, almost carbon shadows; teeth and jaws gaping up at the sun down there in the damp darkness of hellish ground. The flesh – what little there was left – was winter pale and off-yellow, like hardened cheese in a darkened cupboard. Colourless eye sockets glared at him from their dark passages.

Suddenly wilting to his knees, the man bowed his head, as if praying, retching violently.

The man was no expert, but as he buckled over in the filthy nightmare, he suspected from the braces gating the teeth that this was probably the skull of a child barely in its teens.

Chapter Seven

"He knows death to the bone."
W. B. Yeats, "Death"

"Hello, Tom," said Karl, standing at the office doorway of best friend and forensic pathologist, Tom Hicks.

Glancing up from his computer screen, Hicks looked slightly on edge.

"Karl? What the hell are you doing here?"

"Lovely greeting. Haven't seen your grumpy old gob in months, and that's what I get?"

"Don't you know Wilson is upstairs in his office? For God's sake, man, show some common sense – even though I doubt you have any."

"That's what I always admire in you. Your honesty. Anyway, my delightful ex-brother-in-law is way down my list of priorities, right at this moment."

"I'm serious, Karl. I don't know what's going on with you two, but I've heard through the grapevine that he hates your guts."

"The day I worry about a wanker like Wilson is the day I stop being a private investigator. You more than anyone should know I'm not easily intimidated, Tom."

"I'm getting too old for old men acting juvenile."

"Speak for yourself when you say old. Anyway, I brought you a present," said Karl, handing Hicks a book.

"Don't tell me you finally got one of those books of yours published?" said Hicks, taking the book, looking at the cover. "Peter Mullan? Why does that name ring a bell?"

"It should. We were in the same class for about a year. Looked a bit like a weasel. Always complaining."

"Oh, yes . . . now I remember him," said Hicks, smiling. "He's an author?"

"A bestselling one, the bastard. Had to buy that in Eason's this morning where he was signing. Fifteen bloody quid it cost. Is it any wonder people don't buy books any more? Got him to inscribe it to you. That's your birthday covered, next month. So don't be asking for anything else."

"Did he remember you?"

"Of course he bloody remembered me. I saved him from a couple of hidings in school, you know. He owes me," stated Karl. "That's why I gave him a copy of my new manuscript and asked him to have a look at it. Hopefully, he'll give me a cracker blurb. Sometimes that's all it takes to win a publisher over."

"I'm embarrassed for you."

"Don't be. I'm not. Besides, the squeaky wheel always gets the oil. If you don't ask, you won't get."

"You still haven't told me what caused all this bad blood between you and Wilson."

"Best you don't know."

"The last I saw you two together, I had to separate the both of you, rolling in the muck, punching the daylights out of each other – and at a funeral of a murdered officer, into the bargain," said Hicks, looking at Karl in such a way it made Karl's neck itch. "That poor girl, Jenny Lewis. What a horrible tragedy – her and the mother. Not forgetting Detectives Cairns and McKenzie, of course."

"Of course."

"They never did find the killer – or killers. You'd think Wilson would have made the murder of three of his detectives a priority, wouldn't you?"

"Has he recruited any new members of staff?" asked Karl, carefully evading the question.

"So far, he's hired one young detective. Extremely wet behind the ears, by the cut of him. There's talk Wilson is after two more to fill the ranks of his depleted crew, but is refusing to take on a female, after what happened to Jenny Lewis."

"Has Wilson tried to heavy-hand you?" replied Karl. "Remember, he more or less threatened you at the funeral?"

"That was all in the heat of the moment. We give each other a wide berth now. If we happen to stumble into each other in public, we nod professionally as if nothing ever happened."

"Glad to hear you two are so cushy-wushy, now. Which reminds me. Fancy going to a birthday party tomorrow night?"

"Whose party?"

"Ivana's."

"I . . . I can't. I've tickets to *The Thirty-Nine Steps* in the Grand Opera House tomorrow night."

"What a strange coincidence."

"Stop making everything out to be a conspiracy. Anne's been waiting months to see it. Tell Ivana happy birthday and that I'm so sorry I can't be at the party."

"I bet you are."

"What's that supposed to mean?"

"I'm simply saying that you've never approved of Ivana's lifestyle." Karl began grinning. "Perhaps if you give it a go, you'd feel differently towards Ivana."

The normally stoic Hicks looked momentarily knocked off balance. "If you saw the number of victims of sexually related diseases that I have, you wouldn't be standing there grinning like a damn buffoon or taking such a deadly subject so lightly."

"Okay. Point taken," conceded Karl, the grin slowly fading. "Shall we change the subject? Something less deadly?"

"How's Katie doing in Edinburgh?"

"Seems to be settling in fine, though I hate the thought that she's so far from home. I'm always worrying about her."

"Young people are very resilient, Karl. Believe it or not, we were young once," stated Hicks, attempting a smile.

"I can't remember an old dinosaur like you *ever* being young. Even when we were in school together, you were old."

"Always tell Katie that her godfather is watching her progress. Who knows? She might even want to take over from me, when I retire."

"You're like Cliff Richard. You'll never retire," replied Karl, quickly sidestepping the suggestion. The thought of his beloved Katie following in Hicks's footsteps, chopping up the dead, held little appeal for Karl. "What can you tell me about the body found in the Black Mountain area, yesterday?"

"Not much. I'm backlogged by almost four reports, so I'm badly behind schedule. I've no assistant to help me, due to more cutbacks, and I'm still examining a body of a young woman discovered last week near the city centre."

"I didn't read about any body being found last week in the city centre," said Karl, looking slightly puzzled.

"Yes . . . well . . . this particular body was found in the vicinity of Victoria Square."

"That new shopping centre?"

"Yes."

"And? Why wasn't it reported?"

"Your guess is as good as mine; but let's just say I'm becoming almost as cynical as you."

"What's that supposed to mean?"

"They spent what? Almost a billion, or close to, on building Victoria Square? The city council apparently spent almost three hundred thousand advertising its importance for the city. Do you think it would look good discovering a body two days before the grand opening, one street away from their field of dreams?"

Karl's face reddened slightly. "Bastards . . . so it was all hushed-up in the interests of the caviar and champagne brigade?"

"Those are your words, not mine."

"Nice bunch of scumbags we have running this great town of ours," responded Karl, removing the photo of Martina before handing it to Hicks. "I'm searching for this young girl. Her name's Martina Ferris. I'm hoping you tell me it isn't her whose body was discovered in the Black Mountain or the city centre."

"I'm still working on the reports and waiting on dental records," said Hicks, studying the photo. "Her left eye. What happened?"

"Lost it to a pen wound, a few years back."

"Definitely not the body in the city centre."

"Why?"

"No indication of an eye replacement," said Hicks, reaching for a beige-coloured folder and extracting a single page from a family of others. "Having said that, there are similarities."

"Such as?"

"Female. Sixteen or seventeen years of age. Officers at the scene wrongly classified her hair as red, when in fact it was blonde."

"Had it been dyed? Martina could be classified as a punk, from her photo."

"No. Not dyed. So much blood had escaped from the head wound, transforming it into strawberry red."

"Horrible . . ."

"It gets worse. Parts of her insides were missing, surgically removed."

Karl's face knotted slightly. "What? You're saying someone murdered her for body parts?"

"It's a possibility."

"You think someone's selling the parts on the black market?"

"Initially, yes. But only the liver and kidneys are missing." Hicks rubbed his red, sore-looking eyes before continuing. "Are you familiar with the word 'vorarephilia'?"

"If it isn't in Kid's Scrabble, I haven't heard of it. I suspect you knew that before you asked. Showing off again."

"Vorarephilia is the sexual attraction to being eaten by, or eating another person. It's also known as phagophilia or simply called vore for short."

Karl made a face. "I thought that was cannibalism."

"Cannibals eat for survival and tribal domination – not sexual perversion," corrected Hicks. "The fact that the kidneys and liver alone have been removed is an indication – though not conclusively – of possible vorarephilia. The word 'vorarephilia' is derived from the Latin *vorare*, swallow or devour, and the Ancient Greek word *philia*, meaning love."

"How sick is that? You really believe that this is some sort of ritual killing for sexual gratification?"

"We may only ever find that out if the killer is apprehended and confesses. Other than that, it's an educated guess. There was one glaring inconsistency, though."

"What?"

"Her body weight."

"What about it?"

"Not enough calcium to support the fat contents of a normally developed body."

"What's that supposed to mean?" asked Karl.

"Accelerated formation of cells and protein."

"In layman's terms?"

"The young girl's body was carrying too much weight for the skeletal system to support. Similar to placing a ton of metal on a cardboard box. It was only a matter of time before it collapsed." Hicks began hitting a few keys on the computer's keyboard, and suddenly the screen transformed from black and white text to a colourful three-dimensional illustration. "This is the skeletal system. Look inside this bone. See how it works?"

Karl studied the screen, the open bone and the traffic of colours mixing with coded lineage references.

"What exactly am I looking *at*, Tom?"

Hicks sighed impatiently. "Bones are composed of tissue that may take one of two forms. Compact or dense bone; and spongy or cancellous bone. Most bones contain both types. Compact bone is dense, hard, and forms the protective exterior portion of all bones. Spongy bone is inside the compact bone and is very porous. Spongy bone occurs in most bones. The bone tissue is composed of several types of bone cells embedded in a web of inorganic salts, mostly calcium and phosphorus, to give the bone strength, and collagenous fibres and ground substance to give the bone flexibility."

"And . . . ?"

"It takes time for bone build-up. Nature is very patient, knowing calcium can only accommodate precise weight-values through longevity.

However, the bones of the young girl were fooled into believing they were strong enough to withstand this sudden impact of alien matter suddenly thrust upon them. What should have taken years was accomplished in days, possibly weeks."

"She was thin, then suddenly became fat?"

"That's not very PC, and it's certainly not how *I* would phrase it, but yes."

"How is that possible?"

"I don't exactly know. I've sent some of the bone and skin tissues to Queen's. Professor Ashley Kelly at the science lab is looking at them as we speak. Hopefully, she'll have an answer soon."

"If that is how she died, why the horrendous blow to the head?"

"Possibly a hate-induced frenzy. The killer wasn't satisfied with simply murdering the victim, he wanted – *or needed* – mutilation as well, probably thinking that if –"

Hicks suddenly stopped speaking, tilting his head slightly.

"What? What is it?" asked Karl.

"The lift. Someone's coming down. I think you'd better leave now, in case it's Wilson's new man looking for a report on the young girl."

"You think I'm frightened of Wilson?"

"You? No! Not *you*. Everyone knows how tough you are."

"No need to be so sarcastic."

"In case it's slipped your mind, I've got to work here."

"Will you keep me informed of any developments concerning the body in Black Mountain?"

"Yes! But go – *now*. Use the back entrance."

The lift door opened just as Karl walked by. A fresh-faced young man stepped from the lift, staring.

Karl stared back.

"How's it going?" asked the young man, smiling.

Karl glanced at the anxious face of Hicks before answering.

"Not too bad. Haven't seen you about before. You must be new, Detective . . . ?" said Karl, extending his hand.

"How did you know I was a detective?"

"I didn't, but I do now," smiled Karl.

"Detective Chambers. Malcolm Chambers." The young detective's smile broadened as he shook Karl's hand. "Only been on the job for a week, but already I feel like a veteran. I'm working for Detective Inspector Mark Wilson. Do you know him?"

Karl nodded. "I've heard of him. A bit of a legend, apparently. They say he's one of the best detectives in town."

"You got that right," beamed Chambers. "You part of the pathologist team?"

"Not really. I'm from . . . the private sector."

"I didn't catch your name?"

"I didn't throw it," replied Karl. "No doubt I'll be bumping into you in the future, Detective Chambers. Take care."

Outside, Karl was about to climb into his car when a voice asked, "Still driving that old piece of shit, Kane? Thought I recognised it."

Karl turned to see Edward Phillips, one of Wilson's ex-detectives, walking towards him.

For a second, Karl thought about getting in the car, simply driving off. Instead, he decided to stand his ground.

"I heard you'd retired, Phillips."

Phillips stopped directly beside Karl, eyeballing him.

"Retire like my old pals Bulldog and Cairns? You wish, Kane."

There was a strong stench of whiskey escaping from Phillips's mouth, and Karl immediately regretted not getting in the car and leaving. He had heard the rumours of Phillips's dismissal from the force two months ago, accused of shaking down drug dealers and pimps in the north of the city. He wondered what the hell Phillips was doing at headquarters?

"Well, I'd love to reminisce with you, Phillips, but have to go," said Karl, easing into the car.

"Can't you take a joke, Kane? What happened to your sense of humour?"

"Have to check my drawers when I get home. Could've left it there."

"Ha! That's more like the Kane I remember," said Phillips, removing a half bottle of Bushmills whiskey, taking one long slug before offering it to Karl.

"No thanks. That Irish puts hairs on a man's chest. I just had a Brazilian done on mine."

The joke was lost on Phillips, who asked, "How's that sour-faced brother-in-law of yours doing?"

"Oh, you know him. That sour face never sweetens. Must be all that power he has, being the famous detective inspector."

"You can say that again, that I know him," replied Phillips, tapping the side of his nose twice before winking at Karl. "In fact, I'm going in right now to see old Sour Puss, to remind him that I *know him*. If that bastard thinks he can kick me out of the force without my retirement pension, he's got another think coming. Too many secrets stored up here in the old noggin." Phillips tapped the side of his head, and winked again.

"Secrets? What kind of secrets?" asked Karl, suddenly interested.

"Don't be smart, Kane. They wouldn't be secrets any more if I told you, would they now?"

"No. I guess you're right," replied Karl, grinning. "And there's me trying to be smart again. Never seems to work when dealing with cops."

"Cops are different from the rest of you mere mortals, Kane. Most of us believe that we are in a life and death struggle against everyone else, and we're all in it together." Phillips swayed drunkenly before continuing. "Being a cop requires us to be members of a union, a union forged of blood, governed by laws that go beyond the laws that govern the rest of you. It's hard to go against that union. It's also dangerous."

"Look, I really do have to go, Phillips," said Karl, no longer willing to listen to Phillips's incoherent blabbering.

"Ever hear of the King David Syndrome?"

"Can't say I have. Why?"

"Tell you what. I'll do a deal with you. I don't get my pension, you get my secrets concerning our very own King fucking David. How's that? And I'll even make sure my solicitor posts them to you, should an unfortunate *accident* happen to me."

"What are you talking about, unfortunate accident? What kind of unfortunate accident?"

"Accidents always seem to happen when you don't have insurance.

But both you and I have insurance. Don't we, Kane? The trick is, make sure that your insurance policy is up-to-date." Another mysterious wink. "I always liked you, Kane, despite what the others thought of you. You're not the fool you pretend to be."

"I appreciate your encouraging words, Phillips," said Karl, closing the car door, rolling down the window. "Those are the kind of compliments that make my day."

"See you about, Kane," waved Phillips, staggering towards the entrance before disappearing.

"What I would give to be a fly on Wilson's wall," whispered Karl, starting the car and driving away.

CHAPTER EIGHT

*". . . the companions of our childhood always possess a
certain power over our minds which hardly any later
friend can obtain."*
Mary Shelley, *Frankenstein*

"It looks like it's going to be a cracker of a day," said Karl, buttering toast for breakfast the next morning, while glancing out the window at the early morning sun licking over the grey city centre rooftops.

"Yes," agreed Naomi, looking up from the magazine in her hands. "They said all this week should be good."

"One or two slices?"

"One, please." From the magazine, Naomi removed an envelope. "I've something to ask you, Karl, but first you must promise not to be mad."

"Too late. I already am mad. You know by now that I make the Hatter look sane," said Karl, his lips smiling but his eyes the opposite as they settled on the envelope. "*Hmm.* That looks vaguely familiar."

"I . . . this morning I was going through old magazines to dump and came across this letter in an old shoebox. I opened it by mistake . . ."

"That pert little nose of yours always grows when you're fibbing."

"Well . . . I sort of let curiosity get the better of me."

"Remember what happened to Lot's wife? Go on. Ask what you're going to ask. Don't keep me in suspenders."

"It's the title deeds to a house. This house, I suppose," said Naomi, producing an old black and white photo, holding it out for Karl to examine.

"Ten out of ten. Next question, please."

"Why didn't you tell me you owned a big house in the country?"

"Technically speaking, it's my father's. I have what's called enduring power of attorney, because my father is incapable by reason of mental disorder of managing and administering his property and affairs. Knowing he's probably never going to get better, I guess the house is mine. Though I'll probably never see the inside of that place again."

"Why do you say that? It really looks the part. I'd love to go and have a look at it," replied Naomi, smiling. "Our own place in the country. Sounds good to me."

"It's where my mother was murdered and I was attacked, left for dead," said Karl matter-of-factly.

Naomi looked stunned. "Oh my God, Karl . . . I . . . I'm so sorry . . . how could I have been so stupid?" Seconds later, tears were streaming down her face.

Sitting down on the sofa, Karl put his arms around her. "I've been trying to persuade Dad into moving out of that care home he's currently residing in. I was hoping he would move in with us, some time in the future, once we get a bigger place."

"What . . . what did he say?"

Karl sighed. "When I visited him last week, he threw a shoe at me, screaming I was a burglar and a murderer. He tried grabbing a pair of scissors while leaping at me, saying he was going to protect his son."

"Oh my God, Karl."

"The staff finally managed to sedate him. It was heartbreaking to watch. I feel so guilty about where he is, even though it's probably the best place he could be, with his mental problems. He was never the same after my mother was murdered. He's a broken shell of the man I knew when I was growing up, as a kid."

"My poor Karl," said Naomi.

"What's with the tears?" he said, kissing the side of her head.

"I brought back all those bad memories," she sniffed, wiping her nose and eyes on his shirt. "I'm so sorry."

"You didn't bring back anything. They're always there; always following me, everywhere I go."

This piece of information only encouraged the tears to come even faster. "Oh, Karl . . ."

"Stop crying, Naomi. Please . . . you know I don't like to see you crying. Come on. Give me a smile," he soothed.

She attempted one. Failed.

"Call that a smile? Look, perhaps we *can* go. Perhaps there'd be no better way to exorcise my childhood demons than facing them, head on. What do you think?"

"No," sniffed Naomi, shaking her head. "I don't want you to torture yourself. I'm going to put the deeds somewhere safe. When you're ready, we'll go. But only when you're ready."

He kissed her chin. And then her mouth, whispering, "Soon. Soon I'll be ready. Now, you still haven't told me what you bought Ivana for her birthday tonight."

"Oh! I almost forgot. Let me show –"

Karl's mobile rang. It was Hicks.

"Tom? What's happening?"

"The bodies in the Black Mountain and the city centre."

"What about them?"

"Definitely weren't those of the young girl you're searching for. The young girl in Black Mountain was Tina Richardson, a runaway from a home in Larne, two years ago. She was fourteen."

"Terrible."

"The body found in the city was that of Eileen Flynn, another runaway, this time from Belfast itself. Eighteen years old."

"Shit."

"Bodies were mutilated, exactly in the same method."

"That vora rep thing?"

"Vorarephilia," sighed Tom. "Yes, kidneys and liver removed, surgically. Both bodies were overweight – forcefully so."

"Did Professor Kelly over at Queen's get back to you with any explanation?"

"Not yet. She seems as baffled as me. Anyway, it'll probably be all over the news this afternoon. I told Wilson I'm no longer willing to keep this from the general public. Oh, almost forgot to mention: I hear Phillips got his full retirement pension. Even got a recommendation from Wilson."

"Are you serious?"

"Got it from the horse's mouth, so to speak, yesterday."

"Funny, now that you mention it, there is a strong resemblance between Wilson and Arkle," replied Karl. "What happened to the investigation? Wasn't Phillips being investigated for corruption or some other sort of bullshit?"

"He was accused of shaking down pimps and drug dealers in the city, as well as being involved in two controversial shootings. Investigation found no evidence of wrongdoing, *allegedly.*"

"Ever get one of those feelings in your piss that things just aren't kosher at the House of Wilson?"

"No, never in my urine, but I know exactly what you mean," said Hicks. "Something's going on between Phillips and Wilson."

"Out of all of Wilson's crew, Phillips was the one I always got on well with – most of the time, at least."

"With the way he's turned out, why am I not surprised at that statement? To be honest, I never liked the man. I always suspected he thought himself like the rest of his associates – above and beyond the law."

"You always suspect someone of something. It's your suspicious nature, Hicks."

"What was that all about?" asked Naomi, who had beeen waiting for Karl to end the phone conversation.

"That was Hicks. It appears that Belfast has a serial killer on its hands, and the shit is about to hit the fan."

Chapter Nine

"I prefer women with a past.
They're always so demmed amusing to talk to."
Oscar Wilde, *Lady Windermere's Fan*

Considered by many to be Belfast's best gay/transsexual bar, Billy Holiday's was buzzing when Karl and Naomi entered, passing a sign at the doorway stating: **Never mind just *one* good night out. We'll make your hole weak.**

A woman, dressed in tight black leather and uncannily resembling Freddie Mercury, sang from an irritatingly loud karaoke machine. Sweat was escaping from every pore in her muscular body as she swayed, running the mic seductively up the inside of her thighs. The fake moustache glued to thick lips was the only thing that looked real.

Accompanying her on stage was a tall, bald man covered in tattoos, grinding an air guitar, his face a mixture of anguish, pain and ecstasy.

"Naomi! Karl! Toot-a-loot! Over here, darlings!" shouted a voice from a darkened far corner.

"Ivana!" Naomi immediately smiled, waving back enthusiastically. Karl, less so.

"I didn't think you were coming, Naomi," claimed Ivana, kiss-kissing Naomi's cheeks falsely.

"We wouldn't have missed it for anything, Ivana," said Naomi, handing a small birthday-wrapped box to Ivana.

"Oh, you lovely person. You really shouldn't have," gushed Ivana.

"That's exactly what I told her, Ivana," said Karl, slapping his hand with a baton made from rolled-up posters.

"Don't listen to him, Ivana," replied Naomi. "You know what he's like."

"Thankfully, my dear, I *don't*. And neither do I *want* to," retorted Ivana, unwrapping the present. "Oh! Naomi . . . this is too much . . . it's beautiful."

A small gold necklace centred with a large pearl rested in the opened box.

"Here. Let me clip it on for you," volunteered Naomi, circling the necklace on to Ivana's neck. "Oh, Ivana, *that* is so you."

"It's beautiful, darling. Thank you . . . both."

"Vodka and orange, Ivana?" suggested Karl, while a waiter, attired in nothing other than a leopard-skin thong and a banana bulge, hovered at the table, menacingly close to Karl's face.

"*Large*," replied Ivana, winking at the waiter. "I always take it *large*."

"A large vodka and orange, Bacardi and Coke and a *small* glass of Hennessy, please," said Karl, emphasising the small, while doing his best to avoid looking at the semi-naked young man. "Wow, that lady singer has a set of pipes on her. She doesn't even need the mic."

"Freaky Muckery?" spiked Ivana, acidly. "She and her sidekick, Ben Gay, have been on the karaoke machine all night and doing my head in. Did I say karaoke? Derrieroke, I call it. Freaky pulling a song out of her arse and trying to sing it. C'mon, Freaky and Gay! Stop hogging the karaoke!"

Defiantly, Ben Gay immediately brought the invisible guitar to his teeth and ran his mouth along it like a beaver munching a log.

"What's got up the old queen mum's bum!" retaliated Freaky, garnering much laughter from the crowd.

"Not you, anyway!" responded Ivana, lightning fast.

Ben Gay went sliding along the stage on bent knees, knocking over Freaky and the karaoke machine in the process, his head landing between Freaky's legs.

"Shouldn't that be the other way round, Freaky!" shouted Ivana.

"Oh, Ivana," giggled Naomi.

"Well, serves her right. She's a cheapskate, and if there's one thing I hate, it's a cheapskate," replied Ivana. "She's so cheap, she charged her children for the breast milk they consumed."

Even Karl had to grin at that one.

"And as for Ben Gay? Don't get me started! He's a twin. I went out with both of them, years ago, just to see if their dicks were identical."

Karl cringed. His armpits suddenly felt clammy. Wished semi-naked Tarzan would hurry the hell up with the drinks.

"You're cruel, Ivana!" giggled Naomi. "And were their dicks identical?"

"Totally. Right down to the last blue vein, darling!"

Naomi burst out laughing.

"Any bloody chance of that waiter?" asked Karl, trying to catch Naomi's attention.

On a roll, Ivana asked, "What did Freddie Mercury's mother say as his coffin was being lowered into the cold ground?"

"I don't know," replied a giggling Naomi, shrugging her shoulders.

"That's the cleanest hole he's been in for a while!"

"Oh, Ivana. That's not nice," said Naomi, sternly, no longer smiling or laughing. "You shouldn't make fun of the dead."

"You're right. Of course, you're right, darling," replied Ivana, sounding slightly contrite. "It was a cheap joke and I apologise. Actually, I've always been a great fan of Freddie."

Thankfully for Karl, the waiter returned and deposited the drinks on the table. Karl left it to Naomi to tip, not knowing where it might end up.

"Do you think the owner would mind if I put a poster up on one of the walls?" asked Karl, taking a much-anticipated sip from the Hennessy.

"Poster? Depends, I suppose," replied Ivana, sipping on the vodka and orange. "What's the poster of?"

Karl unrolled the group of small posters of Martina Ferris. The young girl's sad face seemed even more forlorn coming out eyes first.

"I had a few of these made this morning, hoping the local bars and cafés wouldn't mind putting them somewhere the general public can see them. Her name is Martina Ferris. She's been missing for almost a month."

"Poor thing," said Ivana, her voice almost a whisper. "She's so sad-looking."

Naomi nodded in agreement.

"She was last seen in and around the Custom House Square area," continued Karl. "Her last fixed abode was –"

"Ivana?" cut in Naomi. "Are you okay? You've become pale."

"What? Oh! No, I'm fine, darling. I think it's the orange in the vodka. Doesn't taste right. That's all . . ." Ivana pushed her drink to the side. "They never use fresh fruit in this place."

"You're leaving yourself wide open with that remark, Ivana," said Karl, a wry smile appearing on his face.

"Enough, Karl," said Naomi.

"Okay. That *was* tasteless. Would you like me to order another one for you, Ivana?" asked Karl reluctantly, not too sure how much money was left in his skinny wallet.

"No . . . no, I think I've had enough. I've been drinking most of the evening anyway. Time to call it a night. Give me one of the posters. I'll make sure it gets a prominent display." Standing, Ivana hugged Naomi. "Thank you for making this a very special birthday, Naomi – both of you. I'll see you during the week. Goodnight."

Naomi waited until Ivana had left before asking Karl, "What do you make of that? She looked terribly sad once she saw Martina's poster, didn't she?"

Karl nodded, his thoughts the same, only darker.

CHAPTER TEN

"There are no secrets better kept than the secrets everybody guesses."
George Bernard Shaw, *Mrs Warren's Profession*

"Karl? We have a visitor," pronounced Naomi, her face a mixture of surprise and pleasure. "Bet you'll never guess who."

"You're right. I'm all guessed-out. So why don't you tell me?" deadpanned Karl, eyes not moving from the horse racing section in the morning's *Irish News.* There were four-legged certainties inked somewhere in these Monday morning pages, but the only certainty at the moment was Karl having a difficult time sniffing them out. He hadn't picked a winner in over four weeks, and forced himself to believe that the law of averages – like fortune – would eventually favour his braveness.

Before Naomi could reply, a voice from behind her said, "I don't know how you stick him, Naomi. He's such an ignorant bastard."

This time, Karl's eyes did move, before registering shock at what stood before them.

Ivana was wearing tight, expensive Italian washed-out jeans, a T-shirt with the distinctive red and white cursive Coke swirl emblazoned on it and a pair of purple-striped Nike tennis shoes, tied with red laces. Her hair was done in a bun, shamelessly exposing a professional make-over done less than an hour ago.

Karl did a wolf whistle.

Ivana seemed quite pleased at the response.

"You really look stunning, girl," enthused Naomi, giving Ivana a loving hug.

Karl nodded in agreement. He had never seen Ivana looking so lovely, almost feminine.

"You shouldn't have got all dolled-up just to come here to see me, doll," said Karl, doing his very bad Humphrey Bogart impression. "It's been what? All of three days since we last locked eyes at your birthday gig."

"Very funny, Karl Kane. For your information, I have a date on Thursday night. These are just casuals," stated Ivana, parking her arse on a table like she was taking up permanent residence.

"A date? Tell me quickly!" gushed Naomi excitedly. "Who is he?"

Ivana's face beamed. "Vincent Harrison."

"*Ohhhhhhhh!* That new waiter in Billy Holiday's, the one who served us on your birthday?"

Karl had a sudden vision of Tarzan swinging through the room, dangling on vines, peeling his banana.

"Do you think he might be a bit too young for my taste?" asked Ivana.

"Well . . . no . . ."

"You can't lie to save your life, Naomi! All those old bitches are saying I'm a baby snatcher. The cheek of them!"

"And the cheeks on him!" responded Naomi, smiling. "They're jealous of you, Ivana."

"I didn't hear you, dear. What did you say?"

"I said – Ivana! You heard me perfectly!"

"I know dear. I know," smiled Ivana.

"He really has a nice arse, hasn't he?" said Naomi.

Ivana nodded. "*Very* nice arse, darling. Very nice *everything*."

"That's *nice* to know, Ivana," cut in Karl, quickly returning to his newspaper. "Did you come here just to tell us about Vincent with everything nice?"

Suddenly sitting down on the chair next to the desk, Ivana hooked the newspaper from Karl's fingers and said, "No . . . actually . . . I've come to talk."

The immediate sombre tone of her voice stopped Karl from snapping the newspaper back.

"Go ahead. I've got two good ears and a head full of nothing. Just don't tell me that you're pregnant," said Karl, smiling. "Or that you're trapped between a cock and a hardener."

"That isn't funny, Karl," said Naomi. "Apologise to Ivana, right now."

"My apologies for my crass humour, Ivana. Now that you have the full attention from a fool, what's on your beautiful mind?"

"I'll go and make some coffee," volunteered Naomi.

"I would much rather you stayed, Naomi," said Ivana. "I have to get this off my chest and need you to hear what I have to say. You may not think much of me when you do."

Naomi shook her head. "Don't be silly, Ivana. You know how much I've always admired you, your bravery. Isn't that right, Karl?"

Karl nodded, noticing for the first time that Ivana's T-shirt did not say Coke, at all, but Cock.

"Would you like something stronger than coffee, Ivana?" offered Karl, pulling his eyes away from the disconcerting T-shirt. "Make you feel a bit more relaxed, perhaps?"

Ivana's face tightened, then quickly loosened as if remembering the price of the make-over. "No thank you. I wish to remain clear-headed," she replied, looking directly into Karl's eyes. "It's concerning . . . it's concerning those young girls found murdered in the Black Mountain and city centre. The news hasn't stopped showing their faces on TV the last couple of days. Terrible . . ."

"Absolutely horrible," agreed Naomi.

A thick silence swiftly entered the room. Naomi glanced at Karl, who kept his face professionally expressionless.

"Yes? What about her, Ivana?" enquired Karl, eventually breaking the silence.

"I think . . . I think I know who could have *something* to do with them."

"What?" Karl's attention went immediately into full swing. "What do you mean?"

"I'm not . . . I'm not one hundred per cent . . . call it intuition. Something just snapped in me when you produced that poster of the young girl with the sad eyes, at my birthday. I can't get her face out of my head. I don't even know if what I have to say is relevant."

"Anything you tell me will be thoroughly checked out, Ivana," encouraged Karl. "Anyway, it's better to be one hundred per cent wrong rather than seeing another young girl brutally tortured and murdered. Don't you agree?"

"That's good philosophy, I suppose." Ivana had an anguished look on her face while picking at an errant piece of cuticle on her middle finger.

Naomi reached out and, touching Ivana's shoulder, said, "Just take your time, Ivana. We are both here for you as friends. Okay?"

Ivana nodded, before sucking in air. "All those years ago when I was a young boy named Frankie Gilmore, my father worked as the game-keeper for a very wealthy family from the Malone Road called Hannah. The Hannah family owned acres and acres of woodland and forest on the outskirts of Belfast. The family consisted of a mother, father and son. The mother, Margaret, had inherited the money from her parents, prominent horsy people originally from Scotland. The father, Paul, was a distinguished and well-known surgeon."

"You're not talking about Sir Paul Hannah?" interrupted Karl. "Used to be the chief surgeon at the Royal Victoria Hospital?"

"Yes . . . yes, that's him. Of course, he wanted his son, Robert – or Bobby, as we called him – to follow in his footsteps, but unfortunately Bobby had no penchant for medicine – *at the time* – and was much more interested in owning his own Hollywood movie studio or messing about with his amateur magician's box, much to his parents' dismay."

Both Karl and Naomi leaned slightly closer to Ivana, as if having difficulty hearing the words coming from her mouth.

"Bobby was a . . . strange boy, a loner," continued Ivana. "He was never without his movie camera, posing as a big shot director, boring the knickers off everyone he encountered. Unfortunately for me, my father forced me to play with him on weekends because he thought it would keep him in his job as gamekeeper."

"That must have been horrible for you, Ivana," said Naomi, reaching out and holding Ivana's hand.

"It wasn't too bad at the start, darling. Bobby was an insufferable bore, but he had lots of money and was always buying buckets of sweets and cream cakes, all of which he used in an attempt to manipulate me into liking him. He was rather plump – like his mother – and always managed to devour more than his share, and even though I had a terrible sweet tooth, his eating habits always put me off. It was like watching a greedy little pig, tiny teeth sawing into the cakes, the cream plastered to his face." Ivana placed her hand over her mouth and coughed loudly. "You're both probably thinking I have a cheek to talk about anyone?"

"For fuck sake, Ivana, you've called me worse things than being fat and a greedy pig," said Karl impatiently, "so let's not get bogged down on childhood sensitivities. What else can you tell us about Bob the Plasterer?"

"Karl's right, Ivana," encouraged Naomi. "We were all probably little snot noses growing up, teasing each other terribly."

"Thank you, darling, though I doubt very much that you would fit into that category. You're just being your usual sweet self. Anyway, one day we were down in the basement of their large house, doing so-called filming with his camera and mucking about with his magic tricks, when suddenly all the lights went out. Fused or something like that. Suddenly, Bobby volunteers to get a torchlight. 'Hold this,' he said. I reached into the darkness and he dropped his magic wand right into my hand, laughing. It wasn't his magic wand, though, but his dick."

Karl almost fell off the chair.

"It was the first time I felt a real dick," claimed Ivana. "I mean, I'd felt my own, of course – before it went for the chop – but it was the first time I had ever held another *boy's*. It was thrilling, and like magic, it changed me for ever, releasing all those feelings I had suppressed. The lie I had been living was finally crushed, and soon I discovered that I liked boys, I liked holding and sucking their dicks."

"*Ahhhhh*. That's lovely, Ivana," responded Naomi, almost motherly, looking as if she had just heard the greatest love story ever told. "Lots of boys go through that stage in their life, but for you it was probably a calling. Isn't that true, Karl?"

Karl remained motionless, sitting in the chair, fixed and hushed, momentarily undone by Ivana's brutal honesty. He wished Naomi would stop bringing attention to him. In all honesty, the thought of sucking a dick, even if that dick had a vagina or would-be vagina parked next door to it like Ivana's, was totally unappealing. For fuck sake, he wouldn't even suck his own dick – not that he was boasting the possibility.

To Karl's great relief, Ivana continued.

"Bobby had a secret shoebox full of photos of naked women. No one was permitted to see them. But one day, I stumbled upon them accidentally. Tiny Polaroid pictures hid inside an old rotting tree at the back of his house. Very shocking and extremely graphic. Dildos, spanking devices . . . things of that nature, all of the same woman."

"Well, at least he liked women, as well," quipped Karl, trying to look on the bright side of things.

"The pictures were all of his mother."

Naomi paled. Karl reddened.

"Then one Saturday, we were all gathered for the annual hunt. It was horrible. All these adults roaming about like mercenaries in their camouflage clothing, shooting and slaughtering tiny defenceless birds. Absolutely disgusting people. My job was to go and chase out the grounded birds along with the dogs, when suddenly I looked back at Bobby, just in time to see him point his shotgun directly at his mother's head and pull the trigger."

"*Dear God!*" whispered Naomi, placing her hand to her mouth.

"Was she killed?" asked Karl, ignoring Naomi's histrionics.

"Yes." Ivana shuddered.

"What happened afterwards, to Bobby?" enquired Karl. "Was he arrested for her murder?"

Shaking her head, Ivana answered, "No. He claimed it was a tragic accident. No one saw it happen – except me, of course. Besides, who would have believed me? His word against mine? I told my father what I had witnessed, and he belted me across the mouth, telling me if I *ever* dared to repeat that disgusting lie again, he would give me the beating of my sorry life. Shortly after that, Bobby was sent away to some posh school to learn medicine."

"And that was the last you heard of him?" asked Karl, not too sure where the connection was being made.

Ivana looked at Naomi and then back to Karl before answering. "Remember about three years ago, when I was attacked and stabbed in the arm and shoulder, late at night outside Billy Holiday's?"

Both Karl and Naomi nodded. Karl remembered it well. Both he and Naomi had rushed to the hospital, fearing the worst.

"You got a busload of stitches," nodded Karl. "I had to take you home in my car. Do you know how long it took me to get the blood off the seats?"

"He's only winding you up, Ivana. Just ignore him," said Naomi, giving Karl a withering look.

"It was some right-wing, anti-gay nutcase," stated Karl. "Isn't that right?"

"That's what the media and the cops said," replied Ivana.

"What *should* they have said?" enquired Karl.

"At first, I didn't recognise the man who attacked me. He kept talking ever so calmly in the most chilling voice I had ever heard. 'As far as I'm concerned you are dead to me, you filthy traitor and cunt of a whore.'" Ivana shuddered before continuing. "It was only afterwards that I remembered his eyes. They were the same eyes I saw on Bobby Hannah when he shot his mother. I *think* it could have been him, even though my attacker was tall and extremely masculine – a far cry from the Bobby of my childhood."

"You *think?* You're not having selective amnesia, are you?" said Karl.

"Don't you dare start accusing me, Karl Kane! I told you from the moment I walked in here that I wasn't one hundred per cent. But when I read in the newspapers about the young girl found cut open, almost surgically, I kept seeing Bobby's face. And it wasn't a knife that was used to stab me, but a scalpel."

There was a moment of silence in the office before Karl asked, "You think he's used his surgical skills to kill these young girls?"

Ivana let out a sigh. Her shoulders appeared to shrink. She seemed on the brink of tears. "It's possible . . . I don't know . . ."

"I was going to ask why didn't you go to the cops, but I suppose I could answer that for you, remembering how they treated you, as if you were the perpetrator instead of the victim, the time you were stabbed."

"I'm so sorry I didn't come here earlier," said Ivana, her voice a whisper. "You probably both hate me because I didn't come with this sooner. I . . . I wasn't sure . . . still not sure . . ."

"We won't hear you talk like that, Ivana," said Naomi, hugging her. "It was brave of you to come forward, trying to help. Both Karl and I are so proud of you. Isn't that right, Karl?"

"Huh? Oh . . . of course we are. It took a lot of . . ." he almost said balls, but quickly decided against that particular word, under the circumstances ". . . courage."

"Look at the state of me," said Ivana, wiping a small gathering of tears away from her face, snot from her nose, as she stood to leave. "All my make-up is running all over the place. I'm a total mess."

"Don't you worry about that," soothed Naomi. "We're going upstairs. I'll have you looking as good as new for Vincent."

"There's something else, isn't there, Ivana? Something you're not telling us," said Karl, standing, looking directly into Ivana's eyes.

"I don't know what you're talking about."

"You came here to clear your conscience by telling us half a story, as if –"

"Karl!" shouted Naomi. "What on earth are you –?"

"A half-baked story, Ivana, that makes *you* feel better? You don't care about the young girls! You couldn't give a damn about –"

"I do!" screamed Ivana.

"Karl! That's enough," threatened Naomi.

"Tell me everything, Ivana! Not the bits that suit, but the bits that you fear, the bits that –"

"Karl! Enough!"

Ivana suddenly crumpled back down into the chair. "No . . . no, Naomi . . . he's right. I haven't been totally truthful."

Naomi's face suddenly reddened.

"Listen, Ivana," said Karl, his voice now calm. "You might still be harbouring feelings for Bobby, for helping you discover the truth about yourself, all those years ago, as a wee boy struggling to face an inhospitable world. But that was then, Ivana. This is now. If you know where he is, for the sake of any future victims, you've got to tell me – now, before it's too late."

Ivana's sobbing began filling the room, as Karl continued relentlessly but calmly.

"You were having a relationship with Bobby, before your sex change, weren't you? Is that why he attacked you? He felt betrayed that you had gone behind his back, become a woman, years later, the ultimate betrayal in the eyes of a very sick misogynist?"

Ivana dipped her head, nodding. "Yes."

"Where is he, Ivana? You must tell me."

Ivana shook her head. "I can't. They'll put him in prison to be killed, and it will be my fault they sent him there. In school, I was a bully's wet dream. I know what it's like to be picked on, day after day."

"He's *not* the victim, Ivana! He could be responsible for the murders of those young girls. You'd rather see more young girls butchered? Is that what you want? Did you really look at that poster of young Martina Ferris, her eyes?"

"Yes! Yes . . . I saw them . . . still seeing them . . ."

"Tell me where he is!"

"I can't!"

"You can and you *will!*" exploded Karl, slamming his fists on the table, making both Ivana and Naomi jump.

"Karl!" shouted Naomi. "There's no need for –"

"*Where* is he, Ivana?"

"I . . . I . . ."

"*Where?*"

"Okay . . . okay . . ." whispered Ivana. "I'll tell you where he might be."

It was a good fifteen minutes before Ivana confessed all that she knew, her face a map of tears and destroyed make-up. Naomi tried her best to comfort her by holding her tightly, whispering soothing words into her ear.

"There now, Ivana. It's all over. It's okay. You've been so brave. It's okay."

"Naomi's right, Ivana. You have been brave to come forward," admitted Karl. "Who the hell knows what I'd have done under the same circumstances?"

"There . . . there's one other thing," sniffed Ivana. "I don't know if it is important or not."

"Yes?" asked Karl, wondering what the hell else could be added to this hellish tale.

"When he was young, Bobby was an expert hunter and tracker."

Chapter Eleven

"Nothing contributes so much to tranquillize the mind as a steady purpose."
Mary Shelley, *Frankenstein*

He sat naked on a mound of sand and scraggy grass, watching the sea drain from the deserted shore. The drainage was leaving behind a solid emptiness weighing heavily on what remained. A bone-white moon kept intermingling with ghostly orange clouds, giving the night sky a dark red hue. The ozone coming off the shore brought a stench with it, not unlike the smell of blood now webbing in his nostrils.

As a boy, he loved visiting the seashore, catching crabs, turning them on their backs while he opened them up, seeing what made the creatures tick. But not tonight. Tonight, he was here for a totally different reason . . .

Standing, he walked back to his car, casually opening the boot, all the while feeling the moon washing over his naked body. Tiny electric shocks ran under his skin.

Delightful.

Hordes of gathering night moths suddenly brought a susurrus whisper to his ears. Their sound was reassuring, calming, and he began removing the carpet topping, exposing the blackness below.

The girl's body was wrapped tightly in black bin lining, like a putre-fied mummification. He could clearly see the nose stressing the texture, and the little "o" made by the startled mouth.

Bending, he leaned into the car's boot and kissed the startled mouth. It gave him fresh, redeeming shudders of electricity. Scooping the body up in his arms, the dead weight made his massive arm muscles bulge with strain. He listened for a few seconds to the quietness before proceeding towards the sandy tongue of shore. His movements were slow and delib-erate, like Frankenstein's godless creation slinking into the night.

The shore's edge was firm, but the more he progressed outwards towards the sea, the less stable the sand became, shifting its wet particles to accommodate his weight. Twice he almost stumbled, but the dead weight in his arms helped him to balance.

It was ten minutes later when the cold sea water finally reached just below his chest. He could feel its deceiving strength while buoying the body on the surface with one hand, ripping the bag open with the other.

She stared up at him from within the bag, one lifeless eye seemingly focusing over his shoulder at the moon. Her other eye was gone, and the empty socket was collecting water that rushed out and ran down her grey cheekbone as she bobbed in the sea. More water rushed to wash away the remnants of blood attached to the body, exposing a pale scar snaking from the hollow of her throat to the middle of her chest: the vestige of a furrow caused by deliberate and cruel hands.

Without warning, a baptismal wave suddenly swept over him, steal-ing the body from his grip. He struggled for control, but lost his balance to the surging water.

A few seconds later, she was gone. Free at last.

Chapter Twelve

"He's an oul butty o' mine – oh, he's a darlin' man,
a daarlin' man."
Sean O'Casey, *Juno and the Paycock*

"What are you going to do about the information Ivana gave us yesterday?" asked Naomi, sitting with her feet up on the sofa, a copy of *Northern Woman* by her side.

"Not much I *can* do except give it to the cops – which I did, early this morning, while you were snoring your pretty head and hangover off," said Karl, handing her a steaming cup of coffee. "I gave the info as an anonymous, concerned citizen, using my best Humphrey Bogart to disguise my own voice."

"You didn't call Wilson personally?" asked Naomi, a puzzled look appearing on her face. "I assumed –"

"You should never assume. Always remember that assume makes an arse out of u and me."

"Ass. It's *ass,* Karl. Not arse. I saw *The Silence of the Lambs,* as well."

"Yes, but this is the Belfast version," grinned Karl.

"What's going on with you and your brother-in-law, Karl? Something isn't right."

"*Ex*-brother-in-law. A family tiff. That's all. The less we see of each other, the better. Anyway, I spoke to Hicks about an hour ago, see if he knew what action the cops took. According to him, they're not going to do shit."

"Are you serious?"

"They said that Mister Robert Hannah is an upstanding member of the business community, and they more or less laughed at the suggestion that he could be involved in anything as terrible as abduction and murder."

"They're not even going to search the address Ivana gave us?"

"Mister Hannah is a generous contributor to the policeman's balls. Bit of a contradiction, policeman's balls, I know, but there you have it."

"Working-class kids against money?"

"You're starting to scare me, Naomi."

"I am?"

"Your thinking is parallel with my own."

"Great minds and all that?"

"Look, I've got to pop out for a little while," said Karl, reaching for his jacket.

"You've been popping out a lot lately," retorted Naomi.

"That's what one nudist said to the other."

"Very funny. Where exactly is it you're popping out *to?*"

"To see a Mister Smith, my dear," replied Karl, smiling, planting a kiss on Naomi's cheek. "Hopefully, I'll be back within the hour. Enjoy that lovely Rio coffee. Cost me a fortune."

"Be careful . . . please."

Seconds later, Karl went out the door carrying nothing but himself. It took him all of five minutes to locate the small, nondescript shop in Bridge Street, sandwiched between a shady-looking café and a dilapidated bakery short of dough. Outside the shop, a large painted sign proclaimed: **We Open the Doors Others Can't.**

Karl entered, immediately spotting a man in the far corner. The man had his broad back to Karl, and tiny sparks were dancing on either side of him as he bent into his work. Dust was everywhere. The heat inside the shop was horrendous. The man's large bulk seemed to be blotting out all oxygen in the room.

"Don't do anything foolish, old man, and everything will be a-okay," whispered Karl, leaning over the counter. "There's a gun pointed right at your back. I want your wife or your money. The choice is yours."

The sparks stopped dancing. The man's broad back stiffened. "You can have the money, but only on condition that you take the wife as well. She's upstairs, shaving her chin," said the man, turning slowly. He had the stocky build of an ex-boxer, his face mapped with tiny scars, missing teeth and a broken-down nose no longer in use.

Karl grinned. "How's business, Willie?"

"It scares the business out of me whenever I hear those words from your mouth, Karl. It always follows with a request," said Willie Morgan, turning to face Karl, a finished key in his hand.

"How's Isabel?"

"I haven't spoken to her in a week; I don't like to interrupt her," said Willie, reaching for his smokes, offering one to Karl before placing one in the V of his fingers. For such a stocky man, he held the cigarette rather daintily.

"I've never had so many offerings of cigarettes since I gave them up," moaned Karl, declining the cig. "How can you stick the heat in here? I've lost a pound just standing talking to you."

"I'm still waiting on your request," said Willie suspiciously, scratching the splinters of the short silvery hair on his well-used face, while doing a quick search of his pocket. Winningly producing a lighter, he lit the cig.

Karl listened to the paper and tobacco crackling, making him pine for the good old, bad old days of lung-staining enjoyment.

"I need a favour."

"I knew it," said Willie, shaking his head before inhaling deeply on the cig. "What is it?"

"It could mean breaking the law," supplied Karl. "No, actually, let me rephrase that. It *will* mean breaking the law."

"How do you know I haven't changed since the last time you saw me? I could be an upstanding member of the community."

"The weather can change, Willie; not you," said Karl, grinning.

"For someone who was going to be a cop and whose brother-in-law is a top detective, you fly awfully close to the sun. One day, your arse is going to be melted, like Icarus. You know that, don't you?"

"Thank you, Socrates, for those enlightening words."

"Now, what's this I hear about you in hospital, a few months back? An operation of some sort?"

"What?" said Karl, feeling his face reddening. "It . . . was nothing. Simply a check-up."

"I heard it was to have your haemorrhoids removed," stated Willie, staring directly into Karl's eyes.

"For fuck sake. Is nothing in this town sacred?"

"Well?"

"Well what?"

"How are they? Your piles?"

"If you really must know, they're a bit like Terry Wogan: extremely unfunny and full of shit," replied Karl. "Now, how about a cup of that infamous coffee of yours, the one they use for tar-and-feathering?"

"Flip the sign and bolt the door. I've done enough trade for today."

"Oh, almost slipped my mind," said Karl, flipping the sign on the door. "Any disposables?"

Willie's eyebrows moved slightly. "Only if need be."

"It's need-be time."

"I can tell there's something hairy coming up," sighed Willie, "and I bet it isn't my arse."

Karl watched Willie heading into a backroom, emerging less than a minute later with a wooden box.

"Something a bit more impressive than a box, please," said Karl, finding a tall stool at the counter before parking his bulk.

"Take a look at this baby," enthused Willie, opening the box, exposing a gun. "It's a beauty. A .357 Colt Python – the Rolls Royce of handguns because of its superior finish, high-quality parts, excellent accuracy and smooth trigger pull. This is the three-inch barrel version, favoured by undercover cops and *dodgy* PI's in the good old US of A – making *you* feel right at home in its company."

"No trace?"

"Not a hope. Serial number's been filed away. Stolen about three years ago from a cop's house. He was too embarrassed to report it missing, apparently," replied Willie, smiling secretively.

Karl held the weapon in his right hand, his thumb depressing the sharply knurled button to release the cylinder. Gentle pressure from the fingers of his left hand slipped the cylinder out of the metal stomach, exposing its contents. Clean light gleamed off the brass rims of the bullets bedded in their metal housing.

"You keep it fucking *loaded?*" asked Karl, taken aback.

"Would you keep a car with no petrol in it?"

"Point taken. What else do you have for me in your bag of tricks?"

"Here. Take a peep into the schoolhouse. Check the sleeping teachers."

"Teachers?"

"They help to teach people a lesson," replied Willie, grinning.

Peering into the box, Karl could see three bleak-looking items nestling snugly together like mummified corpses.

"Blackjacks? I suppose you could say that this brings new meaning to the term jack in the box," quipped Karl.

Removing one of the blackjacks, Willie slapped it hard against the palm of his beefy hand. "These are the best teachers in town. Besides, they're not just any old jacks. These are bludgeoning impact weapons used by the military, security and cops around the world. Professional grade construction, made of smooth black cowhide, loaded with spring steel. The manufacturers advise extreme caution when using. You have to laugh at that. When you hit a man with one of these babies, you don't wrap it in cotton wool or use extreme caution. They're covering their arse, of course. The responsibility is on you."

"You must have a stake in the company, the way you describe those so gleefully."

"I'm letting you know that just because they don't fire bullets, they're not any less lethal than a gun."

"Why three? Aren't they all the same, doing what they say on the label?"

"Are all guns the same?"

"Of course not."

"There you go, then. You've answered your own question. Take this one, for example," said Willie, holding out the jack in his hand. "It's a round jack. It concentrates force on the target and can actually break bones with relative ease. Whereas this one . . ." Willie removed another jack from the box. "This is the flat, spreading its force out on the target, increasing the severity of damage done to the skin but *without* breaking bones."

"You're enjoying this, aren't you?"

"Now this one?" continued Willie, unabated, removing the final jack from its housing. "This is my all-time favourite. The cylinder. Cops in Chicago used these during prohibition to take down the mob's so-called tough guys with one single slap upside the head. This coconut is guaranteed to knock the biggest ape in the jungle out. Your choice."

"So many to choose from. It's almost an embarrassment of riches," said Karl, doing an eeney-meeny-miney-mo with his index finger. "This one, I think. The flat."

"Sure? Do you still need the disposable, even with this?"

"Yes. Just a precaution. I'm like boxers, in that sense."

"What? You like to beat the crap out of people?"

"No," replied Karl, grinning. "I like covering my arse."

CHAPTER THIRTEEN

"A mistress should be like a little country retreat near the town,
not to dwell in constantly, but only for a night and away."
William Wycherley, *The Country Wife*

"W ould you prefer I dimmed the light?" asked Ivana, watching Vincent's anxious face while guiding him into the bedroom.

"I . . . don't know . . . I'm sorry . . . this is kind of new to me."

Ivana dimmed the light – but not too much.

"There's no wrong way to do this," she said smiling, trying desperately to reassure him.

He was blushing and looked on the verge of running from the room. His innocent face made her feel weak at the knees, the urge between her legs growing stronger by the second. She wanted him badly, but was terrified of scaring him away. Wanted it to be so good for both of them.

"Here, let me do it for you," said Ivana, touching his shirt, slowly unbuttoning it from the top down.

A static shock suddenly popped Ivana's fingers.

"Shit! Did you feel that? Are we electric or what?"

He grinned and then nodded. "Right through my chest. It was a cracker."

The shirt fell to the floor and he pushed out of his shoes, fumbling at the socks.

Ivana unbuckled his Levi's, revealing a pair of white Calvin Klein's. The front of the cotton material looked dark, heavy. She almost fainted with anticipation.

His hand went instinctively to holding the underwear. "I . . ."

"Shhhhhhhh. Easy . . ." she whispered, pulling gently but firmly on the offending garment, revealing a large but flaccid cock.

"I'm sorry," he whispered. "It's . . . it's just that I . . ."

Ivana went to the kneeling position, peeling the foreskin back, revealed a bulbous strawberry head. It looked shiny and new, untouched by human lips. She suddenly felt faint again.

"Oh my," she managed to whisper, before taking the shiny new toy in her mouth, taking it all the way to the cock's border where sac and balls meet.

He moaned.

She found it difficult to moan, but did her best while repositioning herself, wiggling out of panties, all the while holding him in her mouth.

He was getting bigger by the second.

Defeated, she quickly came up for air.

"Whoa, big fella! You get any bigger and I'll have to call a lumberjack."

He laughed. There was edgy relief in the laughter.

"That was . . . that was great, Ivana."

"Ha! We haven't even started, lover," said Ivana, quickly removing the remainder of clothing, pulling him headlong on to the bed.

"I . . . don't have a condom," admitted Vincent. "I walked out without one."

"Usually my rule is no glove, no love," said Ivana, grinning. "Luckily for you, I've a larger supply than Boots."

From a top drawer, she removed a box of opened Trojan condoms, and extracted one.

"Lock and *load*," she quipped, releasing the condom from its greasy enclosure, before slipping it expertly over the hardening cock. "Extra large."

Less than a minute later, resting on her back, Ivana watched Vincent's head manoeuvring over her body; felt the texture of his wonderful tongue do wonderful things. It feasted on her nipples, suck suck sucking like some greedy baby, thirsty for milk. On it went, travelling down, exploring the bellybutton before quickly moving to the moist, sensitive area between her legs.

"*Ohhhhhh . . .*" she moaned, closing her eyes, feeling his muscular body gliding upwards before straddling her. There was an urgency to his movement. Slightly awkward. Almost virginal.

While Vincent slipped into her, an idea suddenly slipped into her mind – unwelcome, unbidden, shocking in its content. She wanted to have her cock back, just this once, and fuck young Vincent in the arse. The image was there, so convincing. Sex, like some roaring train: piston halves pumping, motor chugging, everything rattling. She hated to admit it, but at times like this, she missed her old meaty member and its power to fire her up . . .

Just over an hour later, they began dressing. The smell of post-sex was heavy in the room. It smelt like dead flowers and wet talc. A cool breeze filtered in from an open window, bringing with it the hush of traffic faintly humming in the background.

There would be no more sex tonight, much to Ivana's frustration. *The so-called youth of today,* thought Ivana. She had tried stroking and sucking his cock, but she might as well have been handling a wet sock, for all the good it did. Vincent's manhood had disappeared back into the hood and was refusing to come back out, no matter how much tender loving care she promised it.

"You . . . were great," said Vincent, face flushed. "It wasn't what I expected."

"Thank you, Simon Cowell, for your vote. You were curious to fuck a transsexual? Is that what this was all about?" She hadn't intended to sound so bitter.

"No . . . I mean . . . I didn't know what to expect. That's all. I fancied you from the first time I saw you in Billy Holiday's. I just didn't realise you could be so sensitive . . . tender . . ."

"The Ivana in Billy Holiday's isn't the real Ivana, Vincent, dear boy. I play into people's perception of me. It's a game, a charade I play, measuring out my life in perfect coloured pills. They help take away all the nastiness and loneliness."

"You . . . you're crying." he said, his face suddenly anxious. "Did I do or say something you didn't like or want to do?"

She leaned to his face, kissing him lovingly, while harnessing herself back into a silky black bra.

"No. You didn't do anything wrong, dear Vincent, only the joy to make me think one last time of an old friend, dead and gone."

Alone two hours later, after Vincent's departure, Ivana sat listening to the radio's *Oldies but Goldies*.

"Things are finally beginning to look up," she said, wishing it were tomorrow night, when she would be with Vincent once again. "Vincent, Vincent, Vincent . . ."

The thought of his youthful body pouring itself all over her gave Ivana a lovely shiver. She felt a hot flush and wetness coming on between her legs. Thought about the large pink dildo in the top drawer; considered furnishing herself with it and doing some delightful fucking.

"Should I or shouldn't I?"

Blinkingly, something caught her eye. Something on the carpet, round and shiny.

Bending, she picked the item up before studying it. It made her heart beat in a bad way. A wedding ring.

"Oh, Vincent . . . you silly, silly boy."

Suddenly the doorbell buzzed, interrupting her soliloquy.

Quickly fisting the ring, she pocketed it before standing, glancing quickly in the mirror. Lipstick. Hair. Teeth. Everything looked in place. She quickly fanned her face, cooling it down a tad.

The bell buzzed, once more.

There's no fool like an old fool, she thought, opening the door, dreading the lies she would hear, but willing to forgive.

"Hello, Francis."

Chapter Fourteen

"World is crazier and more of it than we think . . ."
Louis MacNeice, "Snow"

K arl entered his office just as the early Friday morning sun began rising over Belfast's dishevelled skyline. Naomi would hopefully be sound asleep – thank goodness – though this time he wasn't dreading a confrontation.

His clothes stank of cigarette smoke and spilt liquor as he began peeling them off before stepping into the shower.

While the water washed away his stench, he kept thinking of his winning hands at the card game, over the past six hours. Three aces. Three kings. Numerous straights. And then the final *coup de grâce:* a royal fucking flush!

He could simply do no wrong. If he wasn't a grown man, he would have wept with joy.

Showered and dried, he counted his winnings, again. Almost one thousand, nine hundred quid – a small fortune, at the moment. And to add to his pleasure, most of it taken from that cheap prick Marty Harrington, owner of a chain of funeral parlours – Heavenly Harrington's – peppered throughout the city. Unlike Karl, though, Harrington *did* weep.

Thirty minutes later, a naked Karl crawled between the bed sheets, squeezing in close to Naomi's deliciously warm body. She stirred and growled in protest at the coldness of his touch.

Disregarding the warning, he snuggled in closer, inhaling her early morning, womanly smell.

"Leave me alone," she hissed, turning away from him, offering up the emptiness of her back. "You didn't mind leaving me alone all night."

Her early morning hoarseness was titillating. He felt an erection stirring.

"It's time to get up, sleepyhead." He nuzzled her neck and stroked her warm bum. "I have an early morning present for you."

"You know where to stick your early morning present, don't you? And it's not near me. Get your hands off my arse."

"Don't be like that, love."

She opened her eyes and blinked a couple of times. "I have to pee."

He pressed hard against her bum, his erection adding an exclamation mark between her buttocks.

Yawning, she tried moving out of his grasp. He held her close, resisting her feeble efforts.

"I *have* to pee," she whined, getting out of bed. "I can't hold it in."

"Be quick, my dearest."

"Get stuffed," she pronounced, walking towards the bathroom, braless breasts bouncing seductively, small buttocks see-sawing mischievously. As she passed the window, morning sunlight wafted in around the curtains and stole through her thin cotton T-shirt, tantalising him with the silhouette of her nakedness hidden beneath.

"Hurry, my dearest . . ." he sang.

She mumbled something nasty before scurrying into the bathroom, slamming the door loudly behind her. A few seconds later, Karl could hear the toilet seat falling, followed by the familiar tinkling sounds. It made him think of his royal flush, again.

Less than a minute later, Naomi re-emerged, poker-faced. He couldn't help but grin at the T-shirt's slogan: **The only Bush I trust is my own**. A glaring caricature of George Bush, depicted as a monkey, looked down upon Karl disapprovingly.

"Your T-shirt's a bit out of date, don't you think?"

"I'm not talking to you, Karl Kane."

"You just did."

"Well, you can put that tiny dick back in its matchbox. It's not lighting my fire any time soon."

"*Oh*. You sure know how to crunch a man's ego," smiled Karl. "How does two nights in Dublin at the Shelbourne sound, with five hundred quid for your good self thrown in?"

"What?" Her drowsy face suddenly looked alert. "What did you say?"

"Thought you weren't talking to me?"

"You won, last night? *Didn't* you?" a smile was slowly emerging on Naomi's morning face. "Tell me you won."

"I won!" exclaimed Karl, suddenly pulling the sheets away, exposing his full meaty erection resting beside a wad of money. "*Big!*"

"Oh, Karl. For little me?" smiled Naomi, falsely fluttering eyelashes, approaching the bed on tiptoes.

"For you! *Come!* And I mean that in more ways than one, you sexy thing, you."

Naomi practically leapt from the floor on to the bed and into Karl's waiting arms, money and erection.

That was when his mobile phone rang on the bedside table.

"Shouldn't you answer that?" whispered Naomi hoarsely into his ears, her hand cupping his balls as if weighing them.

"Answer what? I don't hear a thing except the sound of someone playing 'Tubular Bells' on my balls."

The phone stopped ringing.

Both Naomi and Karl smiled.

It rang again.

"Fucking nuisance! I'm turning it off," said Karl, reaching for the accursed piece of plastic.

"No . . . don't. You better answer it. It could be important."

"What's more important than early morning sex with the woman I love?"

The phone continued ringing.

Naomi reached and handed it to him. "Just answer it. We still have a business to run, despite all your winnings."

Sighing, Karl spoke into the phone. "Yes? Tom? This better be damn –"

For the next thirty seconds, Naomi watched the blood siphon from Karl's face.

"What is it, Karl?" she asked, as soon as he clicked off the phone, two minutes later. "What's wrong?"

The sun spilling into the room accentuated the lines on Karl's suddenly weary face.

"That . . . that was Hicks. It's . . . it's Ivana. She's been murdered."

Chapter Fifteen

"Death must be so beautiful. To lie in the soft brown earth,
with the grasses waving above one's head, and listen to silence.
To have no yesterday, and no to-morrow. To forget time, to
forgive life, to be at peace."
Oscar Wilde, *The Canterville Ghost*

Approximately a quarter of a million people have been buried on the site of Belfast City Cemetery, including politicians, inventors and writers such as Robert Wilson Lynd, one of the finest scribes Belfast has ever produced and friend to J.B. Priestly and James Joyce. The cemetery itself is dotted with beautiful cast-iron fountains and even boasts its own stream running through it. Local myth claims the stream is a purification, washing away the sins of forgotten and lost souls.

Over the years, Karl had attended numerous funerals at the cemetery, some sparsely attended, others labelled "a good turn out". But nothing had prepared him for the gathering crowd from the gay and transsexual community thronging the grounds as Ivana's pink coffin was slowly being eased into the clay on this clear-skied Wednesday morning. Local news reporters – predictors of a circus-type funeral the day before – seemed bitterly disappointed at the dignity of the mourners and onlookers, and suddenly became instrumental in fulfilling their own dark prophecy by acting like clowns, jumping over nestling headstones like horses at the Grand National as they jostled for position using cameras and elbows as weapons.

Granted, a goodly number of mourners *were* dressed in brassy outfits of orange, pink and rainbow-coloured garments, but the vast majority – including Karl and Naomi – wore sombre blacks and greys.

"Oh Karl," sniffed Naomi. "Poor poor Ivana . . . she . . . she never did anyone any . . . any harm. Did she?"

"No. Of course not," replied Karl, his suspicious and cynical mind thinking the opposite.

"But why . . . why poor Ivana?"

"I really don't know, love," replied Karl, wondering the exact same question.

"Has Tom told you anything about how it happened?"

"The cops have stated it was a burglary gone bad. There's been a spate of them in that area over the last two months. They're working on the theory that it's the same person or persons," replied Karl, deliberately omitting the grisly details of Ivana's gruesome murder: her throat had been cut from ear to ear, almost severing the head.

Naomi sniffed more, dabbing tears with a wet Kleenex. "They're evil . . . evil, Karl."

"Hello," said a voice, directly behind Karl and Naomi, interrupting the conversation.

Turning, Karl stared directly into the face of Detective Malcolm Chambers.

"Hello," said Karl, trying to control the rise in his voice. "Naomi, this is Detective Malcolm Chambers, one of Detective Inspector Mark Wilson's *new* and *improved* men."

"Oh . . . hello," sniffed Naomi, reaching out her hand.

"Hello," responded Chambers, smiling, shaking Naomi's hand before directing his attention back to Karl. "This is weird, but I still don't know *your* name."

"What are you doing here?" asked Karl, easing Naomi back, closer, away from the smiling Chambers.

"I've been put in charge of the Gilmore murder inquiry."

"The Gilmore ? Oh . . . Ivana." Hearing Ivana's surname being spoken was almost alien to Karl's ears. "Don't take offence, Detective, but just how many murder inquiries have you been involved *in?*"

"This . . . this is actually my first."

"It's good to see the police are taking this seriously," replied Karl, sarcastically.

"Have you any suspects, Detective Chambers?" asked Naomi.

"Well . . ." Chambers looked uncertain. "Actually, the inquiry is ongoing, and I'm not supposed to divulge anything to the public."

"We're . . . we were Ivana's best friends. Practically family," assured Naomi. "Surely you could tell us?"

Chambers glanced over his shoulder. A police photographer stood a few yards away, snapping pictures of the mourners and gathering onlookers. "We have a suspect in custody."

"Oh my goodness!" exclaimed Naomi.

"That was quick," said Karl, his face knotting slightly. "Who is it?"

"Please, don't breathe a word of this to anyone – especially the media."

"No. Of course not," said Naomi, easing closer to the young detective.

"A Mister Vincent Harrison. He was seen leaving the Gilmore house at the time of the murder."

Naomi's face paled. "Oh my goodness."

"He's denying everything, of course, but it's only a matter of time before he admits it. Initially, we thought it was a burglary gone wrong. But we got a tip from a member of the public on the confidential phone line, stating they saw Harrison leave Gilmore's house at the time of the murder."

"That was nice and confidentially convenient," stated Karl.

"You sound almost disappointed," replied Chambers.

"Forgive my scepticism. Being an agnostic probably has something to do with it."

"Well, *we* know for certain that Ivana had a date with Harrison," cut in Naomi. "She told us that only a few days ago."

"She did? That's great," proclaimed Chambers. "That's a vital piece of information that could strengthen our case against Harrison's denial, Naomi."

"No," corrected Karl. "That's *hearsay*. We don't know for a fact that Harrison ever went to Ivana's. And we certainly aren't *certain* of it, at all. Just what Ivana told us, at the time. It's circumstantial and would be thrown out of any court in the land."

"No need to be so gruff, Karl," admonished Naomi, face flushing slightly. "I'm only telling Detective Chambers what Ivana said to us."

"You seem to know a lot about the law . . . Karl," said Chambers.

"I know a lot about everything, which makes me an expert on nothing."

"Well, the evidence is piling up against Harrison, and that certainly won't be hearsay."

"What evidence?" asked Karl, not expecting an answer.

"I . . . I shouldn't really be discussing it."

"You can tell us," said Naomi. "We won't tell a soul. Promise."

Chambers looked at Naomi, and then at Karl, before returning his gaze back to Naomi. "We found a wedding ring at the scene. It was traced to Lunn's jewellers, in Queen's Arcade. It was one of a pair specifically designed for Harrison and his wife, Sinead."

"He . . . he was married?" asked Naomi, her face failing to hide the shock.

"Two years. His poor wife fainted when she heard the news. Probably more stunned about her husband having sex with a . . ." Chambers's voice suddenly trailed off. "I mean . . . you know . . ."

"A transsexual? You can say the word," said Karl, feeling a bubble of anger rising to the surface. "If the world had more Ivanas, it would be a far better place."

"I didn't mean it in that way."

"No, of course you didn't. Tell me, Detective Chambers. Have you ever heard of a man by the name of Robert Hannah?"

Chambers suddenly looked uneasy.

"I . . . don't think so. Why? Why do you ask?"

"Oh, I don't know. Probably just plucked his name out of the air. Now, if you'll excuse us, we have to go," said Karl, gripping Naomi's elbow before heading off towards the far gate of the cemetery.

"What's wrong with you?" asked Naomi, as they reached the gate.

"He's only trying to find justice for Ivana."

"Who? Charming Chambers with his Tom Cruise smirk? He couldn't find a needle if the thread was still attached."

"He gave us information not available to the public. Don't you believe what he told us about Harrison?"

"I believe Harrison did what most married men would do when confronted with having an affair – especially an affair with a transsexual. He denied it. Now the cops are wasting time, hoping to coerce a so-called confession out of Harrison, when in fact, they should be out there focusing on the real murderer. Want to know something interesting?"

"What?"

"Remember I told you I passed that information about Hannah on to the cops?"

"Yes."

"Well, it was smiling Detective Malcolm Chambers who took the call."

"Oh."

"Oh, indeed. And he just claimed never to have heard of Hannah."

"I think I need a drink."

"You read my mind. Come on. Let's go," replied Karl, easing Naomi towards the car, but not before looking over his shoulder just in time to see Detective Malcolm Chambers instructing the police photographer to aim the camera lens in Karl's direction.

CHAPTER SIXTEEN

"Man is a creature who lives not upon bread alone,
but principally by catchword."
Robert Louis Stevenson, *Virginibus Puerisque*

Karl's mobile rang as he was about to leave the office. He checked the number. "Number withheld", said the screen.

"Hello?"

"Mister Kane?" said an archaic voice. "Mister Karl Kane?"

"Yes . . . who's this?"

"You've been very naughty, Mister Kane."

"Really? Listen, if this is about getting spanked, I'm seriously not into it – at least not by a man. So you take care and –"

"You're involving yourself in things that are really no concern of yours."

"People tell me that all the time, Mister . . . ?"

"I'm not people, Mister Kane. I believe you've already been told quite a bit about me by a passing friend of yours."

"Really?" The hairs on the back of Karl's neck started nipping as he began searching frantically for a tape recorder in the top drawer of the desk. "Friend? What friend would that be, Mister . . . ?" *Where the hell is the damn thing!*

"Oh, I'm sure you know the friend in question – no longer with us,

I'm afraid, buried two days ago. You really need to mind your own business, Mister Kane, rather than mine. Do you watch movies?"

"All the time. It's all I do." *Where the fuck is that piece of crap?*

"Remember what happened to Jack Nicholson in *Chinatown,* sticking his nose where it didn't belong?"

"Vaguely." *Found it!* Karl quickly clicked a button.

"Good day, Mister Kane."

"Who was that?" asked Naomi, just as Karl slammed the tape recorder back into the drawer.

"What? Oh *that?"* said Karl, looking at his mobile. "If I told you, you wouldn't believe me."

"Try me," replied Naomi, folding her arms, waiting.

"Some dirty old dog wanting to spank me. I wouldn't have minded if it'd been a woman."

Naomi burst out laughing. "*I* can believe it. He probably spotted you walking about the town and saw that sexy wiggle of yours."

"You mean this one?" Karl began wiggling his arse.

Naomi's laughter became louder.

"You're such a tease, Karl Kane."

"I know. You wait until I get back later tonight, then we'll get serious about the spanking," said Karl, kissing her quickly on the cheek. "I'm off to see Tom. Find out if he has heard anything through the grapevine."

Leaving the office, he displayed little of the unease he now suddenly felt.

CHAPTER SEVENTEEN

"Of malice or of sorcery, or that power
Which erring men call Chance, this I hold firm,
Virtue may be assailed, but never hurt;
Surprised by unjust force, but never enthralled."
Milton, *Comus*

It was getting late, and Karl was feeling tired as he walked down Hill Street towards home. The day hadn't been too fruitful. Hicks's information had been sketchy at best. What little information there was available about Bob Hannah certainly wasn't being shared – at least not with those outside Wilson's magic circle.

Already darkness was settling in as Karl fumbled for his keys outside the office.

"Got a light?" asked a figure standing in the shadowy doorway, cigarette dangling from his mouth.

Karl was about to reply when he saw – too late – the fist shooting up like a meaty rocket, sparks tailing it before impact. He had never – at least as far as he could remember – been whacked across the side of the head with a frozen Moy Park chicken. If he had, he held little doubt that this was exactly the way it would have felt after being smacked in the face by this great slab of hand and knuckles.

It wasn't the pain so much as the surprise. Karl quickly tried steadying.

Tried balling fists into defensive mode. Tried. Failed. His knees began buckling.

Another rocket hit him in the chin. He felt a bone in his face snap.

"I said, do you have a light?" asked Mister Moy Park, calmly, landing another frozen chicken rocket to Karl's solar plexus.

Struggling to keep the lights on in his head, Karl reached for the wall, trying desperately to steady himself. He failed, hitting the ground, banging his head off the pavement, bloodying.

Suddenly, darkness came running at him.

"You don't look so bad," said Mister Moy Park, hovering his boot over Karl's face before crunching down on it.

Karl felt the impact on the bridge of his nose seconds before Darkness took him into its loving arms.

Chapter Eighteen

"It's an odd job, making decent people laugh."
Molière, *La Critique de Pecole des Femmes*

K arl? *Karl?*
Voices in my head. A whirling of maimed thoughts. Been having a lot of that lately.

"Karl? *Karl?* Can you hear me?"

"Huh?" *Terrible pain. Feels like a train wreck.*

"Karl?"

"Where . . . where am I?"

"Karl!"

"Naomi?"

"Oh, Karl," whispered Naomi, practically throwing herself on top of him. He tried wrapping his arms around her, but his arms felt lethargic. He didn't recognise his surroundings.

"Where . . . where am I, Naomi?"

"You bastard, Karl Kane! Don't you ever do this to me again!" she exclaimed, kissing his battered face. "Scaring the fucking shit out of me."

"You . . . you just used the 'f' word, Naomi Kirkpatrick. That's the . . . that's the first time I've ever heard you swear like that. What's gotten into . . . you?"

"That's you rubbing off on me. I could kill you, for what you've put me through."

Karl tried desperately to chisel bits and pieces of information from the block of nothing in his mind. All he could conjure up were frozen Moy Park chickens, flying at him from every direction.

"You still haven't answered my question, Naomi. Where the hell am I?"

"In hospital."

"What? You know I hate bloody hospitals. Get me the hell out of – *ohhhhhh* . . ." He shifted the weight from his aching ribs. "My ribs? Are they busted?"

"No, thank goodness. Just badly bruised. The doctor said you were lucky that you didn't –"

"Yeah. Lucky's my middle name – *ohhhhhh,*" moaned Karl, easing out of the bed. "Where're my clothes? Get my stuff, Naomi. I'm getting out of here."

"But the doctor said –"

"To hell with the doctor. He doesn't have to pay the bloody medical bills. Where are my clothes?"

Reluctantly, Naomi opened up the door of a tiny metal locker adjacent to the bed and began removing Karl's clothes.

"You're going nowhere, Mister Kane," said a nurse, appearing as Karl's bare feet touched the floor.

"I'm going home, sister, and there's nothing you can do. Naomi? Give me those pants."

"Karl, listen to Nurse Williams. Please," replied Naomi, holding the bundle of clothes in her arms.

"You've been very badly beaten, Mister Kane."

"That's a revelation?"

"You have a possible hairline fracture in your chin."

"My hairline is going thin?"

"Stop being smart, Karl," admonished Naomi.

"You need to stay here for at least a day, Mister Kane, in case of internal bleeding."

"I appreciate your concern, Nurse Williams, and all that you've done, but if I don't leave now, my wallet will be the one having internal bleeding. I really must get going."

"But . . . but the police? They want to interview you, see if you can give them any information on your attacker."

"Tell them he had long flowing blond hair, a winged helmet and goes by the name of Thor. He's the one who gave me the hammering."

Nurse Williams looked taken aback.

"Please forgive his ignorance, Nurse Williams," pleaded Naomi. "He's still a child at heart – a very spoilt child."

"Naomi, for the last time," replied Karl, "will you *give* me those pants, or do I walk out of here commando style?"

"Did you get a look at him, Karl?" asked Naomi, helping Karl ease on to the sofa near the window, an afternoon sun brightening up an otherwise gloomy setting.

"Well, his name could have been Campbell, because his hands were huge soup plates and he hit me with fifty-seven varieties," grimaced Karl. "Can you hand me some of those painkillers, please, my loveliest love? And a glass of Hennessy to wash away the hospital aftertaste in my mouth."

"Hennessy and painkillers? I don't think so. You'll take water or have them dry."

"You're a bloody torturer. Know that?"

"What did he steal from you?"

"Huh?"

"Have you checked what he stole from you, this mugger?"

"I can do all that, later, once I get –"

"I checked. He took nothing. Isn't that a bit strange, a mugger leaving your wallet and mobile phone?"

"Who's the private investigator here, Naomi? You looking to take my job?" replied Karl, forcing a grin while licking at a swollen upper lip.

"Is that an answer?"

"Look, he was . . . he was probably surprised when he heard you opening the door. Now, can I have those painkillers, *please?* You're starting to act like Kathy Bates in *Misery.*"

"Don't insult my intelligence. We both know he wasn't a mugger, Karl."

"Do we?"

"Belfast is becoming so dangerous," said Naomi, filling a glass with water at the sink before handing it along with two painkillers to Karl.

A wry smile appeared on Karl's battered face. "You mean compared to the days when the IRA and British army topped the bill, shooting the hell out of each other? Nowadays, we have Westlife and Boyzone topping the bill at the Waterfront – though to be totally honest, I don't think they're much of an improvement."

"I'm serious, Karl."

"Ironic, isn't it? Bombs and bullets as an everyday occurrence, and bizarrely we felt safer than we do now with packs of marauding thugs looking to beat the fuck out of any poor bastard in their way."

"He had to know you, Karl. This wasn't random."

"Didn't fool you, eh?"

"Look. I've something to say. Don't get angry. Okay?" said Naomi, looking slightly uncomfortable. "You know my parents are thinking of retiring soon, don't you?"

"You've mentioned it," replied Karl, popping the painkillers into his mouth, followed by a sip of water.

"Well . . . we could take over from them."

Karl coughed loudly. The painkillers almost popped back out. "Run their motel in Derrybeg?"

"Why not? You make it sound like a fate worse than death."

"Is my name Basil?"

"What?"

"Could you imagine me running a motel? It would end up like Fawlty fucking Towers – a complete disaster. Please, don't make me laugh. It hurts too much."

"No, it wouldn't be a disaster. You'd be great at it – you're great at everything you do."

"Have you been drinking Bacardi? If getting beat up on a regular basis makes me great, then you're right – I'm the Einstein of Belfast."

"At least I wouldn't have to worry about you each time you leave, wondering what's happened when you're late coming home at night." Naomi looked away.

"What on earth are you crying for?"

"I'm not crying!" proclaimed Naomi, quickly wiping her eyes. "I'm tired. That's all!"

"C'mere you," said Karl, patting the sofa.

"What?"

"C'mon. Sit beside me for a wee while. I can feel the kick of those painkillers you gave me. I'll be asleep in a minute. Sure they were painkillers?"

Naomi sat down, and Karl pulled her tight to him, kissing her eyes, her nose, mouth.

"I love you so much," he said. "If that's what you want, we'll pack up and leave this dirty auld town. Whadda ya say, kid?"

"You wouldn't be happy." She began sniffling again. "You love Belfast, no matter how much you moan and complain about it."

"Ha! You really have been on the Bacardi, my dear. I hate this old whore with a passion. Love to see the back of her." Karl stole a glance in the side table mirror and was immediately shocked by the wasted look on his face. Thankfully, the pills were starting to kick in, flattening his feelings.

I'm cursed to stay here for ever. I'm Belfast born, bred and buttered, were his last thoughts as sleep stole him away.

Chapter Nineteen

"Everyone lives by selling something."
Robert Louis Stevenson, *Across the Plains*

"Karl? A Mister Lennon to see you," said Naomi, standing at the office door.

Glancing from this morning's *Racing Form,* Karl asked, "John or Vladimir?"

"Pardon?"

"His name. How's it spelt? Like one of the Beatles or the communist?"

"What on earth are you mumbling about?"

"Nothing. Just showing my age," replied Karl, sighing. "Show him in."

"Are you sure you're up to seeing anyone? It's only been a week since the assault. The hospital said it should be a fortnight, at least, before you start doing any sort of work."

"In the private investigating business, one week *is* a fortnight. Perhaps I should take a Polaroid of my face and send it to that decent, all-loving landlord of ours? Think he'll let us skip rent for a few months until my mug heals? Perhaps he'll pay the hospital bills while he's at it?"

"You can be very ignorant and nasty at times."

"Only at times?"

Seemingly on the verge of a verbal joust, Naomi simply shook her head and walked out of the room, muttering something inaudible under her breath.

A few seconds later, a stocky, well-built man entered and, sitting down, placed a black leather briefcase on Karl's desk. The man's face looked soft and spongy, with big acne holes drilled into his drinker's plum-coloured nose and ruddy cheeks. His hands were large, with crescents of dirt under his fingernails.

"Good day, Karl. I'm Stanley Lennon. As in Beatle, to answer your question. How's it going?" he said with a broad smile, seven o'clock shadow crawling over it like a raw nappy rash.

"Must get thicker walls installed," semi-smiled Karl, resenting immediately Lennon's excessive familiarity.

"Did you get the name of the driver?" A smell like battery acid kept emanating from Lennon's mouth, each time he spoke.

"What driver?" asked Karl, puzzled.

"The bus driver who did that to your face!" Lennon slapped his legs, grinning, the nappy rash spreading quickly.

"What exactly is it you want, Mister Lennon?" asked Karl, testily.

"Stanley. Call me Stanley, Karl. Everyone does."

"Okay . . . Stanley. What can I do for you?"

Lennon's smile suddenly relaxed and there was something about the smothering smirk that needled Karl.

"It's what *I* can almost certainly do for *you*, Karl," said Lennon, opening the lips of the briefcase. "Do you know what I have in here?"

Shrugging his shoulders, Karl replied, "Your briefs? If so, I hope they're clean."

"That's funny. I was told you were funny."

"Okay. I give up. What do you have in your briefcase, if not your briefs?"

"The best painkiller known to man," replied Lennon, removing five tiny bricks of twenties waist-banded with fat, red elastic bands. "I represent a client wishing to remain anonymous," said Lennon. "There's five thousand in twenties, Karl. Count it."

"I've seen enough movies to know the amount is probably correct.

I've also seen enough movies to know it isn't free and usually ends up costing more than its sum," said Karl, leaning slightly over his desk towards Lennon. "This is the part when the good guy – usually Humphrey Bogart – says whatever you're selling, pal, I sure as hell ain't buying."

Lennon's smile widened.

If his greasy fried egg smile gets any broader, it'll slip from his face, thought Karl.

"You don't have to buy a single thing, Karl. These are free samples. Take away all your debts and pain."

"What exactly is it this anonymous client of yours wants?"

"He wishes you to take a little holiday," grinned Lennon, winking. "Somewhere sunny and good for your health."

"*Hmm.* I see . . ." replied Karl, scratching his chin before looking at his watch. "I'm sorry, Stanley, I can't stand the sun. I'm easily burnt – been burnt quite a few times, truth be told. Now, if you don't mind, I've other clients to see. Tell Mister Anonymous that he might be the one taking a holiday soon. A very long holiday."

Standing, Lennon returned the bricks to the briefcase, snapping it shut. "For such a street-smart person, you seem rather dumb, Karl. Good day."

"Sorry for being so *brief,* Stanley."

Less than a minute later, Naomi appeared at the door.

"What was all that about?"

"Just a salesman trying to sell."

"What was he selling?"

"Dirty underwear and uncertainties."

"Well, he certainly wants to change that aftershave he wears. Must have bathed in it." Naomi waved her hands about, distilling the air. "*Phew.* What a stink."

"Yes, he certainly had a smell of trouble about him," said Karl, reaching for his haemorrhoids cream. His arse was tingling terribly, just like *Spiderman.*

Chapter Twenty

"Be nice to people on your way up because you'll meet
the same people on your way down."
Wilson Mizner, *The Legendary Mizners*

Stanley Lennon pushed open the door to his Lisburn Road home, shortly after midnight, placing his briefcase on a small mahogany table residing in the hallway. Bending, he retrieved the morning's mail languishing on the mat. Bills, mostly, mixing with the unbearable wastage of junk.

"Damn junk mail. They should get a –"

"Hello, Stanley," said a voice, emerging from the living room.

"What the –!"

The blackjack slipped expertly down the sleeve of Karl's coat, into his curved fingers. The blow struck Lennon on the side of the head as he turned, sending him spiralling to the ground.

"My father always said that the mightiest oak can be felled by the tiniest of blades," said Karl, admiring the jack in his hand while towering over the moaning Lennon. "He obviously wasn't bullshitting."

"Oh," groaned Lennon, hand instinctively touching the side of his large head.

"Don't worry. No leakage of blood – *yet.*"

"Kane? Have you . . . have you gone insane?"

"You can call me Karl, *Stanley.* Everyone does. And to answer your question, yes, I'm insane in the membrane," replied Karl, whacking Lennon again, this time on the shoulder.

"*Argghhhh!* . . . God the night . . . You fucking mad bastard!"

"Language! Didn't your parents – if you had any – teach you about swearing, you fucking bastard?" *Whack! Whack! Whack!* Lennon's legs the target.

"*Ahhhhhhhhhhh!*"

"You got everything in reverse, Stanley. The carrot and the stick. You were supposed to offer me the money first; then the beating."

"I . . . I don't know what you're fucking blabbering about."

"You said this morning that the money in your briefcase would take away my pain. Remember? Well, I kind of like my pain. Over the last few days, I've actually grown quite fond of it. Even given it a name. Want to know what I call it?"

"No. Just keep away from me, you sick bastard."

"*Can't-wait-to-find-the-prick-who-done-this-to-my-face-so-that-I-can-kick-the-shit-out-of-him pain,*" hissed Karl. "I know it sounds kind of longwinded, but I'm working on an abbreviation."

"What . . . what's this all about?" Lennon's anguished face was quickly imploding within itself. "This . . . fucking pain's unbelievable."

"I never did see the prick who attacked me that night, but he had obviously taken a swim in Brut aftershave. Funny, but isn't that the same shit you almost suffocated us with in the office this morning? Also, he suffered from halitosis. His breath stank like rotting battery acid. My intuition tells me the attacker wasn't a kick-in-the-arse off six two, weighing in at about two hundred and forty pounds of solid muscle. Big Coco the Clown shoes, just like the ones you're wearing right now. Probably had a seven o'clock shadow dripping from his face, and a grin of a paedophile."

Lennon's face tightened. "I wouldn't sully a man's reputation by accusing him of being a fucking paedo, Kane."

"You're *working* for one, scumbag. Want some more information? You used to be a cop. One of the so-called heavy-squad from Glenfield, in Carrickfergus. See? I know everything there is to know about you, Stanley, even have your new home address in Ballymena." Karl whacked Lennon across the ankles.

Lennon screamed like a banshee with its hair caught in a mangle.

"Scream like that again and I'll stuff a pair of briefs in your mouth, tough guy." *Whack!* The left shoulder blade.

"*Ohhhhhhh . . .*" groaned Lennon. "*Please . . .* why are you doing this? Money? You want more money?"

"Listen carefully, Mister Moy Park. You made a trilogy of errors the night you attacked me. Don't compound them now by lying. Otherwise, I'll have to get serious," said Karl, producing the .357 Colt Python before pressing it tight against Lennon's quickly perspiring forehead.

"*Please . . . don't . . .*"

"I want you to inform Mister Anonymous that I'm coming for him. I know the scumbag murdered Ivana, and I won't rest until justice is done – one way or the other." *Whack!* The back of the neck with the jack.

Lennon bit down on the sleeve of his coat, groaning, his fingers curling inwards.

"What's wrong, tough guy?" asked Karl, perspiring badly, bending on one knee while inspecting his handiwork. "Don't mind dispensing it, but hate being the recipient?"

Blood was flowing from Lennon's mouth. He spat, and a thick wad landed at Karl's feet. "You better . . . better kill me, Kane . . . you bastard . . ."

"Oh, *I* don't need to kill you, Stanley. Do you know what profession my brother-in-law represents?"

"He . . . he's a cop."

"A cop?" Karl laughed. "That's a bit like saying the pope's an altar boy. No, my dearest brother-in-law isn't simply a cop. He's the chief of fucking detectives, and unfortunately for you, *Stanley,* my brother-in-law loves me like a brother-in-law. If you want to stay healthy, my advice is to pack all your earthly possessions and get the hell out of Belfast – *pronto.* Go back to Ballymena or whatever hillbilly town you now reside in."

"Fuck you," moaned Lennon.

"That's appreciation for you. Do you know that I had to do everything in my power to stop my brother-in-law sending a couple of his associates to have a less-than-friendly chat with you? Trust me. This is a picnic in Utopia compared to what their chats are like. The River Lagan can be a very lonely place, Stanley, and rats like you gnawing recklessly at mousetrap cheese have only one place to go."

"Fuck you!"

Turning Lennon over, Karl inspected the defeated man's face. For all his bravado, Lennon appeared edgy, assessing. Karl did not need to be a psychologist to detect, in the face of another, terrified eyes struggling desperately to anticipate what was coming next.

"You don't look *too* bad," said Karl, menacingly running the warm jack over Lennon's sweating face. "Just be grateful I don't leave you the way you left me."

He whacked Lennon over the head, for good measure.

Lennon never saw it coming . . .

"Good night, sweetheart," whispered Karl, standing, before exiting the house.

Outside, the night air was cool. Soulless. Soundless. Karl walked steadily to the car.

"You okay?" asked Willie, watching Karl get in.

Karl nodded. "That was called a transfer of pain."

"You did what had to be done. Bet he had no qualms about the beating he gave you. End of story. You'll not see him again."

"I hope you're right, Willie, my friend," replied Karl. "Here. Put this in the back."

"A briefcase? What's in it?"

"My medical expenses," replied Karl, starting the car. "And briefs."

CHAPTER TWENTY-ONE

"Frisch weht der Wind, Der Heimat zu, Mein Irisch Kind,
Wo weilest du?"
"Fresh blows the wind, To the homeland, My Irish darling,
Where do you linger?"
Richard Wagner, *Tristan und Isolde,*
translated by T.S. Eliot for *The Waste Land*

The phone rang just as Karl began pouring some early morning coffee. He hated early calls. They never brought good news. He hesitated before picking up the phone. The incident with Lennon, two nights ago, suddenly flashed in his head, but he erased it quickly, believing Lennon would not want cops poking their noses into his messy business dealings despite the beating.

"Tom? What's wrong?"

"The body of a young girl was washed ashore three nights ago in Scotland, over beside the Mull of Kintyre. Been in the water for some considerable time, apparently. Scottish police believe it's Martina Ferris. They've asked me to send her dental records to confirm it."

"Ah shit."

"They've faxed me photos of the body. I would say it's her, Karl. The eye wound is prominent in the pictures. I'm sorry."

"Did . . . did they say how she died? Was it an accident? Drowning?"

There was a momentary silence before Hicks responded.

"No. No accident. She was murdered, the same way the other young girls were murdered."

Karl felt blood rise all the way from his feet, before settling in his eyes.

"Karl? You still there?"

"What? Oh . . . yes. Still here . . . listen, thanks for calling me. I won't tell Martina's sister, until you confirm everything. Will you call me as soon as the body is returned, or if you hear anything relevant?"

"Yes. Of course."

"Thanks, Tom. Talk to you later," said Karl, ending the conversation with a push of a button.

"What is it, Karl?" asked the groggy voice of Naomi, blinking out the early morning tiredness from her eyes. "Who was that on the phone?"

"Tom Hicks. The police in Scotland have found a body. Possibly that of Martina Ferris. Not yet confirmed."

"Martina . . . oh the poor girl," said Naomi, shaking her head with disbelief. "Did they say how she died?"

"More than likely murdered."

"Oh my God . . . how?"

"We'll have to wait and see the autopsy report," said Karl, not wishing to disclose the grisly details to an already distressed Naomi.

"What about Geraldine? She'll have to be told."

"We'll wait until we get a definite answer from Tom. No point jumping the gun."

Naomi nodded in agreement. "You're right. There's still the possibility it's not Martina. Isn't that right?"

Karl did not answer.

CHAPTER TWENTY-TWO

"Cruelty has a human heart . . ."
William Blake, *A Divine Image*

Late afternoon, and Karl tapped aimlessly at the Royal Quiet DeLuxe's keys, trying desperately to finish the chapter of his latest manuscript. The phone call from Hicks this morning had unsettled him. Each time he tried typing a word, Martina's face appeared on the page, derailing his train of thought.

"It's no use," he sighed, loudly, hoping to catch Naomi's attention. He needed a bit of comforting and used the oldest excuse in the book. "Writer's block."

She ignored him, her face glued to the TV set.

"It's no bloody use," he repeated, louder. "I can't focus."

"Huh? Did you say something, Karl?"

"I said . . . forget it."

The doorbell began buzzing just as Karl placed his fingers back on the keys.

"It's okay. You sit there, Naomi. I've nothing else to do," he said, lightly sarcastic, journeying downstairs.

Opening the door, Karl was greeted by Sean, his regular postman.

"On time as usual, Sean. I could set my watch by you – if it had six hands."

"Definitely not my fault today, Karl," replied Sean, sheepishly. "The queue in McDonald's was terrible. You'd think they were giving the Big Macs away, the crowd in there."

"Aren't you supposed to deliver the mail first?"

"On an empty stomach?"

"Okay. You win. What goodies have you for me?"

"It's what I haven't got for you."

"I love cryptic postmen. What have you *not* got for me?"

"A bulky big package representing one of your rejected manuscripts."

"Hilarious. Everyone in this town is a comedian. Just give me the mail and go back to your Happy Meal. Make us all happy."

Upstairs, Karl checked the mail, junking the junk, wishing he could follow suit with the three bills weighing heavily in his hand.

"Anything, Karl?" asked Naomi, taking her eyes off the screen for a few seconds.

"Yes. Three letters for you from a guy called Bill, and one big mysterious brown envelope for me," said Karl, ripping the head off the large brown. It took Karl less than ten seconds to read the letter contained within:

> *Dear Carl* (Name spelt wrong. Deliberately? Was paranoia taking hold?)
>
> *I found your writing to be very funny and original. Unfortunately, that said, I am going to disappoint both of us by saying I am sorry I will not be able to do a blurb for you. My agent does not allow it. I must warn you that you do not have permission to use either 'funny' or 'original' – or indeed mention this correspondence in any of your future work with the exception that if said future work should make it into the best-selling list, then please do mention it, by all means. My new book,* Dead Man's Grave, *is due out in March and will be available in all good book stores and competitively priced. Please enjoy the enclosed promotional clippings. They are free and yours to cherish for ever. I should mention before closing that I still have a very limited number of signed copies of my last massive seller,* Forward to Darkness, *available and at a competitive price,*

also. Furthermore, anyone buying two of my best-selling books will be sent a beautiful black and white photo of yours truly, taken by the world-famous photographer, Miles O'Rourke. A better deal for the Mullan fan would be purchasing four of my best-selling books. They get a signed *photo, absolutely free.*

Yours truly, Peter T. Mullan, author of six best-selling novels including the critically acclaimed Her Deadly Son, *soon to be a hit movie starring Mel Gibson (or Harrison Ford).*

PS: Yes, that really is *my signature on the photo! Feel free to trade it on eBay.*

"Who's it from, Karl?" enquired Naomi.

"From this wanker," said Karl, holding the large black and white photo for Naomi to view.

"Who's that?"

"That is the bastard I stopped from getting a good hiding in school, numerous times. I wish now I had joined in. This is Mister Bestseller himself, Peter Mullan."

"Why'd he send you a photo of himself?"

"Probably because he hadn't one of me to send."

"Isn't he the writer you went to see down in Eason's?"

"Yes, well . . . let's not linger on the past," said Karl, ripping both letter and photo up before making his way to the kitchen area. "Would you like some coffee?"

"Huh?" said Naomi, returning her attention back to the screen.

"I said would you like . . . what the hell is that you're watching? Are you crying? What the hell are you crying about, now? I hope it's not because of that wanker's letter?"

"I'm not crying!" snapped Naomi, dabbing a Kleenex at her eyes.

"Must be a weepy you're watching, then. Please don't tell me it's *Titanic,* again?"

"It's . . . it's the highest cruelty on earth," stated Naomi, indicating the screen, while scribbling on to a notepad.

"What is?"

"That horrible torture. *Foie gras.*"

"I love it when you speak with a French accent. Which reminds me. *Wee wee, Mademoiselle. I must go to zee lava-tor-ee,*" grinned Karl, doing a terrible Peter Sellers.

"This isn't funny. I'm writing a letter to the papers about it," scolded Naomi. "*Foie gras* should be made a crime."

"I fully agree with whatever it is you're talking about. What did you do with the *Belfast Telegraph?* There's a couple of horse racing results I need to check . . ." Karl's voice suddenly trailed off. A goose on the screen was being roughly manhandled, a ten-inch steel tube being forced down its throat. The bird was making an almost-human sound of anguish as the tube went further down its throat. It was appalling to watch, but like the scene of a car wreck, Karl's morbid curiosity refused to allow him to draw his eyes away. "What . . . what's happened to that goose?"

Naomi sniffed. "The poor thing is being force fed with filtered corn through a metal tube placed in its esophagus."

"Why? Is it sick?"

"No, of course not. The inhumane technique of gavaging – or *foie gras* – dates as far back as 2500 BC, when the ancient Egyptians began keeping birds for food, deliberately fattening the birds through force-feeding."

"What's the point?"

"Do you know the translation for *foie gras?*"

"Fat liver?"

"That's right. The rich livers enlarge three or four times their normal size. It's a supposed delicacy loved by so-called chefs and greedy connoisseurs."

The goose was screaming a high-pitched *herr-onk onk, herr-onk onk* of distress. To Karl, it sounded almost frighteningly human. It was starting to give him the shits.

"Can't you turn that bloody sound down just a tad, Naomi?"

"Does it upset you?"

"Well, yes."

"Good," she replied, pushing the volume up via the remote. "Everyone should hear this before they sit down to a meal!"

Herr-onk onk, herr-onk onk, herr-onk onk, herr-onk onkkkkkkkkkkkkkkk kkkk.

"What the hell's gotten into you?"

"This torture goes on for the last twelve to twenty-one days of the birds' lives, before they are finally slaughtered. Can you imagine being tortured like that, screaming when no one gives a shit? Horrible horrible horrible . . ."

Luck sometimes followed Karl like a dog. Sometimes it ran a little too far ahead. Other times it fell a little too far behind, but it was always within calling range, and if he paused long enough, he knew it would eventually come. Without warning, his doggy luck suddenly hit him, like a rubber band snapping against his forehead. The idea grew so large in his mind that he could think of nothing else.

"I've got to go out, Naomi. Shouldn't be long," he declared, quickly grabbing his coat.

"But . . . it's late. Look, I'll turn this off, if it's upsetting you, and –"

"No! No, just keep watching it. I'll need to ask you some questions when I get back."

CHAPTER TWENTY-THREE

*"There is something haunting in the light of the moon; it has
all the dispassionateness of a disembodied soul, and something
of its inconceivable mystery."*
Joseph Conrad, *Lord Jim*

Dusk was settling into Belfast, curling cat-ways for the night.
The streets were deserted – everyone already where they wanted to be – and the city was fast becoming a startlingly quiet
wasteland.

The iron smell of rain was in the warm, muggy air.

Karl stood beneath the arch and halo of steel streetlamps before finally entering the building, a ghostly moon the only witness.

"I had a feeling you'd return," said Cathy, smugly. "Did you find your
precious Martina? Has that particular little goose started laying more
golden eggs for you again?"

Cathy seemed to have physically deteriorated since last he saw her.
Her face's mottling had spread like an unmanageable rash, making her
look ill, sallow and sweaty. Bizarrely, she was wearing a too-small bathing
suit, breasts swelling above the wire-rimmed top. Below, her bottoms
rode up on the insides of her thighs. Karl caught a glance of menacing-
looking pubic shadow.

"I need you to tell me about the young girls, Cathy – all of them."

"You like them young, eh? Plump and delicious like little naked geese? Can't handle someone your own age, ripe like me?"

"You know what he's doing with them."

"Who?"

"He's fattening them up like geese to the slaughter. The first time we met, you asked me if the fat golden goose fled its cage. Remember? And a moment ago, you mentioned goose again."

Cathy smiled, uttering not a word.

"You lure them here, Cathy, for him. Don't you? All the little girls? They've all been here, at one time or another. Haven't they?"

"I . . . I don't know what you're talking about."

For the first time since meeting her, Karl thought he detected hesitancy in Cathy's usual certitude of manner.

"You don't want to be an accessory to murder, Cathy. I believe you were trying to stop him, his sick murdering game. You were throwing little clues at me, but I was too thick to understand. I didn't catch on at first, but I have now. Where or what is the cage?"

"I . . . you should leave . . . I don't want to talk to you."

"They found a body in Scotland. More than likely it's Martina Ferris. Do you want that on your conscience, Cathy? Murder and torture of young girls?"

"This could be some sort of trap, to put me back in prison."

"It's no trap. I can assure you that I'm not a cop of any description – undercover or otherwise. I need this information. I need to stop him murdering more young girls. Your name won't be brought into this. I promise you."

"You . . . you still haven't convinced me that you're not really an undercover cop."

"How the hell can I prove it to you? Go on, test me."

"Well . . . I do have a . . . tester. Just to prove you're not a cop . . ." From a stack of battered suitcases directly to her right, she began extracting a small, metal box. Removed a tiny, fat package wrapped in cling film from the box. The package's content was brown. Resembled a lone turd. Cathy suddenly grinned secretively at Karl.

"What's that?" asked Karl.

"This? This is a the best type of lie detector test." Her grin straightened into a knife slit.

Rummaging through another box, she produced a wrinkled apple and a rather battered but fully functioning Victorinox Spartan Swiss army knife, expertly selecting the correct blade from the metal housing. With the blade, she beheaded the stem of the apple before flipping the fruit sideways, tunnelling halfway into its stomach, vomiting out the contents. Her movements were fluent. An expert's touch.

"Do you like apple pies?" she asked.

"I don't have time for nonsense, Cathy. Can you help me or not?" stated Karl, his patience long gone.

"This recipe can't be rushed. Give me that pen on the top of that suitcase," she instructed, holding out her hand like a doctor performing an operation.

Karl quickly located the item, handing her a yellow Bic ballpoint.

She removed the disused pen's blue cap before expertly biting the golden nib and extracting the inky inner via her shadowed teeth. Spat the inner out. Blew through the plastic body like a kid with a peashooter. "Perfect. No blockage."

"Are you going to tell me what this is all about?"

"Soon!" she exclaimed, scooping out more of the fruity sludge. Repeated three more times before unwrapping the cling film from the fat package, plugging the brown waxy substance into the apple's stomach. Entrenching the Bic's plastic body permanently in the top of the apple, she provocatively ran her tongue along the Bic in a way that made Karl shiver in a bad way. "This is what you call a real pipe. Give me a lighter."

"I don't have one. I've stopped smoking."

"You'll find one over there, beside the shoes," she said, watching him scout until he found it. "Good. That's it. Bring it over."

"Now what?" he asked, holding the lighter.

"Light me up," she commanded.

"You're going to smoke out of *that?*"

"And you."

Karl shook his head. "No, I'm not."

"This isn't a pantomime where I say oh yes you are, and you say oh no I'm not." Her face suddenly shut down. No expression. "It looks like you can't be trusted. My instincts *were* right. You *are* a cop. Going to arrest me for possession, Mister Pig?" Cathy oink oinked twice, close to Karl's face, wetting his skin with spittle.

For the longest few seconds of his life, Karl calculated his options, understanding that there was but one. He flicked the wheel, the flame skinny and sharp in the dim light. He held the flame towards her. She guided his hand closer until the flame connected to the apple's contents, making it glow a bright orange speckled with red and black. Without warning, the flame caught the hairs on his fingers, scorching them.

"Fuck!" Karl pulled his hand quickly away.

Cathy sniffed the aroma of burnt flesh, smiling. "That isn't bacon I smell? Oink! Oink!"

Fuck you, he wanted to say, but said nothing while watching her sucking on the Bic pipe, gently but with purpose. Within seconds, the entire room was suddenly filled with the sweetness of baked apples and a less than subtle smell of something less homely, the reek cutting hard and clean to his brain.

"My apple pies are the best," smiled Cathy, watching him beyond lowered eyelids, smoke filtering through her chipped teeth, clinging to her face.

Slowly opening her eyes, she proffered Karl the pipe. He reluctantly took it. Glanced at her face, the way it was imploding like a sagging balloon, before staring at the madness nesting in his hand. The Bic's entrance was thick with Cathy's saliva. Unappealing. Quickly obstructed it from his thoughts. Went for the jugular of the deep dive by taking a brave toke of the pipe. Coughed. Spluttered wildly. Disgorged smoke and greenish snot from his nose. Disgusted. Quickly wiped.

"You really *are* new to this," laughed Cathy. "Don't worry. The first cut is always the deepest – and *sweetish*. Now, this time, inhale like you mean it; as if your very life depends upon it. *Don't* waste it."

Reluctantly, he sucked it in, no longer trying to block its dark journey into his lungs and bloodstream. Its power hit him, right in the neck. An invisible voltage hardwired to his brain. His arms were suddenly humming with electricity. His legs felt empty, like papier mâché. He needed to sit.

"Take another hit," said Cathy, studying his eyes. "Don't you trust me?"

"Of course . . . I trust . . . you. Very much . . ." he muttered, little seconds too late, his timing out of kilter. The room was slowly swooning. He closed his eyes to stop the vertigo. It took more than a moment to shake his eyes away and pull them back to Cathy. "Just . . . just tell me . . . tell me where the cage is . . . ?"

"What a beautiful journey you're going to have. I hope your passport and visa are all in order, Karl?" chuckled Cathy, the laugh sinister and dark.

"Journey?" His head was becoming swampy. He could feel his face screwing inward like a bathtub draining.

"We're both in the same head, Karl. Don't you understand that?"

"Same head . . ." The room was swelling, in and out, breathing like a concrete lung. He could hear its heart beat. *Beat. Beat. Beat.* "Heart . . . is on fire . . . I need . . . air . . ."

"Don't stress." Cathy's eyes widened slightly, speckling with instant delight. She kissed him gently on the cheek, bringing her mouth to his. Her mouth widened, her sweaty face becoming flushed and big-pored. She murmured something inaudible but foul in his ear.

Karl could smell her pungent body odour; could see his distorted reflection on the surface of the bulbous studs rooted in her tongue. To Karl, something bizarre was happening to Cathy's lips, causing them to swell up and look like female genitalia. She pushed the bizarre lips forcefully against his. He resisted.

"If you're not willing to help me," she hissed inside his mouth, "then I'm not willing to help you. If you disobey one more time, you'll no longer be welcome. Do I make myself clear? You'll never find the cage."

Karl tried to respond. "My tongue . . . it's . . . all rub . . . rub . . . rub-be*ryyyyyyyyyyyy*."

"Am I clear!"

"Yes . . . per . . . fect . . . ly . . ."

"My apples are the best on the market," said Cathy, placing Karl's hand on one of her breasts. "Know why?"

Karl shook his head, his tongue no longer forming words. He was sinking fast in dark quicksand and madness.

"Once you're done, you simply eat the evidence!" exclaimed Cathy, her laughter vulgar, unexpectedly loud, her other hand pushing the smouldering apple tight against his mouth, hurting his teeth. "Bite. Make the evidence vanish. We don't want the cops arresting us. Do we?" Her eyes were suddenly wide and vacant like a window forced open.

Karl nodded in slow motion. Opened his mouth. Bit down on the apple. It tasted like mushy sawdust. He swallowed the hot contents in his mouth. He was invulnerable.

For a brief, cogent moment, he saw sparks dancing before him. Cathy was removing what little clothing there was attached to her body, her eyes never leaving his.

He could now see, for the first time, that Nature has been careless in its disregard for her anatomy. Her body was misshapen, bent scoliotic. Blue veins mapped the entire expanse of her exposed skin. Yet, despite all the imperfections, there was a repulsive beauty for any eye willing to look.

"You lying bastard! If you're not a cop, what was this doing in your fucking coat? *Eh!* Answer, you bastard, before I blow your lying skull off!"

The .357 Colt Python being held tight against his head was wobbling in her trembling hands.

"No! Don't! Just . . . just let . . . just let me explain. P . . . p . . . please . . . C . . . Cathy . . ."

Suddenly, everything developed into a still-life framed negative. Cathy's knuckles became bone-white. Her finger tightened on the trigger. Karl held his breath. He imagined the trigger being pulled, the bullet tearing half his ashen face off.

"I'm listening, but I can't guarantee for how long," replied Cathy, breaking the deadly silence. "It better be good, otherwise it'll be bad – for you."

Karl tried bringing saliva to his mouth, but it remained dry as cotton. "I . . . I keep it for protection. I've made plenty of enemies, over the years as a private investigator. Just for protection . . . that's all . . ."

"I don't believe you," she hissed, adding pressure to the trigger.

She's going to do it. The mad bastard was going to do it. "Just look at the barrel, for fuck sake! Look . . . look where the serial number was. It's been filed off. The gun's illegal. Think the cops would allow me to carry that about with me? You've got to believe me, Cathy."

"Don't got to do anything, except pull this trigger! Lay down, face to the floor!"

"Look, Cathy, there's no need –"

"I won't tell you again – *get on the ground!*"

With a free hand, Cathy produced a needle, its syringe filled with polluted brown liquid. Drops fell from the needle's tip leaving a creeping trail. She made a movement, bringing herself closer to Karl. There was heat, tremendous heat, shifting from her body. She reached and touched his shoulder.

He recoiled.

"Don't," she whispered, moving her tongue around the word as she slipped the needle into Karl's neck.

Initially, he couldn't feel it, but then came the rush, a cold rush of exhilaration and power invading every pore and blood cell, confusing his senses.

Tiring, Karl closed his eyes to the profane madness. He could feel Cathy pulling him on to his back, sliding on top, her oily skin as slippery as a snake. He tried pushing her off, but his arms had become impotent.

"Don't fight it," she whispered. "Easy . . . that's right. Nice and easy . . ." She began removing his clothes, gently at first, then with purpose, ripping them.

"Please . . . don't . . . do this, Cathy . . ."

He could feel her fingers guiding his penis into her wet darkness.

Then everything went bizarre . . .

Someone began painting tar over his eyes. Everything was changing from bone-white to night-black. His brain slowed down to an absolute crawl. Wobbly. *Rubberisssssssssssed.* The table in the corner was moving towards him, its wooden legs now suddenly human flesh, rubbing up against him, panting like a sexual dog. The curtains covering the window formed into giant tongues. They licked his naked skin tenderly. Everyone and everything was his friend. The room was changing colours: a kaleidoscope of pyschedelic rainbows. Naked cherubs went sliding down the rainbows, giggling and waving at him to join in. He waved back in slow motion, watching their shoulder-blades see-sawing with movement, their tiny buttocks grinning with pleasure. Soft music permeated his cranium. The entire place was becoming a petri dish of weirdness.

Cathy was grinning, holding a collection of syringes the size of knitting needles, rubbing them against each other. *Klick Klick Klick,* they sounded.

"You really think I gave a fuck about some little whore?" asked Cathy, eyes widening, a sinister smirk taking over her entire face. "Oink Oink!"

Karl thought of *Les Tricoteuses,* of Madame Defarge's smirk of death. It chilled him to the bone.

"You . . . you've got to help . . . help them . . . please, Cathy . . ."

Suddenly, without warning, the entire scene began speeding right back up to normal. Karl felt his insides pulling tightly together. Something tangible began climbing into the back of his mind, switching his entire world off. Seconds later, he dissolved into a rolling sea of darkness, punctuated by flashes of white light. The darkness seemed endless. The floor opened up, swallowing him. The room went into hiding.

The last thing he saw was the figure of a man, standing beside Cathy, grinning.

Chapter Twenty-Four

"If God did not exist, it would be necessary to invent him."
Voltaire, *Epistle to the author of the book, The Three Impostors*

"Karl?"

"Huh?"

"Open your eyes, Karl," said a man's voice.

Somewhere in Karl's head, a buzz saw was cutting through his skull as he slowly began opening his eyes. Bleached light stung like acid. He closed them quickly, shielding eyes with an arm.

"Shit!"

"Sorry," replied the voice. "I keep forgetting about that. Let me dim myself down a tad. There. How's that?"

Gingerly, Karl willed his reluctant lids open. He was in a room of some sort. All white, washed-out, lacking a focal point of colour for the eye to concentrate on. A stranger was looking in through the windows of Karl's eyes. The stranger's skin was almost fluorescent, eerily not unlike the room itself.

Momentarily disorientated, Karl blustered, "Where . . . where the hell am I?"

"Hell? I hope that was just a slip of the tongue, Karl," replied the stranger, smiling slightly. "Don't you remember? You puffing away like a kid behind the bicycle shed in school, before taking the needle? This is my House – or it *was*."

The room slowly began morphing into colours and shapes and smells – smells of incense and melting candles quickening the air.

"The old church . . . ? Who . . . who *are* you? You're not the one I saw standing beside Cathy."

"You can't guess who I am?"

"Not in the mood for guessing, friend. Just tell."

"I'm Jesus, Karl."

"Of course you are. You can tell me who's going to win the Grand National, then?"

"I never encourage gambling, Karl."

"Did Cathy tell you my name? Where is the man who was with her? Was that Bob Hannah?"

"Cathy and Bob?" Jesus laughed. "They are not on my team. Sin drips from every curve of Cathy's seductive body. That's not the first time Cathy's done the old apple and needle trick. That goes way back to the Garden. And I mean *way* back." The laugh became secretive.

"Who the hell *are* you?"

"You really shouldn't use that imprecation in my presence. Good job I have a sense of humour, Karl. So don't go listening to all those crazy followers of mine telling you different. I can't stand those born-again Christians, void of all humour."

For the first time, Karl noticed that the large crucifix dangling from the ceiling was now vacant of its lone occupant. Quickly he began scrutinising the man a bit more closely. Bearded and scraggy-looking, partially clothed in rags and wearing a filthy T-shirt stating: **I was an atheist until I realised I was God**. To Karl, there was a borderline familiarity about him, a sliding sense of recognition.

Attempting to stand, Karl suddenly felt his knees turning to rubber. *"Oh . . ."*

"Steady," encouraged the soothing voice of Jesus.

Karl could feel burning bile bubble in his throat. Without warning, he collapsed to the ground, vomiting violently. His world began spinning and spinning. He hadn't felt this sick in years. Wondered if he was dying – or simply dead?

"Oh God," he moaned.

"Yes?"

"Don't. Okay? Don't be an annoying bastard," said Karl feebly, trying to sound threatening, wiping sour spillage from his mouth. "I'm not in the mood for any of this shit."

"Why?"

"Can't you see? I'm stoned."

"Where I come from, being stoned takes on an entirely different meaning. A lot more sinister."

"Hilarious. A real Frank Carson. Just leave me alone . . . *oh* . . . my head . . ."

"Your features look tired and battered, Karl. What you really need is a *faith* lift. If you want, I can turn that frown upside down and make your soul all aglow," replied Jesus. "Here, let me give you a hand up."

Karl reached for the hand, immediately noticing the drilled wound. It appeared to be damp, the leakage slightly thick. Instinctively, he recoiled slightly.

"What's . . . what's wrong with your hand? It's bleeding."

"Stigmata," responded Jesus, smiling a weird and wonderful smile. "You can't pretend to ignore it, Karl. It demands your attention."

"Of course," replied Karl, sarcastically. "Have to get one, the next time I do party tricks for Naomi."

From a click of Jesus's fingers appeared lit cigarettes – two. Jesus eased one towards his mouth while offering the other to Karl.

"No thanks," said Karl. "Trying to give them up."

"Lead us not into temptation, eh?" said Jesus, smiling a wonderful, blindingly white smile that any ad man would die for.

"Something like that."

Sucking gently on the cig, Jesus closed his eyes, seemingly taking in the taste.

"It's been a *very* long time since I had one of these. I really needed that – bad. *Oops.* I guess I shouldn't really be associating bad with me, should I?"

Karl said nothing, watching the cigarette slowly eat itself, disappearing in a crackling wisp of smoke like a lonely spectre.

"Take my hand, Karl," commanded Jesus, his voice strong yet gentle. "Don't be afraid. It won't bite you."

Stifling an impulse to ignore the request, Karl reached and

reluctantly grabbed the extended hand. *Pow!* A tactile shudder, quickly followed by a surge of a thousand little jolts shooting through his nervous system began railing and rattling along his spine, before exiting his mouth and ears. He staggered, his feet feeling as if floating inches from the ground.

So real. Sooooo realllll. Surrealllllllllllll.

"Easy, Karl. Don't rush the rush. There's no hurry. We have all eternity."

"Who . . . who *are* you . . . really?" Hesitancy had now entered Karl's voice. He quickly released his grip on the stranger's strange hand.

"Really? I've already told you who I am: I Am the Great I Am."

"That must be nice for you. You sound more like the Cat in the Hat. Now, if you don't mind, I've got to get going. It was nice meeting you, and all that."

"I can help you, Karl. Always remember, Jesus saves."

"Is that so? Where? The Bank of Ireland or Ulster Bank?"

"You really know how to turn the knife, Karl. You're a bigger doubter than Thomas. We've a lot in common, you and I. We've both been crucified for one thing or another," said Jesus, pulling his T-shirt up, turning and revealing an exposed back. It was horribly scarred with hundreds of deep cut lines, raw and damp as sliced bacon.

Karl involuntary grimaced at the scarred back. "Who the hell . . . who *done* that?"

"Everyone. Read between the *lines,* Karl. Don't allow cynicism and guilt to cloud your judgement."

"Guilt? What guilt?"

"Your mother."

Karl could feel the blood draining from his face. His legs were rubberising again. "You keep my mother out of this."

"You didn't murder your mother, Karl. You didn't facilitate it in any shape or form. You were barely nine years old. Don't you understand that, after all these years?"

"You better stop talking like that, if you know what's good for you."

"You were hurt by her, as a child. You witnessed her having affairs with other men, while your father was at sea. You hated her because –"

"You're a liar! I didn't hate her! I never hated my mother. I loved her. She never had affairs!"

"You also blamed her for bringing the monster into your house. When she was murdered and you were attacked and left for dead by the same monster, you believed that your thoughts somehow played a part in that brutal slaying. That's how unjustifiable guilt operates, sitting in a corner like a spider, weaving silently in the dark, making you doubt, questioning your conscience, your faith."

"Liar! I don't have any so-called faith. I stopped believing in God's falsehood a long time ago. God's all smoke and mirrors. I even spell his name in lower case when I'm typing."

"Oh, *that* hurt, Karl," replied Jesus, a small smile on his face. "*Believe* in me. I *can* help. Allow me to oil your rusted faith. Perhaps I should introduce you to Jude? Now *there's* an optimist for you. He's in charge of all lost and hopeless causes."

"I don't need *anyone's* help. I'll figure it all out. I always do."

"It must be terrible, being so perfect. Next you'll be trying to walk on water when you have all that Hennessy in you."

"Leave me alone! I need no one! I've *no doubts* about that!" Karl squeezed his hands tight against his ears, but the voice still penetrated.

Suddenly, a crackling black and white film began playing, flickering ghostly on the far wall.

"What . . . what are you doing?"

"Thought you might like to watch an old silent movie with me, for old time's sake."

Creepy piano keys began playing *Stormy Weather*. The hairs on Karl's neck began to prickle.

The screen came suddenly to life with bursts of interrogating flashes dancing on the darkness of the ceiling, revealing a large country kitchen of some sort. A man, sitting at a table. Karl could only see his back, but it sent shivers down his spine. The man was staring down along the dark paradise of a gun's barrel, pressed tight against his head. The gun was held by a stocky gunman of brawny beef, a skin-peeling smirk pencilling his leering face.

Lightning was flashing through windows. Everything was in monochrome except a pool of blood oozing from a girl's body on the floor.

The blood was the reddest red Karl had ever seen. It resembled Superman's cape. Another gunman stood over the body, throwing his head back with laughter, like a hyena on two legs.

"What the . . . ?" Karl attempted to kick his brain into gear, but everything was in slow motion.

The hyena was now semi-naked, its hairy penis stiff while mounting the body. Saliva began pooling round the hyena's mouth.

The gunman at the table was talking but no words were forming. He placed the gun tighter against the man's head, and slowly pulled back the hammer. He grinned.

Weirdly, parts of the tabletop splintered outwards, leaving a newly formed deadeye in the centre of the table. The gunman's head suddenly jerked back violently, his chin immediately developing a tiny cavity, not unlike Kirk Douglas's famous dimple. A track-line of smooth blood inked from the cavity, causing a miniature bib of dark red to form on his chest. He didn't move. He didn't utter a single word. His eyes resembled glass.

A thumb of lazy smoke oozed from the table's deadeye.

The man at the table now stood, pointing his concealed weapon at the hyena on the floor, firing twice, killing it.

"Turn that damn thing off!" screamed Karl. "Turn it off!"

The screen suddenly evaporated.

"You had no qualms about killing Bulldog. Or Detective Cairns," stated Jesus.

"They . . . they deserved it. Bulldog and Cairns both murdered . . . many people . . . murdered Jenny Lewis . . . her mother. I was . . . I was only . . . was . . . defending myself . . ."

"Yes, I know you were. But it tasted real good when you shot them, didn't it?"

"They were thugs . . . bullies, picking . . . always picking on the weak." Karl cupped his hands against his ears. He wanted this accusing voice to stop tormenting him. "They murdered . . . anyone standing in their murderous way."

"All very true," acknowledged Jesus. "But you brought yourself down to their level, Karl, didn't you? You love scratching at the outer skin of Darkness. The relief is tremendous. Isn't it?"

"Leave me alone!" His hands squeezed tighter. His skull felt ready to explode. "You're not real!"

"If you don't believe in me, I can't help you." Jesus reached out his bloody hands. "Ask and you shall receive, Karl. I can help."

"Don't touch me with your creepy hands! I don't need you!" Karl's head began spinning. "Don't need you. Don't . . . need you . . . need you . . ."

"Okay. If that's your final word?" said Jesus, glancing towards the heavens. "Let's give a round of applause to Karl for his stubborn unbelief. Let's give him Jericho!"

Despite the annoying voice penetrating his head, Karl could detect other sounds, ripping and scratching sounds, sounds like ribs violently expanding, tearing through their encasements. Without warning, the walls of the old church began crumbling. The naked cherubs immediately flew to the safety of the ceiling. The large crucifix dangling from the ceiling began melting at an incredible pace, pooling on to the floor in a Daliesque bloody puddle before shaping into a question mark.

From Jesus's wounds, blood came flooding out in a great deluge.

The colour red was everywhere. Wine. Blood. Candles. Eyes. Karl needed to escape, get away from all the madness. He tried staggering out, just as he heard the sound from above. A part of the ceiling caught him, smack dead centre in the forehead.

Everything suddenly became dark as concrete rained down from the heavens, and immediately all hell broke loose.

CHAPTER TWENTY-FIVE

"Night, the mother of fear and mystery, was coming upon me."
H.G. Wells, *The War of the Worlds*

Karl staggered down Hill Street, feeling like a drunk as he headed homewards. He slipped twice on the cobblestones underfoot, cursing their giant-knuckle unevenness, before finally reaching the door of his office.

His hand was shaking so badly he found it difficult to work the key into the door. All about, night shadows were quickly coming undone. Soon it would be dawn.

"Come on, you bastard. Get in," he hissed, glancing to his left and then to his right, the key seemingly getting bigger and fatter, becoming more awkward to hold.

Thankfully, the narrow street was empty – as far as he could detect – but the feeling of eyes watching him never left as the key finally hit home.

Inside the darkened hallway, he leaned against the door and held his breath.

Footsteps? Someone walking; nearing?

Thump thump thump went his heart.

The hallway seemed to be getting darker, swaying like a boat on unfriendly waters. Vertigo was kicking in. He feared being on the verge of a blackout.

Breathe, for fuck sake! Your bastarding imagination's interfering with reason.

He quickly breathed, allowing air to fill burning lungs, until it chased everything from his head.

"Easy . . . easy . . ." The dizziness began easing.

Steadying, he entered the bathroom, gently locking the door before hitting the light switch.

"Fuck the night . . ." Clothing bloody and tattered.

Hesitantly, he consulted the wall mirror, directly to his left.

"Shit!" The face looking back at him was a stranger; a bloody, ashen-faced stranger, puckered skin covered in blood. He looked lost, like a mourner at the wrong funeral.

Quickly turning on the water tap, cupping hands beneath the faucet, Karl began channelling the water into his mouth. Finished, he squeezed some toothpaste from a tube on to his index finger, rubbing the gooey contents hard against his teeth.

Discarding his bloody clothing, he stepped out of their puddle and into the shower, its cold-water propulsion jolting him into alertness.

"Karl? Is that you?" asked Naomi's muffled voice, close to the door.

Shit! "Yes . . . yes, love . . ."

"Why's the door locked?"

He could hear her pushing against the door, fiddling with the handle.

Think! "I . . . I just took a terrible shit. It stank all the way to Bangor."

"Too much information, thank you," returned Naomi's disgusted voice. "It's almost five in the morning. Where've you been?"

"To . . . to the been place."

"I'm not in the mood for your sarcasm, Karl. Why the shower at this time of the morning?"

"I . . ." *Think, for fuck sake!* "I . . . slipped and fell against a skip, over beside Saint Anne's Cathedral. Some silly bastard left it filled with planks of wood and broken glass sticking out. Almost broke my bloody neck. Busted my face, a bit . . ."

"Oh my God, Karl! Are you okay?"

"Yes . . . just a few bloody scratches and on-coming bruises. I'll feel a lot better when I sip that Hennessy you've got waiting for me in the bedroom," he replied, desperately trying to make his voice sound jolly and calm.

"Want me to come in and scrub your back?"

Karl quickly glanced at the pile of bloody clothes. "Er . . . I'm . . . I'm almost finished. In a few minutes, you can scrub my front, in bed."

Naomi giggled. "Okay, but don't be long."

"Only a few more minutes."

He listened to her walk away before bending over and vomiting into the shower's enclosure. It was a full-bodied vomit, shaking most of the upper body, face instantly contorting in pain.

It was a good ten minutes later before he felt confident enough to stand, and step out of the shower's enclosure.

Checking his naked body, he looked for major cuts. Nothing. A few scratches, but not enough to warrant the blood-covered clothing on the ground.

Where the hell did all the blood come from? Suddenly, a foggy flashback of weirdness. A man pretending to be Jesus, laughing as he self-inflicted knife wounds to his wrists, claiming to be able to bring the house down – literally.

"Headcase," mumbled Karl, less than confident.

Cathy's smirking face suddenly appeared at the mirror. He quickly wiped it away with the foggy condensation.

Balling the clothes, he quickly deposited them in a large black garbage bag from underneath the sink and stealthily made his way downstairs, stepping out into the cold street, naked. He glanced left and right before dumping the clothes in a bin huddled together with others for the morning collection.

Without warning, a mangy cat jumped from its filthy hideout, scaring the shit clean out of him.

"*Bastard!*" he hissed.

Closing the door quietly behind him, he tiptoed up the stairs towards the bedroom. Inside, Naomi was sound asleep, his glass of Hennessy parked beside the table lamp.

He swallowed the lovely liquid expertly with one gulp, dreading what the next few hours would bring.

Chapter Twenty-Six

"Is there no way out of the mind?"
Sylvia Plath, *Apprehensions*

"You still haven't told me where you went last night – or should I say this morning?" said Naomi, pouring a steady ribbon of black coffee, before handing it to Karl.

Background music from Downtown Radio's afternoon show lilted over the room. Fleetwood Mac's "Go Your Own Way".

Cupping the mug, Karl considered how the coffee's blackness resembled his mood perfectly.

"This fair trade coffee tastes like bloody muck. Can't we just get our normal coffee? Where the hell's all that expensive Rio coffee?" moaned Karl, trying desperately to sidestep the looming interrogation. His brain was still quaking with the drainage of whatever shit Cathy had injected into his body.

"You're just in one of your hate-the-world moods, finding fault in everything. Anyway, you were just about to tell me where you were at five in the morning and how you got all those mysterious scratches on your face."

Trying desperately to come up with a feasible story, Karl's brain suddenly began kicking into gear. Hated the thought of lying to Naomi, but could find no other escape route. Truth be told, he was still somewhat confused about last night, almost as if it had all been a bad dream.

"I already told you: I banged into a skip, over beside Saint Anne's Cathedral. If you must know, I met up with an old schoolmate from years back. He happened to be at that cocksucker's signing down at Eason's and – *arrghhhh!*" Some of the coffee spilt from the cup on to his left leg. "Fucking bastarding coffee!"

"Karl!" screamed Naomi, rushing towards him. "Get those pants off, quickly, before the coffee burns through to your skin! Hurry!"

"It's nothing," said Karl, grimacing. He hadn't meant to spill so bloody much.

"Don't be silly. Get your pants off – *now.*"

"I love it when you talk dirty."

"This isn't funny, Karl. You could have scalded yourself, badly."

"Another inch, and I'd have done more than bloody scalded myself."

As Karl peeled off the offending pants, he reluctantly agreed with himself that the pain was worth it, if only to keep Naomi's mind away from last night.

"Oh, you poor thing," soothed Naomi, seeing the red welt quickly forming on the wounded leg. "I'll have to get some ointment from the medicine cabinet. I'll be back in a sec."

The words of "Go Your Own Way" faded quickly, train-rushed by a news jingle.

"This is the news on Downtown Radio," stated the newscaster's bland voice. "Police have confirmed that the body of a woman was found floating in the River Lagan, in the early hours of this morning."

Karl did not make an immediate association with the words.

"Initial reports suggest the woman was one of the homeless people living in and around the old church at Custom House Square . . ."

"Karl? Are you okay?" asked Naomi, entering the room, startling him.

"What? Oh . . . yes . . ." He suddenly felt dizzy.

"What was that about a woman's body being found in the Lagan?"

"I . . . I'm listening to it." He needed air. Everything spinning.

"Karl? What's wrong? You don't look too good. Perhaps we should go to the hospital? That burn could be a lot worse than we realise."

"*. . . shot in the head . . .*"

The words caught Karl like a meat hook to the throat.

CHAPTER TWENTY-SEVEN

"The truth is rarely pure, and never simple."
Oscar Wilde, *The Importance of Being Earnest*

It was two days later when Karl finally decided to make his way to Hicks's office, dreading what he might hear concerning the body found floating in the Lagan.

Inside, he found Hicks spreading ketchup over a flat-looking hamburger and tired salad.

"How the hell can you eat in this place?" asked Karl, trying to block the cloying stench of dead bodies from entering his nostrils.

"There was no need for you to come here. I told you that on the phone. I could just as easily have brought you the damn report, Karl," said Hicks, bringing the hamburger to his mouth. "Seems as if you're almost spoiling for a fight with Wilson."

"I'm not looking for a fight, Tom, unless it concerns getting justice for Martina and Ivana."

"They've already arrested someone for Ivana's murder, so you can stop dragging her name into your crusade."

"Vincent Harrison? Come off it. The cops are trying to squeeze a round peg into a square hole. The lad's obviously innocent."

"Really? I believe that when enough murky patterns emerge, one can make a clear enough picture out of them."

"What murky patterns?"

"Harrison's numerous court appearances, as a juvenile."

"What for?"

"Well, at fifteen he was charged with GBH against his then girl-friend. Charges were later dropped when the girlfriend changed her story. Two other times he appeared in the dock, and both times violence was involved. This time the victims were men – gay men."

"I see," said Karl, hating being caught wrong-footed by his best friend. "So, Harrison is now a homophobic stalker?"

"Sometimes you've got to open your eyes to the obvious, Karl. Murder isn't always complicated."

"You still haven't told me if the body out there is Martina's," said Karl, stealing a quick glance towards the main room. Two bodies lay side by side in sheet-covered gurneys.

"It's definitely hers. The dental records confirm it. When the body arrived late last night, I wasted no time in conducting my own autopsy, working through to the wee hours of this morning. The kidneys and liver were missing, and once again we had accelerated formation of cells and protein."

"It's the same bastard doing this?"

"I never jump to conclusions, no matter how easy the leap. Keeping all options open is my preferred policy. Her sister will have to come and identify the body, of course, just to make it official."

"I haven't told Geraldine yet. I'm not looking forward to it. What do you say in a situation like this? I feel I let her down."

"That's all very laudable, but I always warned you about keeping your emotions detached from the cases you get involved in. Once you become personally involved, you can't remain objective. I don't have that luxury and need to retain a clinical detachment."

"Easier said than done."

"Well, if it helps, I've no doubt Martina Ferris wasn't killed in Scotland," said Hicks, pouring coffee into a cup.

"What makes you so certain?"

"When I conducted the autopsy, I discovered particles of seaweed had coagulated inside the body. The seaweed in question is indigenous to the Antrim coast."

"Trying to throw the cops off the scent? Do you think he's panicking, thinks someone knows who he is?"

"That's feasible, I suppose. Interestingly, there were tiny splinters of paint trapped between her fingernails."

"Paint? What kind of paint?"

"Specialist paint called Neo X2. It's used to paint barracks and places of that nature."

"Barracks?"

"For the military and police. And don't give me that look."

"What look?"

"The there-must-be-police-involved-somehow-in-these-murders look."

"Well? Who knows?"

"Your paranoia will end up sending you in the wrong direction," said Hicks, sipping his coffee. "Do you want to see the body before you go?"

"Stop trying to be smart. You know I don't have a strong enough stomach for that sort of thing. I take the hint. I'm going now."

"Good. If there are any more developments, I'll *phone* you."

Turning to go, Karl hesitated. "Tom . . . there was a woman's body found floating in the Lagan, two days ago. What can you tell me about her?"

Nodding, Hicks indicated his nose towards the bodies. "Cathy McGlone. That's the body over there, beside Martina Ferris's."

Karl fought the temptation to look. "What . . . what are the cops saying?"

"Not too much, other than she ran some sort of Fagan homeless gang, over near Custom House Square."

"Just because they're homeless doesn't make them criminals."

"What the hell's eating you? I never said it makes them criminals, so there's no need to be so defensive. I'm simply stating what the police report said."

"I'm sick of people pinning everything on homeless people. Pin it on the fuckers with money."

"Calm down," replied Hicks, looking at Karl curiously. "Why the interest in McGlone?"

"How . . . how did she die? The news said something about her being shot."

"She was murdered. Shot in the head four times. Quite brutal, almost like a frenzy."

Karl felt his stomach do a trapdoor sensation. His haemorrhoid began burning the arse off him. He needed to take a shit.

"Any . . . any clues about her attacker?" asked Karl, poking a finger in the offending area.

"Don't do *that*, Karl. It's disgusting. Can't you see I'm eating?" Hicks swallowed another well-chewed chunk of meat, washing it down with coffee. "No, no clues as such, but there are some fingerprints imprinted upon the neck. Vague prints. Time will tell if we can capitalise on them."

"That's something." *Fuck!*

"One thing, though."

"What?"

"Cathy McGlone had a record as long as Gerry Adams's face."

"What . . . what the hell is *that* supposed to mean?"

"McGlone used to be nicknamed Yo-Yo because she had been in and out of prison so many times."

"Oh?"

"Police were looking for her six years ago when she suddenly and mysteriously vanished," continued Hicks.

"What . . . what did the cops want her for?"

"Attempted abduction of a child, over near the Malone Road. Luckily, an alert neighbour spotted something suspicious and immediately called the police. McGlone escaped, but the police found her fingerprints at the scene. They've been searching for her ever since."

Fuck! "Wow . . ."

"At least it gives the police something to work on, as far as the killings are concerned. I would say that when all this comes out in the wash, McGlone's name will be plastered all over it."

"Everything nicely tied up in a bow, eh?"

"What's that supposed to mean?"

"Nothing."

"Are you sure?"

"Am I ever sure of anything?"

"There's something you're not telling me, Karl, and I know from past experience that you won't unless you have to. A little bit of advice from your best friend. When you walk into a coalmine and see the canary, feet up, common sense should tell you it's time to get the hell out of there. Understand?"

Look, I . . . have to go . . . the smell . . . can't stick the smell of hamburgers and death any more."

Outside, Karl began retching, his entire body shaking with pain. Shockwaves radiated from the base of his spine.

Suddenly, he felt terribly unclean.

CHAPTER TWENTY-EIGHT

"See how love and murder will out."
William Congreve, *The Double Dealer*

Early next morning, Karl shocked himself awake, momentarily disorientated and saturated in sweat. He was frightened, not by last night's nightmare; instead it was the devastating fear of a man whose world has suddenly grown completely beyond him and out of control. His stomach felt tight, as if he'd been performing crunches all night. Cathy kept appearing over and over again in the nightmare, laughing, telling Karl what a great fuck he had been.

Thankfully, Naomi was still sleeping, her breathing coming deep and slow. She had managed to nearly twist her way out of the sheets. They were pulled all the way down to her waist, her bare breasts exposed. Karl reached, pulling the sheets over her, before exiting the bed.

In the kitchen, waiting for the coffee to brew, he thought about his choices, their limitation.

You should have acted sooner, said an accusing voice in his head.

"Couldn't have. Not enough evidence."

Ha! That's never stopped you before. If anything, it encouraged you.

"This is different."

Bullshit! You had sex with Cathy. Possibly killed her with all those drugs fucking your head about.

"Don't talk shite!"

"Karl? Who're you talking to?" asked Naomi, suddenly appearing at the doorway, startling him. She looked as unnerved as Karl.

"What? Oh! Myself. I've . . . finally flown over the cuckoo's nest." He forced a smile. "Coffee?"

"You've been acting strangely, ever since that night you claimed to have banged into a skip. Have you something you want to tell me?"

Something in Naomi's voice was warning Karl that this was a new level, almost an accusation. The word *claimed* sounded ominous.

Believing that the best defence is a wimpy offence, Karl stuttered, "Claimed? What the hell is that supposed to mean?"

"Cathy. Who is she? You kept saying her name, over and over again, in your sleep. You must think I'm stupid, Karl Kane! You're hiding things from me. Terrible things. I can tell. I know you too well." Naomi's bottom lip began trembling. It made her more beautiful, that look, and precious, and fragile, and the bastard in Karl made him feel an even bigger bastard. "We haven't made love in almost a week. Think I didn't smell her on you, despite your late night showering that night? I don't care what you think of me, but don't *ever* think of me as a fool."

"It's not how it looks, Naomi," said Karl, scratching at the nicotine patch on his arm, wishing for a cigarette. "You've got to believe me."

"Believe *you?* That's a joke. Tell you what. Take a deep breath, Karl Kane. Get your tongue in gear, but so help me God, if one lie slips out of your mouth, you'll never see me again. And that's a promise."

"I need a cigarette."

"You can smoke your head off as soon as I walk out of here – for good."

No longer able to contain it, Karl released all the pent-up air trapped in his lungs. Bullet-biting time had now arrived. There was no escaping it.

"Okay . . . look, I should have been up front with you from the start, Naomi, but as they say, there's no fool like an old fool. I didn't know how you'd react."

"I knew it!" declared Naomi, tears forming. "I knew it! You cheating bastard!"

"No! It's not like you think. Just listen. That's all I ask . . . please."

For the next twenty minutes, Karl did his best to relay all past events concerning Cathy.

"I went to the hospital the next morning," continued Karl. "I told you it was to get a check-up about my cuts, but it was a check-up for sexually transmitted diseases . . . that's why I haven't tried to make love to you. I'm sorry, Naomi."

Naomi's face was ashen. She didn't speak.

"McGlone more or less raped me, Naomi. Can't you see?" pleaded Karl, the tone of his voice becoming frantic. "Once she stuck that needle in me, I was totally powerless. What could I have done? Answer me, for fuck sake, instead of standing there, judging me with those accusing eyes."

"Did you kill this . . . McGlone, dump her body in the Lagan?" Naomi's emotionless voice sounded like ice sliding down a glass.

"What? I can't believe you're seriously asking me that. How can you even think I'm capable of such a thing?"

"How? At night, over the last few months in bed, you've been tossing and turning in your sleep, mumbling . . ."

"Mumbling? What . . . what kind of mumbling?"

Naomi's face reddened.

"You . . . you keep mentioning the two police officers who were killed a few months ago. The bad one, Bulldog . . ."

Karl's heart moved up a notch.

"What . . . what did I say?"

"Mostly incoherent babbling."

"Stop bullshitting me. What the hell did I say?" The question came out harder than he had intended.

Naomi suddenly looked frightened. "You . . . you said you were glad you killed him – killed them both."

Karl suddenly felt light-headed, feeling as if someone just cracked his skull with an iron bar. The room moved slightly. "I . . . I . . . ." He looked away from Naomi, no longer able to hold her stare.

"Karl," said Naomi, her voice a whisper.

"What?"

"Sometimes . . ." her voice slipped away.

"What? Sometimes what, Naomi?"

"Sometimes good people have to do bad things," replied Naomi, silently turning before leaving the room.

Chapter Twenty-Nine

"Meredith, we're in!"
Fred Kitchen, *The Bailiff*

"And you simply lost it?" asked Willie suspiciously, staring at Karl, who was desperately searching for an inconspicuous parking space. "How could you simply lose a gun?"

"Simple. I simply lost it. I'm a simple person," stated Karl, bringing the car to an abrupt halt outside a closed café. *Oh, I lost it in an old church while having a yarn with Jesus, and a woman was possibly murdered with it.*

"Well, I'm not getting you another one, if that's the cavalier attitude you have."

"Look, you're right, Willie. I should have been more careful. I'll make it up to you, somehow."

"Just hope it's not one of your notorious horse tips," replied Willie huffily.

"I'll think of something nice, for Isabel. Okay? Now, come on. We've got to get moving before it gets bright."

A waxy moon resting its chin on the scabby rooftops cast an eerie shadow over husks of buildings, as Karl and Willie entered the area. Jaundiced streetlights spilled long shadows. The echoing street, the handbills blowing by and the absence of any sign of life – not even the ghostly reflection of an onlooker in the dodgy nightclub near the end of the street – all managed to convey a strong sense of abandonment and loss. Only the large distribution centre for Royal Mail held a semblance of activity.

"The street's not exactly buzzing, is it?" said Willie, more to himself than Karl.

"It's almost three in the morning. What else would you expect?" offered Karl, suddenly pointing at a battered-looking building. "That's our place."

"Looks like it's ready to collapse."

"Don't jinx us."

"And you don't know what's inside, what the building's being used for?"

"Nope. Not an iota. Only that Mister Bob Hannah has been seen frequently emerging from it. Could be a warehouse or storage area, even his home."

Karl's immediate impression of the building reinforced the casual wariness he felt along the narrow, bare-bone street flanked by skeletal remains of derelict shops and offices. Beyond the measurement of night, the ugly-looking building had the intimidating structure of a large concrete phoenix ripping through the ground, reinforced with iron-barred windows and daunting metal doors. Only the mansard roof gave some semblance of shape. A coagulated growth of corrosion had collected on the building's drainage, overlapping down the side, as if haemorrhaging rusty blood in tiger stripes.

"C'mon. Let's head to the back of the building, see if we can find a way in," said Karl. "The front is too exposed."

The lack of proper lighting added caution to the greyness of the night, making it difficult for Karl and Willie to manoeuvre casually, forcing them to stumble constantly over discarded wood and old bricks from a nearby building site.

"Careful you don't break your bloody neck on all this crap," advised Karl.

"So dark. Are you sure your friend got the address right?" said Willie, tripping over a piece of protruding timber.

"Yes," assured Karl, anything but assured.

On the waste ground, a child's discarded bike was balled into a metal fist and formed parts of a gluey, catarrhal bondage of dried muck and powdery, cemented dust. Numerous other pieces of junk, mostly old furniture and plastic crates, were strewn haphazardly in a heap. Empty booze bottles and used condoms were everywhere, mixing with sticky, water-damaged pages from porn magazines. Black-painted zodiac and hex signs scarred every available wall, mingling with badly spelt words praising Satan and all things dark. Corpses of dead rats, flattened and bloodied by breezeblocks, resembled strawberry pancakes. But it was a gutted lifelike sawdust doll, its damp intestines vomited on the ground, that gave Karl the shits. Its weird eyes seemed to be daring him. They were godless and disconcerting.

"Nice area. The kind of place that gives Willie the willies in his willie," whispered Willie, clutching a tiny leather bag to his chest like a talisman. "Tomb Street. You can't make these things up. Wasn't there a graveyard or something like that here at one time, years ago?"

"No, it's because by the time the mail gets delivered to your door, you're a long time dead," replied Karl, omitting that he believed the graveyard was actually beneath their feet.

"Is that a dead chicken, over there beside that weird doll? It *is* a dead chicken, isn't it?"

"I don't know if it's dead or not, only that there won't be any more eggs popping out of its arse any time soon. Anyway, it's probably just the antics of bored kids with nothing better to do," claimed Karl, trying to sound calm and casual. "It makes them seem dangerous and daring."

"When I was a kid, rapping someone's door and running like hell was considered dangerous and daring," mumbled Willie, suddenly coming to an abrupt halt at the back door, extracting a miniature torchlight from his pocket. A few seconds later the tiny beam of yellow focused in on its intended target: a large brass locking system on an impressive, graffiti-scarred iron door.

"Well?" asked Karl, impatiently. "Can you do it?"

Willie shook his head. "It's a mother-in-law bastard of a lock. A Claymore DX with Scandinavian oval cylinders."

"For fuck sake." Even the name impressed Karl, sounding like the tag for a machine-gun.

"These things take security to the next echelon, offering the highest possible level of protection against unlawful key duplication," praised Willie. "This bastard differs from a normal lock, in that it has at least one thousand key indents, an anti-drill plate *and* anti-saw rollers in the bolt. Not forgetting a security curtain and anti-pick defences."

"An awful lot of anti in there, Willie. Why am I not hearing too many uncles?"

"This lock is almost impossible to pick and the bull's balls to drill. It's a virtual Fort Knox."

"That's that, then? You're more or less telling me that our short excursion in the night is over?" Already Karl was running his eyes over the building, trying to gauge any possible weaknesses that could be exploited to help facilitate access. A last resort would be trying the front. He dreaded the thought of it, the unnecessary exposure it would bring.

"I said *almost* impossible to pick. Hold this flashlight. We're not leaving here without a fight," insisted Willie, rummaging through his bag, removing a family of tools and a device shaped like a tiny horseshoe. "I designed this little by-pass tool a few years ago. Cross your fingers that it works."

"I'll cross my toes and legs as well if it helps to –"

Suddenly, Karl felt the hairs on the back of his neck beginning to tingle in a bad way. A *very* bad way. His haemorrhoids began aching. Glancing slowly over his right shoulder, he watched the lone vehicle cruising towards them at snail's pace, its lights dimmed suspiciously.

Oh fuck. A squad car. He wondered if Willie had spotted it; wondered how to alert him without causing panic. He quickly turned the flashlight off, plunging everything into darkness.

"What the hell are you –" Willie managed to say, before Karl's hand clasped his mouth.

"*Cops,*" whispered Karl, his stomach doing tiny somersaults as he removed his hand from Willie's mouth.

"Some sneaky bastard must have seen us," muttered Willie sneakily.

The menacing-looking car came silently to an abrupt halt, its dimmed lights extinguishing completely. It sat there in the dark like a block of distorted plastic.

"What the hell are they up to?" whispered Karl.

"Calling reinforcements, no doubt."

Seconds turned to minutes before the car's door opened. A cop stepped out.

From the advantage of diluted light, Karl could see the bloated-nosed cop devouring a sandwich in such a way that it looked like he was playing a harmonica.

"He's staring straight at us," insisted Willie, practically reading Karl's mind.

"Keep quiet, for fuck sake. He's walking in our direction."

Thoughts began rushing Karl as the cop neared: *If he's on his own, we could make a run for it, across the waste ground. By the time he manoeuvres that squad car, we could create a good distance between us. How is Willie's ticker? Could he manage to sprint across all that rubble without collapsing in a heap? Get serious. You'd be attending his funeral on Friday. Explain that to Isabel.*

The cop stopped a few feet away, wiping his hands on the sandwich's wrapper before tossing it on the ground. Suddenly, he seemed to freeze, his head tilting back slightly as if a pungent stench had attacked his nostrils.

He is staring directly at us, thought Karl, shoulders tightening with crosshair tension. A rush of unpleasant heat began foresting up through his face. His mouth went completely dry. He couldn't swallow.

The cop made a movement, his right hand reaching for the obscene-looking gun on his hips. Seconds later, the sharp sound of a zip could be heard, and then something like a drizzle followed by a more confident burst. The piss hissed and steamed on dead leaves. A loud fart sounded, followed by a sigh of relief. The cop re-zipped his zipper and then turned before quickly walking back towards the squad car, farting twice more in the emptiness of the night.

"Disgusting bastard," whispered Willie. "If that had been me taking my truncheon out, pissing and farting in public, I'd have been arrested by the same dirty bastard. Bet he doesn't even wash his hands."

"Look on the bright side, Willie."

"What would that be?

"Farting and pissing at the same time. Despite all the criticism direct-ed at them, cops can multi-task, after all."

The car's headlights abruptly came on, chalking the waste ground with a half-moon wash before slinking away, just as slowly and menac-ingly as it had arrived.

Karl suddenly realised that for the last few minutes he had been holding his breath like a child passing a graveyard late at night. His heart hadn't stopped thumping in his skull. *What the hell are you doing here, you big fucking eejit, getting Willie and yourself into all sorts of shit? If stupidity ever becomes a currency, you'll end up becoming a fucking millionaire.*

"Tea break over," said Willie, returning to his work in progress. "Hold that light."

Five minutes turned to ten, but in Karl's head it felt like hours. On the brink of surrender and searching for an alternative, two beautiful words suddenly brought redemption to Karl's bones.

"Got it!" exclaimed Willie, easing the door open while nesting his by-pass tool triumphantly in the fat of his palm. "God, if I could legal-ly patent this wee number, I'd make a fortune."

"You really *can* open doors others can't, you old rascal," praised Karl, standing in the shadows, unmoving.

"C'mon. What are you waiting for? We've got to close this door quickly."

"You've done enough, Willie. I'll take it from here. No need to get involved any further."

"What? You invite me to the party, force me to do all the hard work, and now you're trying to prevent me seeing the fruits of my labour? Somehow, I don't think so. Are you coming or not?"

Defeated, Karl shrugged his shoulders. "I guess we better get in before Officer O'Leaky returns with another full bladder."

Inside, the building's interior was heavily dark, funerary, like the lining of a painted jar. From his bag, Willie removed another torchlight

– heavy-duty, this time – and began scanning its yellow circular beam over the entire area, bringing instant revelations.

"My God," awed Willie. "It's . . . it's a movie house."

Karl remained speechless, luxuriating in what the yellow beam revealed.

The movie theatre was decorated in a congregation of cardinal colours, inspired by ecclesiastical raiment: crimson, royal blue, amethyst, gold and silver. Large doors of mahogany and brass were lavishly decorated with sculptures and murals depicting various actors from the silent movies era. Framed original posters took pride of place. Classics such as F.W. Murnau's *Phantom*, Joe May's *Asphalt*, Clarence Brown's *Flesh and the Devil* and G.W. Pabst's *Die Freudlose Gasse* mingled with the controversial: Richard Oswald's *Different From the Others*; Carl Theodor Dreyer's *Michael* and William Dieterle's *Sex in Chains*.

A separate poster of acclaimed Belfast actor Stephen Boyd, racing Charlton Heston in the famous chariot scene in *Ben Hur*, held pride of place in a separate alcove.

"Boyd used to work in this street when he was growing up, strangely enough," supplied Karl, taking the heavy-duty torchlight from Willie. "From Tomb Street to Easy Street. Some jump, eh?"

"Doesn't this place take you back to Saturday afternoons, slapping the arse off yourself after watching a cowboy movie?" smiled Willie.

"Not the fleapit I went to in Duncairn Gardens, known lovingly as the Donkey," said Karl, a sharp ache of recognition in his gut, of a kind of innocence somehow irretrievably lost; of a distant memory suddenly recaptured with subtle elegiac quality. "This is almost like the Moulin Rouge."

The seating arrangement was similarly elaborate and lush, with a sweeping crescent of a balcony directly overhead. But it was what occupied each second seat that sent a quick shudder up Karl's spine: bizarrely lifelike mannequins decked out in the appropriate dress code of an F. Scott Fitzgerald novel, staring frozen-eyed at the silent screen directly ahead.

"All we need is Mrs Fazackalee lovingly playing her piano accompaniment to a silent film," smiled Willie.

"Who?"

"The old lady played by Margaret Rutherford in that classic Peter Sellers film, *The Smallest Show on Earth*."

"C'mon. Let's head over to the stairs," said Karl, suddenly realising that time was slipping away. "That looks like an office of some sort, near the top."

A few seconds later, both men stood outside the office, its metal door triple-locked.

Willie laughed an insane laugh. "*Three?* Give me a break."

"Just do your best."

"What exactly are we looking *for?*" asked Willie, worming a tiny lock pick into one of the locks.

"I don't exactly know. Something. Anything. Sometimes not knowing what you're looking for helps you find something you never expected to find in the first place. Hopefully, something incriminating belonging to a double-barrelled palindrome by the name of Hannah."

It took Willie ten minutes to defeat the first lock and six more minutes to defeat the other two.

They quickly stepped inside, Karl closing the door behind them.

The large office was glutted with a mixture of papers, books and various unkempt knick-knacks. A collection of keys dangling from metal loops were attached to a protruding nail. A photocopier resting in the corner was watched over by fluorescent lights dangling from creaking chains, appearing ready for collapse. A solid mahogany desk ruled the room, topped with a tiny lamp neighbouring an open-style Rolodex.

"That looks like a skeleton key," said Willie, looking at the rings of keys. He reached over and removed a set, and then nodded. "That's what it is."

"Do such things exist? I thought that was all movie bollocks."

"No, they do exist. This one, for example? A Kingston U90. Used by cops, screws or military for locking up prisoners and –"

"Used by cops and military?"

"Saves them running about with a ton of metal in their pants. Did I hit on something? Your eyes suddenly lit up for second."

"I don't really know. Just thinking."

Karl began rifling through a stack of drawers. Nothing much.

Rubber stamps and stationery. He sniffed the aroma of pencil shavings and dried ink. The smell made him think of bad school days.

That was when he spotted the safe.

"Willie?"

"What?"

"Can you do anything with that?" said Karl, indicating the safe.

"Hmm . . ." Willie ran his hands over the safe as if conducting a séance. "It's a Burton Eurovault TG-3 Grade 3. Floor bolted and concrete filled construction with reinforced steel fibres and bars."

"Can you *do* anything with it?" repeated Karl impatiently.

"For an extra hundred quid, he could have had an electronic combination lock, and the answer would have been a resounding no." Willie removed an item from his bag of tricks and knelt down beside the safe. "Thankfully, the cheap prick is penny wise and quid foolish. Two minutes is my all-time record on one of these. Let me see . . ."

One minute crawled by.

Karl checked his watch.

"Forget about it, Willie. We don't have a lot of –"

"Quite a bit of stuff in here," said Willie, smiling, pulling back the door on the safe. "Mostly paper and a few DVDs, by the looks of it."

Quickly bending down, Karl reached into the safe. A folder, choc-a-bloc with pages. He disturbed it, scanning the pages for any clue to what he was searching for. The pages contained what looked like foreign movie titles – French, mainly – all alphabetically sequenced.

"*Observez sa matrice.*"

"What? Did you say something?" asked Willie, sitting in a fat leather chair, his work done for the day.

"*She Must Die.*"

"Who must die?"

"I'm trying to sound-out these French titles."

"From here you sound more like Peter Sellers doing a very bad Inspector Clouseau."

"*Les femmes sont la mort. The Women Are Death,* perhaps?"

"Not Disney, then?"

"I have the sneaking suspicion that they're all snuff movies."

"Snuff movies?"

"People – usually women – tortured and murdered for so-called pleasure."

"What kind of sick bastard would watch those disgusting things?"

"The sick bastard who normally sits in that chair, no doubt. Our Mister Hannah."

Willie quickly eased from the chair.

"Check these DVDs out," instructed Karl, grabbing a handful, before handing some to Willie. "They look like soft porn, but go through them, just in case."

"*Shaving Ryan's Privates*," grinned Willie, looking at the cover. "You have to admit that's a funny title."

"Hilarious," said Karl, quickly scanning some of the DVDs. "This one's called *E-Three: The Extra Testicle*."

"Not bad. Eight out of ten."

"*The Lord of the Rings*."

Willie looked puzzled. "*The Lord of the Rings?* You've got to be kidding me. That's one of my all-time favourites."

"Not this one, I can assure you."

"Why?"

"The rings on the cover have hairs sprouting out of them."

"Sick bastards."

Karl quickly placed the DVDs back, and on doing so, discovered a small collection of wrapped papers nestling at the back of the safe. He removed the papers.

"If I'm not mistaken, these are deeds to properties," said Karl. "Must have a right few bob, our Bob."

"What do you want me to do?"

"Search the rest of the room. We don't know when Hannah will return. See if there is anything of interest over in those boxes in the far corner."

While Willie worked the boxes, Karl placed the deeds on top of the photocopier's bed face, immediately pressing the copy button. Waiting for the copies, he flicked through the Rolodex, reluctantly switching on the table lamp for better viewing. Puzzlingly, the Rolodex held no names or addresses, just initials and phone numbers.

Quickly removing some of the cards in the Rolodex, he gave them the same treatment as the property deeds.

"*Karl!*" hissed Willie, pointing directly towards the far entrance down below the office. "*We have visitors.*"

Almost instantly, Karl reached and turned off the table lamp. Peeping through the office curtains, he studied two figures in the theatre talking to each other.

"*Who are they?*" whispered Willie, his voice barely audible.

"*From the couple of photos I saw, the taller of the two is Bob Hannah. I haven't a clue who the other one is.*"

Hannah was tall, extremely muscular, with hair cropped down almost to the bone. The other figure was harder to make out. A lot smaller than Hannah and thinly built.

Suddenly, the photocopier jerked noisily in the corner, making both Karl and Willie jump slightly.

"Shit, damn, fuck!" hissed Karl, rushing quickly to the machine. "The bloody paper is jammed!"

"He's looking up, Karl. Your man's looking directly up here," said Willie, panic in his voice. "Oh no. He's walking this way . . ."

Karl felt his nerves tightening like guitar strings.

For such a tall and muscular man, Bob Hannah walked lightly, as if on cushioned soles. He walked calmly and confidently up the stairs, stopping directly outside his office. He listened. He did not hurry. He placed his keys in the locks, opening them one by one in a timely fashion, and then pushed open the door before walking in, turning the light on in the process. He allowed the semi-silence of the room to settle before studying the table and then the safe. Nothing amiss. He glanced at the photocopier. Something. What? Reaching over, he touched the top of the machine with his hand. He removed his hand and looked at his palm strangely, as if wondering where it had come from. Warm? Or was it simply the stifling heat in the room? His leather office chair looked out of place. What? He placed his hand on the soft leathery indent made by Willie's arse less than a minute ago. Warm, also? He glanced at the side door. He walked to it and checked that it was closed.

It was. He opened it and journeyed down the stairs, but not before removing the fire axe stationed on the wall. The exit sign gave off a green hue, and he followed it obediently without turning on the lights on the stairway.

At the exit doors, he leaned his body inwards, placing an opened palm on the metal skin as if sucking in its energy. He placed his right ear against the door and listened, his grip on the axe tightening. He balanced his body like an ancient god awaiting a sacrifice.

Karl and Willie remained motionless, their backs to the exit doors. They did not speak. They were one mind in two bodies, stifling all breathing, like unholy offerings preparing to meet their god. Karl felt something grabbing his intestines, knotting them.

With each silent second, the dread grew. He tried relaxing the muscles in his jaw. He could hear breathing. Not his. Not Willie's. It was discharging from the other side of the door. It seemed to have a life of its own. Tangible. Evil. He felt the door move slightly, as if it were breathing also. Someone pushing against it? He held his breath. Waited.

Hannah stood there, listening to the outside world created by a god of accidental ability. He listened to the night sounds of cats frolicking and fucking; of unhurried traffic in the distance; the night hum of dead silence only, a sleeping town in a tunnel of glass. He held little doubt that someone was out there, close. Very close. He thought about the foreign smells in the office and the eerie feeling of a presence not too long gone. The thought disturbed him momentarily, then was gone, just as quickly. He thought of other things. The thin thread between life and death, and what fate can bring if tested. He tried stifling the urge not to tempt fate and its unpredictability, but he failed, pushing the doors quickly open, sucking in the warm clammy night air as it rushed at him.

He stepped back, preparing for fate, the axe held high in striking mode. He gritted his teeth. Waited. The night was there, watching, like one black sheet of nothing, waiting patiently for him. The night seemed darker than usual. He held his breath and stepped out, as if in a time machine, not knowing what he would find.

It startled him, the two drunken brutes rolling on the ground a few feet away, fighting over cheap wine evidently wasted from one of the many smashed bottles littering the filthy waste ground. They were cursing, threatening unspeakable wrath upon each other, as they tossed and turned in all the shit of the night. One of them had pissed his pants. He could see that clearly, even in the heavy shroud of night.

Disgusting creatures, he thought. "Animals . . . scum . . ." he whispered, fearful that they would hear him, hoping they would, his hands tightening, his knuckles protruding from their encasement. He wished the dirty animals each had an axe, just like this healing, no-nonsense harbinger in his able hands. They could hack each other to pieces, and their deaths wouldn't even be counted, their insignificance in this world washed away with their cheap wine and filthy piss.

Closing the door quietly, he retraced his steps all the way back to the theatre, leaving the axe standing guard at the top of the stairs.

"You can open your eyes, Miss McCambridge," he said, a thin smile scrawled on skinny lips.

Obediently, the young girl opened her eyes, gawking in sweetie-shop awe. "It's . . . it's . . . this isn't yours . . . it can't be . . . is it, Mister Hannah?"

His thin smile fattened into a healthy grin of pride. "Yes. Isn't it beautiful?"

She nodded, her open mouth saying nothing.

"Let me undress you," he said, walking to her, his hands displayed openly.

"Here?" Her face reddened slightly. "In the middle of the movie house?"

"*Theatre,*" he corrected, an edge to his voice. "Movie houses are for barbarians. Here, we are in the company of gods, Miss McCambridge. Allow them to feast on your beauty. If you please the gods, wondrous things will happen. Don't you know that?"

The redness on her face deepened. She smiled awkwardly, while he removed her grubby sweater. The sweater fell to the ground, her hands instinctively covering the tiny dirty bra she wore. She began shaking. The theatre was extremely warm.

"You do have a way with words, Mister Hannah."

"Bob. Call me Bob. May I call you Judy?" He smiled.

Judy nodded shyly. "Yes . . . of course . . . Bob."

"Tell me, Judy, why on earth have you cropped your beautiful hair? It makes you look rather boyish – in a very sexy way, of course."

"I . . . it keeps them from wanting me. At night, in the streets . . . they're always watching me, trying to take without paying. You're not like that, Mister – I mean Bob. You're a kind man. I knew that from the way you spoke to me, bought me McDonald's and cigarettes, last week, and today."

"There will be plenty more surprises awaiting you, Judy. Now, remove your bra. The gods are eager to see what hides beneath."

Nervously she removed the bra. The breasts were buds. Nothing more.

"No . . . don't cover your breasts," he said. "They're beautiful, not meant to be covered."

She obeyed, bringing her hands slowly down to her sides.

"How old are you, Judy?"

"Four- I mean sixteen. I'll be seventeen next week."

"Really? Then we must have a *very* special party for you. I'll invite some *very* important people to it. You would like that, wouldn't you?" He touched her breast, his nails skating over the tiny nipples. A pleasing but disturbing sensation took him by surprise, despite the strong stench of unwashed skin coming from her. She would need to take a bath – perhaps more than one.

"Remove the rest of your garments. I have new clothing waiting for you. We can't have a beauty like you seen in such tattered rags."

Hesitantly, she began slipping out of the battered shoes and badly stained jeans, revealing a pair of oversized boxer shorts, bony hips protruding over the waistband like tiny anchors. She removed the shorts and stood naked, bony chest and girdle of ribs a chalky grey colour in the artificial light. A hatching of small scars and red pockmarks covered her upper arms.

"This will help you relax, Judy," said Hannah, producing a needle and syringe.

"What . . . what is it, Bob?"

"It'll take all your suffering and pain away, for ever."

CHAPTER THIRTY

"They fuck you up, your mum and dad.
They may not mean to, but they do.
They fill you with the faults they had
And add some extra, just for you."
Philip Larkin, "This Be the Verse"

Friday afternoon, and Karl stretched his legs on to the edge of the table, leaning back on a chair while reading a magazine article about travelling to Belfast. Once lumped as one of the four bastarding B's to avoid when travelling – Beirut, Baghdad and Bosnia being the other Horsemen of the Apocalypse – Belfast was now receiving a more favourable, if somewhat belated, press.

"Tourists have been told they no longer need to bring their bulletproof vest with them, when coming to Belfast," said Karl loudly through the open door, hoping to capture Naomi's ear.

Naomi continued to work at the computer in the next room, ignoring him.

"It's been almost a week, Naomi," said Karl. "When are you going to at least acknowledge me and start thawing out?"

Glancing up from the screen, Naomi presented Karl with a snarling did-you-dare-say-something look?

Unfortunately for Karl, he was quickly discovering that Naomi was fast becoming singularly skilled at ignoring him while going about her normal business. Deep down, he wished for a few hard slaps to his face as punishment for Cathy McGlone instead of this tortuous unresponsiveness.

Thankfully, his mobile rang on the desk. Picking it up, he asked, "Hello?"

"Dad?"

"Katie! How's my favourite daughter?"

"Fine. How's the weather in Belfast?"

"If you've called all the way from Scotland to ask for money, I'll suddenly feel under the weather." Karl detected a giggle in Katie's reply.

"You're so suspicious, Dad."

"Goes with the territory, my wee love. Anyway, enough preamble. How're you doing?"

"Doing really good, Dad."

"Hope you're keeping an eye on those Scotsmen. As I've told you a hundred times before, I never trust a man who wears a skirt," replied Karl, scratching an annoying imperfection on his nose.

"That's disgusting."

"It's the truth."

"I'm not on about Scotsmen, Dad. I'm talking about you picking your nose."

"I'm not picking my . . . how the hell . . . ?" Karl's legs dropped immediately from the desk, springing the rest of his body forward. Katie's smiling face was staring at him from the office's outside window. She was waving.

Before Karl could make a move, Naomi was already heading towards the office's front door. A few seconds later, Katie appeared at the doorway and rushed to give her father a hug, totally ignoring Naomi.

"Why didn't you tell me you were coming? I'd have baked a cake," smiled Karl, kissing his daughter's head.

"I wanted it to be a surprise." Katie's squeezed harder. "Surprised?"

Karl felt that the squeezing and show of emotion was a bit of a show for Naomi.

"Pleasantly so. You've said hello to Naomi?"

"How about you and me heading over to Nick's Warehouse?" replied Katie, brushing off the question. "It's been over a year since I was last there."

"Okay," agreed Karl. "Naomi? Fancy something to eat?"

Katie's face tightened.

"No, thank you," replied Naomi, rather stiffly.

"Okay . . . I shouldn't be too long."

Naomi returned to the screen without answering.

Outside Nick's Warehouse, a troupe of jugglers on a tiny tricycle pedalled past Karl and Katie. Six colourful clowns ran behind, honking horns and throwing animal-shaped sponges at onlookers.

"Clowns. They give me the creeps. They're like fascists in those rigs and pointed hats," said Karl disdainfully. "They should be called Ku Klux Klowns."

"Don't be such a killjoy, Dad," said Katie, smiling. "I forgot the circus is here for a week. Remember how you used to take me, when I was a kid?"

"You're *still* a kid. Even when you're sixty, you'll still be a kid to me. Always remember that."

"That's embarrassing, Dad."

"No, that's a parent."

"So many clowns," said Katie, shaking her head. "I've never seen so many in one place."

"Always someone clowning around in this town," quipped Karl, his face suddenly hit with a rhino-shaped sponge.

"I think it's great. Makes the city more of a metropolis."

"Metropolis is where Superman lives. Here we have clowns. There's a weeklong convention of them going on at the Waterfront. They mustn't have heard that we have a permanent circus of them up at Stormont."

Inside Nick's Warehouse, Karl made his way to his favourite spot at the window. From here he could see the office, a short distance down the street. He pictured Naomi tapping away at the computer's keyboard. Felt a terrible ache in his stomach.

"That was very rude of you, Katie, back at the office," said Karl, guiding Katie to her seat.

"I don't know what you're talking about." A half grin appeared on Katie's face.

"You know precisely what I'm talking about. Ignoring Naomi the way you did."

"*Naomi?* Oh, is that her name? She's ugly. What do you see in her?"

"Don't be cheeky."

"Well, I don't like her."

"No one said you have to, but don't be rude. Now, how come you didn't inform me that you were coming home for the summer?"

"I'm not home for the summer."

"What's that supposed to mean?"

"I'm home for good, Dad. I finally got my transfer to Queen's."

"Oh, Katie! That's brilliant!" responded Karl, delighted, reaching over and holding Katie's hand before kissing her cheek. "Hold on a minute. Why am I so bloody happy? That means you'll be able to find me easier now when you're looking for money. I can't win!"

Katie laughed, throwing back her head slightly, and Karl saw – as if for the very first time – that his daughter had turned into a very beautiful young woman. She would be a heartbreaker, just like her mother.

"It's Mum's birthday on Monday," said Katie, eyes sparkling.

"And?"

"I thought we'd surprise her. Bring her to The Edge. She loves that restaurant."

Bring her to the edge. A horrible flashback of ex-wife Lynne entered Karl's head. He had returned unexpectedly from a business trip to Dublin and, upon entering their bedroom, was shocked to find a naked stranger in his bed.

"Fuck," said the naked stranger, tapping weirdly on the bed sheets.

It took a full second for Karl to realise that the stranger was tapping his wife's hidden head, trying desperately to get her attention. It took another few seconds for Karl to realise that the stranger tapping his wife's head was a woman.

Lynne's head slowly emerged from beneath the bed sheets, the area around her large mouth slick from cunnilingus, or mouth-to-vagina resuscitation, as Karl aptly, but drunkenly put it, days later.

"You're not supposed to be here," whispered Lynne, rather hoarsely, wiping her wet mouth.

"And you're not supposed to be *there*," answered Karl, calmly, in shock, about to turn and leave.

"Karl, please . . . please let me explain . . ."

"No need to. I'm gone. Stay and finish your meal."

"You bastard!' screamed Lynne, charging from the bed, a threateningly large, lance-like dildo strapped to her waist and groin area. "You fucker!"

No thanks. You fuck her.

"Dad? Are you listening to me?" asked Katie, bringing him back from self-torture.

"I'm sorry, Katie, but there won't be a reconciliation, if that's what you're planning."

"I can't believe you're willing to throw away twenty years of marriage because of a kiss from an old boyfriend."

"An old . . . ? What *old* boyfriend?"

"Mum told me all about it; how an old childhood friend kissed her, and you walked in on them. She admits the kiss lasted longer than it should have, but blames the gin and tonic."

"Really? Simply a lingering kiss alongside the old G and T? Very original."

"She assures me that she'll never look at another man again, for the rest of her life, Dad."

"I can believe that."

"Well?"

"Katie, I know how much it would mean to you, for your mum and dad to get together again, but it's not going to happen, my wee love."

"It's her, isn't it? Her with the fancy name. You dumped Mum because your fling is a lot younger. Isn't that it?"

Karl could detect a slight hardening of Katie's voice.

"No, it's not that, Katie. It's not a fling. It's much more complicated. Give your old man some credit for being a bit more complex than that. Be appreciative that I have found someone I care deeply about, and who cares deeply for me."

"I can't believe this! You'd rather have that . . . that *secretary* over Mum, or over my feelings?" Katie's voice was becoming irritable, rising considerably.

"Calm down, Katie. Please."

"You can't love her!"

"Would you calm down for one –?"

Forcefully pushing the table away, Katie stood, grabbing her jacket before storming out of Nick's, almost knocking down the oncoming waiter.

"Katie!" shouted Karl, rushing after her.

"As long as you stay with that woman, you're no longer my dad!" she screamed, disappearing into the crushing crowd of amused onlookers, clowns and jugglers.

CHAPTER THIRTY-ONE

"Dripping water hollows out a stone . . ."
Ovid, *Epistulae Ex Ponto*

The next morning, Karl's mobile rang on the floor, wakening him.

"Bastarding sofa . . . neck feels broke . . ." he moaned, moving his body awkwardly on the futon.

Groggy-eyed, he checked his wristwatch. 6:30 A.M. "Who the bloody hell . . . ?" He checked the number on the mobile. Didn't recognise it. His head began throbbing from last night's self-pitying intoxication. Mouth dry and distracting.

Placing the mobile to his ear, Karl whispered, "Hello?"

"Karl?" A woman's voice. Edgy. Uncertain.

"Yes?" He thought he recognised the voice, but wasn't one hundred per cent certain. "Who's this?"

"Lynne," said the voice of his ex.

"Lynne? Look, if this is about more bloody money, you can just –"

"Is Katie with you?"

Something about Lynne's voice forced Karl to quickly clear away the sludge in his head.

"Katie . . . ? No . . . no, she's not here. Why? What's wrong?" Karl pushed himself out and on to the edge of the futon.

"She didn't return home last night. Told me before she left yesterday that she was going to surprise you at your office. Did she show up?"

"Yes . . . we went to Nick's for a meal." Then remembering, he quickly corrected himself. "Well . . . we didn't actually start the meal."

"What do you mean?"

Karl could feel his face redden.

"We . . . we never actually got a chance to order it. We had a bit of an . . . argument. She walked out, in a huff."

"You bastard! She came all the way from Scotland, to see you and tell you her great news, and you ended up arguing with her? What the hell's wrong with you?"

"Don't start any sanctimonious claptrap, for fuck sake!" shouted Karl, quickly on to his feet, pacing the carpeted floor.

"Was the argument over *Ni-emm-e?*" exclaimed Lynne in a patronising voice. "Your daughter's out walking the streets, and all you're concerned about is *Ni-emm-e?*"

"All this shouting at each other isn't helping. Katie's obviously staying with her mates. I'll call them now, as soon as you get your bucket mouth off the phone."

"Really? Tell me the name of *one* of Katie's friends, Karl. Go on. Shock me that you even know that much about your daughter."

Karl's face suddenly felt on fire.

"I . . ."

"You worthless piece of shit! You don't even know *any* of your daughter's friends. Bet you know all of *Ni-emm-e's* friends though."

"Calm down, Lynne. Just calm –"

"Find, Katie, you bastard! Just find her."

CHAPTER THIRTY-TWO

"The devil's agents may be of flesh and blood, may they not?"
Arthur Conan Doyle, *The Hound of the Baskervilles*

Katie awoke to a jarring darkness offering no clues as to her whereabouts other than a nocturnal sense of dread. A soggy mattress smelling of piss and vomit was all that separated her from the bare floor.

To her horror, she was naked, and she immediately began pulling her knees up to her chest, hugging them for security and warmth. A smell of dampness filled the air. She could hear noises in the distance, but they seemed tiny, as if down a tunnel.

"Good girl. You're awake," said a voice in the darkness.

The voice startled and terrified her. She tightened the grip on her knees. Burning panic began rising in her chest. If only she could shake herself awake from this nightmare. "What . . . where am I?"

"Do not worry, Katie. You are safe. This is my kingdom. No harm can come to you here, provided you abide by the rules – my rules."

"How . . . how do you know my name? Why . . . are you doing this?" Her voice sounded strange.

"Do you realise how strong-willed you are? You'd be surprised the number of people who die, waking up confused and stressed when they open their eyes to a foreign environment. They become so frightened about their location and purpose that their heart simply bursts open, killing them."

"Don't hurt me, please." *It's okay. The alarm clock will go off, shortly, freeing you from this madness.*

"I need you to stand."

"Please . . . can I have my clothes? It's so cold . . ." *Wake up!*

"Later, if you behave. For now, I need you to stand. Do not make me repeat myself again."

She tried standing, but her knees began trembling so much she had to sit back down.

"I . . . can't stand. My knees are buckling."

Abruptly, something touched her where the small of her back flowed into her buttocks; something cold and clammy like the vinyl skin of a shark. Hands. Large hands.

She screamed.

"Screaming is futile, Katie. No one can hear you. Not down here."

The clammy hands began pulling her up, forcing her to stand. She stood shakily, her knees refusing to stop quivering. Suddenly, like a fog evaporating, her eyes slowly began adjusting to the dark.

He stood there, the monster, silhouetted in the heavy gloom. Tall. Muscular. Naked. Something fashioned from an insane god's hands, his face mangled by knots of darkness.

Her heart began pumping faster. *Wake the hell up!*

"Just do as you're told, and everything will be fine and dandy," he insisted. "Over here, in this direction."

The hands began pulling, guiding her like a person suddenly blinded. The ground beneath her bare feet was wet with puddles, stinking of urine and exposed oil. Without warning, she banged her knees, hard, against something, something with wheels.

"Good," said the voice. "Climb on and stretch yourself out."

"Okay . . . please, don't hurt me. I'll do whatever –" Without warning, Katie leapt at him with such surprising force it sent him skittering backwards against the wall, his head rebounding off it with a sickening thud. Her nails immediately became daggers, scratching and digging, drawing blood and flesh. "Bastard! Dirty filthy bastard!" she screamed, finding his eyes, gorging them, her teeth clenching involuntary with hatred and determination.

He howled a wounded animal noise, the blood spilling from eyes and face.

"Bastard! Bastard! Bastard!" screamed Katie, feeling the rubbery eyeballs shift in the sockets' housing. *A few more seconds. You can do this. Blind the bastard. Rip them out!*

The sudden kick to her groin forced an agonising scream from her mouth. The pain was excruciating. She vomited, struggling through the pain just to breathe the dirty air.

Hands suddenly grabbed, scooping her up from the ground as if she were a wet doll, before thrusting her down violently upon the wheeled object.

She could feel straps snaking around her, tightening like a boa constrictor.

"You broke the rules. Now suffer the consequences," he hissed, tightening the straps until she found breathing difficult.

"You don't . . . you don't know my father. He . . . he'll find you, bastard. He'll kill you." She could see his face clearly now, for the very first time, and it terrified her more than when it hid in the shadows unseen.

"That's where you're wrong, sweet Katie. I know your father rather well. He'll neither find me, nor kill me. Now, I need you to open your mouth. If you refuse, I have ways – *very painful ways* – of making you."

He was forcing something against her mouth. Firm and greasy. It stank like the urine puddles beneath.

His penis? She felt her stomach heave, but ignored it, steeling her determination. *Let him do it, let the bastard shove it in. Bite the pickle off. Let him bleed to death. Bastard.*

"If you resist the tubing, it will rip your throat lining," he said, pushing the tube against her mouth. "That would be very painful and fatal. Better to comply. Far, far better."

She clamped her teeth tightly, willing them to lockjaw.

"Very well," he continued. "You leave me no alternative."

She could hear him shuffling about, moving things in the semidarkness.

"Blame yourself for this, dear Katie."

Some sort of bizarre metal apparatus was being clamped against her face. It felt like a mask with chin support. Turning a small wing nut at the side of the device, he began tightening.

She could feel her jaws caving, the more he turned the wing nut. A tiny clamp was placed on her nose. She tried holding her breath, but could hold it no longer, her mouth suddenly springing open, gasping like a stranded fish.

He coaxed the tube in, lubricating it with a thick, transparent gel. "I warned you."

She gagged, and suddenly her entire body began jerking epileptically.

"Easy, easy," he soothed, pushing the tube further down her throat. "Try not to panic. You will only end up choking . . . easy . . . easy . . . relax . . . good girl . . . soon you'll be ready."

As quickly as it had started, the jerking began slowing, steadying to a normal plateau. Katie felt darkness pouring into her brain, seeping down to her eyes. A blackout was coming. She welcomed it.

PART TWO

THE DARK PLACE

Chapter Thirty-Three

"One hair of a woman can draw more than a hundred pair of oxen."
James Howell, *Familiar Letters*

At the panoramic window of his office, Detective Inspector Mark Wilson stood sipping a cup of coffee, his eyes scanning early morning workers parading off to their jobs in the direction of Belfast City centre. Only a slight beer belly marred the poker-straight frame of his body. His cropped marine-short haircut – shaped like a smoothing iron – accentuated a face badly pitted with pockmarks. Not caused by acne, but by a shotgun blast to his face, many years ago.

A sudden rap at the door brought his attention away from the window.

"Yes?"

The door opened, revealing the weary face of Detective Malcolm Chambers.

"There's a woman here, sir – outside I mean. She . . . she wants to see you immediately. I . . . I told her that was impossible. I don't even know how she got up the stairs without being stopped at the –"

"A woman? Who the hell is she, and what does she want?"

"She told me to get . . . to get you, and for me to –"

Suddenly, Chambers was brushed to the side by the woman, her stormy face menacing.

"Lynne?" said Wilson, almost dropping the cup from his hand.

"What the hell's all this, barging in without –?"

"What have you done about Katie?" demanded Lynne.

"Katie?" Wilson's face knotted into a puzzle. "What do you mean? What's wrong with Katie?"

"You're saying Karl hasn't contacted you about Katie going missing yesterday?" A red flush ran up Lynne's attractive but gob-smacked face. "I don't believe this."

At the mention of Karl's name, Wilson's face did a slight nervous tic.

"Just calm down for a second, Lynne," said Wilson, stepping forward towards his sister, quickly seating her in a chair. "Chambers? Don't stand there gawking, man. Bring in some tea and biscuits for my sister – and another coffee for me."

"Right away, sir!" exclaimed Chambers, backing quickly out of the office.

"Okay, Lynne," soothed Wilson. "Start from the start."

Lynne looked on the verge of tears. It confused and startled Mark Wilson, this unnatural outpouring of vulnerability by his supposedly rhinoceros-skinned sister – a woman not known for showing any sign of weakness.

"Katie got her transfer to Queen's, a few days ago. She starts after the summer," commenced Lynne.

"Queen's? That's great," responded Wilson, smiling. "Now I'll get to see more of my favourite niece."

"She . . . she went to break the good news to her father on Thursday, but when she hadn't come home by Friday afternoon, I decided to call Karl, find out if Katie was staying with him."

"And? What did Kane say?"

"They . . . they had had an argument of some sort. Katie never stayed. The last he saw of her was at Nick's Warehouse, when she angrily left without ordering a meal."

"What was the argument over? Did he say?"

"No. You know him. He can't tell the truth even if it sounds better than a lie, the bastard." Lynne made a face. "Now it's your turn to tell the truth."

"What are you talking about?"

"Why hasn't Karl been in touch with you? That would have been a priority with him, no matter how useless he is."

"How the hell would I know why he hasn't been in touch? Why don't you ask *him?*"

"Your eyes always give you away, Mark. Even as a kid. That's why Mum and Dad always knew when you had just done something wrong. You're not good at concealing."

Wilson seemed to be studying his sister, as if weighing up certain words in his head.

"Things . . . things have happened between Kane and myself. I can't go into the details, Lynne. Not even with you. Your ex-husband walks a very thin line in life. That's all I need to –"

Wilson stopped abruptly. He hadn't noticed Chambers standing at the door, tray in hand. How long had he been standing there, listening?

"Put the damn tray down at the table, man. We haven't got bloody giraffe tongues!"

"Yes, sir! I rapped the door before entering. Sorry."

Waiting until Chambers closed the door behind him, Lynne said, "Now you listen, Mark, and listen good. Do you think for one second that I will allow some bullshit between you and Karl get in the way of my daughter's safety?" Lynne stared at her brother in such a way it made his balls shrivel inside their sac.

"Lynne, you know I'll do all in my power to –"

"Don't. Don't dare give me one of your press releases," hissed Lynne, standing. "Between the two of you, find Katie – and quickly. Do I make myself clear?"

Wilson's eyes could not hold her stare.

"Yes," he finally said, watching her walk to the door, feeling her presence in the room long after she had left.

CHAPTER THIRTY-FOUR

"Memory is man's greatest friend and worst enemy."
Gilbert Parker, *Romany of the Snows*

K arl looked haggard, purple half moons under his eyes. For the past ten minutes or so, since entering Wilson's office, he had been troubled by a miserable feeling of déjà vu. As the minutes wore on, his apprehension deepened, and he more than once wondered if his anxieties were justified or whether they were nothing more than the product of a stressed mind. One thing for certain, though: he wasn't looking forward to this meeting with his ex-brother-in-law, despite the good news that CCTV footage had captured some of Katie's movements before her disappearance.

"I wish Mark would hurry and get in here," said Lynne, pacing the floor. "I need to see this footage."

"He'll get here in *his* own good time. You can be bloody sure of that," sniped Karl. "Probably more important things to do, like breakfast."

"It's hard to believe I was here two days ago, screaming my head off at him, accusing him of doing nothing."

"He hasn't done anything yet, except keep us waiting."

"Don't start, Karl. You didn't help the situation by not informing him immediately. He could have been on the ball a lot sooner."

"Glad you have so much faith in your brother. Wish I could share some of –"

Suddenly, Wilson stepped into the room, nodding to Lynne, totally ignoring Karl.

It was left ultimately for Lynne to scrape at the icy layer of silence between the two alpha males.

"Look, I don't know what the hell is going on between you two, and I really don't care," stated Lynne, glancing from Karl to Wilson. "But from here on in, all I ask is that we *all* focus on one thing and one thing only: the safe return of Katie. After that, you two can continue hating each other until the cows come home. Agreed?"

Karl nodded; Wilson mumbled something inaudible.

"Mark? I couldn't understand one word from your mouth," said Lynne, fixing her brother with a stare of impatience.

"*Agreed,*" said Wilson, giving a mutinous glare.

"Okay," continued Lynne, clearly relieved. "This is your territory, Mark."

All eyes immediately fell on Wilson as he stood, switching on a TV stationed atop his desk. The screen immediately came to life.

"This is CCTV footage obtained less than three hours ago. It's a bit blurred in places. That's why I was delayed, trying to get it as clear as possible."

Karl felt his face redden.

"This was taken on the day Katie went missing," continued Wilson. "It shows her emerging from Nick's Warehouse before walking down Hill Street towards Talbot Street."

"Oh God, Karl, look at her," said Lynne, her voice quivering, tears suddenly forming in her eyes.

Karl's heart went to his mouth, watching Katie walking down Hill Street, cutting across Talbot Street before heading in the direction of Saint Anne's Cathedral. Her tiny figure looked terribly forlorn, and suddenly he was overcome with guilt and the self-inflicted curse of *if only* . . .

Wilson touched a button on the remote, freezing the frame. "We lose her here, at Academy Street, because some of the cameras in that area were not functioning properly, smashed by yobs. Fortunately, the

University of Ulster's security cameras captured her once again, this time heading in the direction of Fredrick Street before she disappears from view altogether."

"Oh God," whispered Lynne. "You've . . . you've got to do something, Mark. Please."

"We . . . we're working twenty-four seven on Katie's disappearance –"

"Abduction," cut in Karl. "She didn't disappear like some magician's trick. She was *abducted.*"

"All resources at hand," continued Wilson, as if he hadn't heard Karl's voice, "are being used to their utmost. I have four detectives working on the enquiry, three of whom are on loan."

"I hope Smiling Chambers isn't one of them," said Karl.

"Right! That does it," declared Wilson, his face turning red. "I'm not standing here to be ridiculed by –"

"Mark, don't you dare!" shouted Lynne, before turning her attention to Karl. "What the hell is wrong with you, Karl? Can't you just shut up and listen for a change?"

"He's talking a load of bollocks!" snapped Karl. "Ask him why they didn't raid the premises of the chief suspect, Bob Hannah, even after getting a tip-off from a member of the public."

The room suddenly fell silent. All eyes refocused on an uncomfortable-looking Wilson.

"Well, Mark?" asked Lynne, breaking the silence. "Is it true, what Karl just said?"

Wilson gnawed at his lower lip before answering. "Bob Hannah is a multi-millionaire businessman. He contributes to numerous charities –"

"How many of those are police *charities?*" asked Karl.

"He contributes to numerous charities," continued Wilson, "and is not the sort of person whose premises you raid simply because some *anonymous* member of the public with a grudge makes a phone call against him, offering no evidence of any sort. That information was passed on to me by one of my men. I told him to disregard it as a crank call."

"You bastard," said Karl.

"It was you who made the call, wasn't it?" accused Wilson. "Didn't have too much belief in your own information if you had to call it in anonymously."

"Stop it, the two of you!" yelled Lynne. "For God's sake, just stop it!"

"You're bloody good at defending him," persisted Karl. "Research on serial killers has shown they are generally intelligent, have often suffered serious emotional trauma in childhood, particularly sexual events, and grow up loners. This is a textbook description of Hannah."

"Serious emotional trauma? You mean his mother being killed when he was young," stated Wilson smugly. "Couldn't that apply to you, Kane?"

"Mark! How *dare* you talk like that to Karl?" said Lynne, coldly composed now, poking her face into her brother's. "Apologise to Karl, right *now.*"

"It's okay, Lynne," said Karl, forcing a calmness to his voice. "I'm neither rising to the bait nor allowing Mark's childish remarks to distract us. What Mark really needs to do is uncork his head from his arse."

"Give me evidence, Kane, instead of slobbers. That's all you're good at!"

"Evidence? You want evidence," said Karl, voice rising. "He murdered Ivana because he feared she would eventually expose his past."

"What nonsense. We have the killer in custody. Evidence is mounting against him as we speak."

"Vincent Harrison? That's another load of bollocks. He's being used as a scapegoat for police incompetence."

"You have evidence to the contrary?" sneered Wilson. "Where is it?"

"You know that Hannah murdered his mother?"

"Now who's talking bollocks? It was an accident during some hunting party, when he was a kid."

"Ivana witnessed it."

"You sure know how to tell whoppers. Conveniently for you, Ivana is dead; therefore you can't back up your wild allegation."

"It suits the cops that Ivana was murdered, doesn't it?"

"What? What did you say? That's a serious allegation to –"

"Not only did Hannah murder his mother, but he was having an incestuous relationship with her also."

"Oh my goodness . . ." whispered Lynne. "Are . . . are you certain?"

"Ha! He's certain of nothing," said Wilson. "It's all hearsay. Where is your *evidence,* Kane?"

"My instinct."

"Perhaps in the middle ages *your instinct* would have carried weight as a witch finder general. Fortunately for the rest of us, it would never reach a court in modern times. The law demands a more solid foundation to convict a person than your bloody *instinct.*"

"Tina Richardson. Body found mutilated in the Black Mountain."

"Evidence?"

"Eileen Flynn. Mutilated."

"*Where* is the evidence, Kane?"

"He abducted Martina Ferris, brutally murdered her –"

"Evidence, evidence, evidence." Wilson was smirking now.

"Cathy McGlone, recently murdered. She was on the run for the last six years for the attempted abduction of a child."

"Yes. I know that. And?"

"The child lived two streets away from Bob Hannah at the time."

"Coincidence never makes good evidence, Kane."

"It's Hannah, and you damn well know it!"

"You have no evidence to show if any of this is –"

Karl slapped the table with such force that Lynne jumped slightly.

"There's your fucking evidence!" declared Karl, opening up a group of folded documents. "Right there. Under your snotty fucking nose."

Wilson lifted the documents gingerly from the table, his eyes skimming over them.

"Photocopies of property deeds? What do these prove?" asked Wilson.

"Check the document in your right hand. See the property?"

Wilson studied the document. "Crumlin Road Prison? And?"

"They all belong to Bob Hannah."

"*And?*" said Wilson. "So, he owns the rights to Crumlin Road Prison. Wish I did."

"Martina Ferris had paint trapped beneath her fingernails. Specialist paint called Neo X2. It's used to paint military barracks and . . . prisons."

"*Oh my God,*" whispered Lynne, placing a hand to her mouth. "You think . . . you think Katie is being held prisoner in Crumlin Road? Oh my God, Karl . . ."

"I have to think something, Lynne, otherwise I'll go fucking insane. There's also a skeleton key in Hannah's movie house. Tell me that's a coincidence."

"Are you listening to this, Mark?" said Lynne. "What the hell are you going to do?"

"I . . . I'm going to have to study these documents carefully . . ."

"Study? *Study!*" screamed Lynne. "You'll do more than study, Mark. By God you will."

"I'm doing the best that I can, Lynne. This isn't easy for me, either."

"Well, your best isn't good enough, it would seem," accused Karl. "That other page you're holding is a photocopy of a Rolodex. Just numbers. No names. But check the numbers like I did. They belong to numerous politicians and judges – including our current mayor, Alan Mosley. No doubt they like watching the same sort of movies as Bob Hannah. Snuff movies. You know what snuff movies are? Women being killed for so-called pleasure."

Lynne paled. Her mouth opened, but no words came out.

"And these documents just happen to come into your possession?" said Wilson.

"No. I broke into his movie house, the same place where he's been living for the last ten years. He has snuff and paedophile movies in there, good enough to warrant a search. Good enough to put the fucker in jail."

"You're admitting to breaking and entering?"

"Shocking, isn't it? Put a hundred unpaid parking tickets along with that crime of the century."

"You've got to go and get this monster, Mark," pleaded Lynne.

"Kane contaminated the evidence," replied Wilson. "The court would simply throw it out. It's going to be hard to –"

"You better damn well do something, Mark – and now," said Lynne, her voice eerily calm. "Stop making excuses. Get the warrant. Bring that bastard in, or so help me God, I'll find and kill him myself."

Chapter Thirty-Five

"All the misfortunes of men derive from one single thing,
which is their inability to be at ease in a room."
Blaise Pascal, *Pensées*

The very next morning, Karl and Lynne waited anxiously in Wilson's office.

"It's gone well after ten. What the hell's keeping your brother? He said he'd inform us as soon as Hannah was brought in at ten," accused Karl, sipping tepid coffee.

"You always think this will happen to someone else's child," said Lynne, ignoring Karl's protestations. "Never your own."

"We can't wrap our kids in cotton wool, Lynne, otherwise scumbags like Hannah have won."

"What if it isn't Hannah? What do we do then, Karl?"

"It *is* him," said Karl, his voice filled with a confidence he did not feel.

Lynne removed a lighter and a packet of cigarettes, easing one out before offering the pack to Karl, ignoring the No Smoking sign resting on Wilson's desk.

"I've . . ." He could smell the aroma from the open pack. It smelt good. He took a cigarette from the enclosure, placing it in his mouth. It tasted damn sweet. *Just one to help calm the nerves.*

Lynne's lighter sparked irritably before breaking flame. She lit her own cigarette before bringing the flame to Karl's face.

"I've given them up," he said, removing the cig from his mouth before handing it back to Lynne.

"You're joking? Oh, Karl, I'm sorry. I didn't know." Lynne looked embarrassed.

"Don't worry about it. I was just testing myself."

"That's brilliant," said Lynne, taking a deep suck of the cig before releasing toxic air into the room. "Wish I could."

"What's the smile for?"

"You've changed."

"Me? Ha! I don't think so."

"No, really. Something I can't put my finger on, but you *have* changed."

"I'll have to tell Naomi . . ." He suddenly felt uncomfortable. "I . . ."

"I'm sorry for making fun of Naomi's name. It was so childish of me," said Lynne, looking away from his gaze. "We had something, Karl, didn't we? Years ago. We *did* love each other."

"Of course we did. How the hell else would we have stuck each other for so bloody long?"

"I . . . I always thought our marriage would last for ever; like a rock."

"So did I. Only thing was, it ended up like Northern Rock," smiled Karl, making Lynne laugh, despite the dire circumstances of the situation.

"Oh, Karl, I do miss you, the way you can make me laugh at life. You know that?"

"I need to take a leak, Lynne," said Karl, standing, quickly changing the subject. "All this coffee is crunching my bladder."

"Try not to be too long. Just in case Mark comes in."

Moving down the corridor towards the toilet, Karl passed two uniformed officers. Both nodded solemnly at him.

Inside the toilet, he waited a few seconds, catching his breath, untangling his mangled thoughts. *Easy. Take it nice and easy. All those visits to this place over the years are starting to pay dividends. You know these corridors like the back of your hand.*

Popping his head out into the corridor, he glanced left and then right. All clear. He moved quickly, proceeding down the corridor, turning left before making a sharp right into a rather dingy-looking area masquerading as a tea-room. Stained cups and unfinished sandwiches lay scattered everywhere. Thankfully, the place was deserted. Quickly, he opened a door, leading him out towards his intended target.

Green lights were glaring in the semi-darkness, directly above two doors.

It hasn't started, yet. Which fucking room are they going to use?

Suddenly, distant voices began filling the corridor. *Fuck! Pick a door. Quickly!*

Slipping stealthily into a room, Karl welcomed its beautiful darkness, trying desperately to steady his breathing.

The voices became louder, clearer. Suddenly, someone began turning the handle of the door.

Karl held his breath. His entire body felt weak with nerves. The door slowly eased open.

"No, we'll use B Room, Detective Chambers," said Wilson's voice.

"Okay, sir," came the reply, and the door closed.

Immediately, Karl released all trapped air from his lungs before walking to the two-way mirror. Four lone chairs filled the room. From listening to Wilson over the years, Karl knew that the salient lack of a table was part of the psychological mind games played out in the room. In such a claustrophobic environment, the removal of a table is the equivalent of removing barriers, the interrogator hoping to be perceived as a friend.

The door to the interrogation room suddenly opened, revealing a smiling Hannah and a well-known solicitor by the name of James Johnson. Wilson and Chambers followed.

Hannah's eyes were shadowed slits.

I wonder how many unfortunate victims saw those eyes before being murdered without remorse or pity, you bastard? And what the hell are those marks on your face? Looks like someone's tore a good lump out of you. To Karl, the scars on Hannah's face looked fresh. No more than a few days old.

Pressing a small green button just below the windowpane, Karl listened as Wilson's voice began filtering through a small pair of speakers recessed into the panelling.

"Mister Hannah. This is Detective Malcolm Chambers. He'll be conducting the interview. I'll be observing. Is that okay?"

Hannah nodded. "Certainly. I know you're only doing your job, Inspector Wilson. As I stated before I came to –"

"Don't say another word, Robert," interrupted Johnson, handing a sheet of paper towards Chambers. "I would like to give you this sworn statement from my client stating that he is not going to make *any* statements to the police, other than this. Now, you can arrest him on some trumped-up charge, but I can guarantee he'll be out on bail in less than an hour. I'm sure you know Mister Hannah's importance in the business community and police benevolent funds?"

Chambers looked at Wilson's blank face before answering. "Yes . . . of course we do, Mister Johnson, and we very much appreciate it. We certainly are not going to arrest Mister Hannah; simply ask him a few questions concerning his whereabouts on certain nights, last month."

"My client will not be answering *any* questions with regards –"

"It's okay, James," cut in Hannah. "I don't mind answering a few questions concerning my whereabouts, if it helps the police with their inquiries."

"Please, Robert, as your solicitor, I am advising you not to make any statements, other than the one we agreed to before we –"

Hannah held up a hand, halting the verbal manure trafficking from Johnson's mouth. "It really is okay, James. I have nothing to hide."

Resigned, Johnson said to Chambers, "Okay, but no tape recordings. Agreed?"

Chambers looked at Wilson.

"Agreed," said Wilson.

"Detective Chambers?" said Hannah, smiling. "Your questions, please."

"Yes, thank you, Mister Hannah," said Chambers, producing a notebook from his pocket. "Can you tell me where you were on the eleventh of last month?"

"Hmmm. That's a toughie. Can you remember where *you* were, Detective?"

"Please just answer the questions put to you, Mister Hannah," said Wilson.

"Yes, you're correct. Sorry, Inspector. If you give me a minute to think . . . Oh! Of course! How could I have forgotten? I was at a fundraiser."

"Is there a name you can give, to confirm that?" asked Chambers.

"Why, yes. There are quite a few. Ian Finnegan, for starters, not forgetting Judge –"

"Ian Finnegan?" Chambers's face paled. "Chief Constable Finnegan?"

"Why, yes. Is there a problem?"

"What? No. No, of course not," replied Chambers, flustered, looking quickly at Wilson.

Wilson's face remained impassive – unlike Karl's, whose own did a peculiar twitching at the mention of the chief constable's name.

"Your next question, Detective Chambers?" asked Hannah.

"Er . . . yes, sir. Let me see . . ." mumbled Chambers, randomly flipping pages from the notebook.

Whatever questions Chambers had initially intended to ask, they sure as hell weren't the mundane ones now being solicited, thought Karl, listening with disgust at the grovelling Chambers.

"Ask him where he got those scratch marks, dickhead," whispered Karl.

As if by magic, Wilson suddenly cut in.

"Those scratches look pretty bad, Mister Hannah. Could you tell me what happened? How you obtained them?"

"What – oh! These?" Hannah smiled, touching the scratches. "Blue Boy gave them to me."

"Blue Boy?"

"My cat. A Russian Blue. Normally, he's of good disposition, but a couple of days ago he attacked me while I was resting in bed. I think it had to do with the fact that I had to have him neutered."

"Neutered?" asked Chambers.

Slowly, deliberately, Hannah craned his neck. Staring intently at the two-way, he replied. "His balls removed."

Chambers winced. Wilson remained impassive.

Behind the two-way, Hannah's remarks flamed Karl's face. *You bastard.*

For the next twenty minutes, Karl listened, barely able to control the rising anger burning in his chest at Chambers's indolent questioning and Wilson's seeming indifference.

"The only thing missing from this walk in the fucking park is the picnic basket," said Karl, easing quickly from the room.

"Karl? What on earth kept you?" asked an anxious-looking Lynne, watching Karl re-enter Wilson's office. "What's wrong? You look sickish."

"It's nothing. Just something indigestible in my stomach."

"There's a bug doing the rounds. That's probably what's hit you."

"You're right. Something is bugging me," replied Karl, walking to the open window for some air. "This bastarding heat can't get any worse."

Five minutes later, Wilson entered the room.

"Well?" asked Lynne, quickly. "What did you find out, Mark?"

Walking to his desk, Wilson filled a glass with water, sipping before answering.

"Not an awful lot. He's given us names of people he was with on certain dates put to him by us. Of course, we'll check everything out first before we –"

"Of course you will," cut in Karl.

"What's that snide remark supposed to mean?" snarled Wilson.

"You know exactly what it means!"

"Karl! Mark! For God's sake, would you two stop this nonsense!" screamed Lynne. "What is wrong with you two?"

"Wrong?" snapped Karl. "Ask your brother why he pussy-footed around Hannah in the interrogation room."

"How the hell would you know what way I . . ." Wilson's voice suddenly trailed off. "You . . . you were in the observation room."

"You really believe that bastard got those fucking scratches on his face because of some cat being pissed at him?"

"You fool! Do you know what you've done by listening in on an interview with a suspect? You've jeopardised all our work!"

"Bollocks! It wasn't so long ago you were allowing me into the interrogation rooms to listen to suspects, so long as I came up with the goods for you!"

"You might be after a Pyrrhic victory, Kane, but we're after something a lot more bloody tangible. Do you know the importance of the interrogation room? Of course you bloody well don't! We have to carefully gather all the verbal details so later it can tie into the physical evidence of the crime. It's critical that those details are clearly stated, accurate, and unmarred, allowing the court to establish motive, opportunity and a proper timeline."

"Fuck, times really have changed from the give-the-fucker-a-good-kicking-in-the-balls days!"

"You really think you're smart, don't you?"

"Smart enough to know when not to be smart."

"Well, think about this, smart arse," said Wilson, voice suddenly icy calm. "If I arrest Hannah, put him in prison, and it turns out he's the abductor of Katie, and acting alone, who's going to feed and give her water? Not him. He'll be locked up, nice and secure. Is that what you really want?"

A bottled stillness suddenly came over Karl as he tried desperately to remember what he was thinking about just a moment ago. Nothing came. A panic attack? That was it, his brain refusing to function.

"I . . ." muttered Karl, unnaturally lost for words.

"I think you've done enough damage here, Kane. You know the way out."

CHAPTER THIRTY-SIX

"Ah, what a dusty answer gets the soul
When hot for certainties in this our life!"
George Meredith, *Modern Love*

Karl stared out the window like a zombie, watching people flowing into work. They all seemed to have the same expressionless face stitched between their ears. He kept trying to refocus his mind, but it kept returning to yesterday's disastrous results at the police station. Wilson was right. What good would it have done, arresting Hannah? A shiver ran up Karl's spine at the thought of Katie starving to death in some darkened hole. What the hell was he thinking of? That was the problem. He *wasn't* thinking, allowing his heart and emotions to run amok.

"Stop torturing yourself, Karl," said Naomi, placing a hand on his shoulder. "Everything will work itself out. You'll see."

"I'm glad you didn't leave," stated Karl, placing a hand on Naomi's. "I'd be a basket case if you had."

"Let's not talk about that, for now."

The phone on his desk rang. He picked it up hurriedly.

"Hello?"

"I'll make this quick," said Wilson on the other end. "I'm not going to press charges against you. But I must warn you, Hannah's not a happy man —"

"As if I give a fuck about his happiness!" snapped Karl, relief suddenly combining with anger.

"If you would just let me finish!" boomeranged Wilson's tetchy voice. "He's not a happy man because as we speak, all of his premises – including Crumlin Road Prison – are being searched."

Relief suddenly flooded over Karl.

"I . . . thanks," mumbled Karl. "I . . . appreciate this . . ."

"I don't want your thanks. I didn't do this for you – or my sister. I did it because Katie is my niece and I love her as if she were my daughter."

"I owe you an apology for –"

"Stuff your apology! Don't think this changes anything between us. I still hold you responsible for the deaths of my detectives. Your day will come, Kane," snarled Wilson, hanging up.

No sooner had the phone stopped ringing when it started once again.

"Hello?" asked Karl.

"You couldn't leave well enough alone, could you?" hissed the voice at the other end.

"Hannah?"

"I would have released her after a while. But you've changed the rules, dear Karl, and I don't allow the rules to be changed. As we speak, barbarians are tearing my theatre apart, all because of you. I have no doubt about that. Do you know how that feels, to be violated?"

"Let Katie go. Please. I'll do anything you ask."

"Too late. Far too late to bargain, dear Karl."

"What is it you want from me?"

"I'm going to kill you, dear Karl, and not in a very nice way. I'm going to kill you with the gun Cathy took from you."

"It was you, that night, wasn't it? It was you who murdered Cathy."

"Cathy had outlived her usefulness. She had become a liability. The good thing is that the gun has your prints on it, not mine."

Karl's stomach suddenly heaved.

"Did you ever see your beautiful daughter naked, sweet Karl?"

The blood went straight to Karl's head. *Bang! Bang! Bang!*

"You've gone all quiet, dear Karl," continued Hannah. "Trying to trace this call? Won't do you any good. I always use a throwaway phone.

Where was I? Oh! Sweet Katie. Did you know she has her little boy nipples and clit pierced? Quite provocative, I can assure you. But you probably knew that already. Eh? I might send you a photo of –"

"Bastard! So help me, you bastard, if you've touched my daughter, I –"

"Just think of this: if I hadn't been watching you, that day in Nick's Warehouse, I would never have guessed Katie was your daughter. You looked right at me when I hit you up the face with the rhino-shaped sponge," laughed Hannah.

"What?"

"The clown. That was me, dear Karl. I even winked at you as I walked by. I was on the lookout for other young . . . companions, when I suddenly realised the resemblance between father and daughter."

"You fucking bastard . . ."

"You brought all this to your own door, Karl. Live with the consequences – for ever."

The phone went dead.

CHAPTER THIRTY-SEVEN

"Soldiering, my dear madam, is the coward's art of attacking mercilessly when you are strong, and keeping out of harm's way when you are weak. That is the whole secret of successful fighting. Get your enemy at a disadvantage; and never, on any account, fight him on equal terms."
George Bernard Shaw, *Arms and the Man*

Karl sat in Wilson's office, feigning calmness, all the while watching Lynne ripping shreds from her brother.

"How the hell can you sit there, Mark, claiming you can't find anything!" screamed Lynne, leaning into Wilson's haggard-looking face.

"Because we *couldn't* find anything, damn it! Perhaps if *someone* hadn't burglarised his premises, it wouldn't have unnerved Hannah enough to move any incriminating evidence stored there!" retorted Wilson, glancing at Karl.

"Or someone in your office tipping him off," said Karl, calmly.

"You would say that, wouldn't you, Kane? All mouth, no brains. Always looking for police corruption, aren't you?"

"I don't think you looked hard enough, Mark," accused Lynne.

"For God's sake, Lynne! The search parties explored every inch of the prison, in a three-day extensive search. They even reopened all of the old covered-in escape tunnels, just to make sure. What else can I do?"

"You can find my daughter! That's what you can do!" Without warning, Lynne suddenly burst into sobs. "Just . . . just find her."

"Easy, Lynne," soothed Karl, suddenly standing beside his ex-wife, holding her tightly in his arms. "Easy, girl . . . breathe easy. That's it . . . easy . . ."

"Oh, Karl, what . . . what are we going to do?"

"Something. I've already made my mind up. Come on, I'm taking you home."

"This something better not be breaking the law, Kane," cut-in Wilson, blocking the doorway. "You won't get any permission or support from me if you do. I warn you well in advance."

Starting from his toes, a lit fuse of burning anger immediately ran up the entire length of Karl's body, heading for the gunpowder in his brain. He stopped it, just in time, preventing the explosion.

"I don't need *your* permission or support for anything, Mark," replied Karl, calmly. "Perhaps not too far in the future, you're the one going to need *my* support, though."

"Your support? Ha! Don't make me laugh, Kane. Why the hell would I need your support in the future or any other time, for that matter?"

Forcing a smile, Karl replied, "A wee birdie told me that Phillips got his pension reinstated. I wonder why? Perhaps I don't need to wonder. Perhaps I already know the reason. Think about that, Mark, the next time you forget to look over your shoulder. Now move out of the way."

Paling quickly, Wilson moved slowly from the door before easing down on to a chair.

Karl closed the door gently behind him and Lynne.

CHAPTER THIRTY-EIGHT

"A man's mind will very generally refuse to make itself up until it be driven and compelled by emergency."
Anthony Trollope, *Ayala's Angel*

Karl was certain the bar – Ramblers – was somewhere in the vicinity. What he wasn't certain of was its ownership; if it was still run by the man he desperately needed to speak to. Yesterday's confrontation with Wilson had galvanised him. Sitting on his arse was a luxury he no longer could afford.

"Who're you looking for, Mister?" asked a little girl no older than ten years of age, angelic face a landmass of freckles resembling rusted nails. Her left hand held a beat-up teddy bear with bizarre glass eyes and both ears missing. It resembled road kill.

"Don't you know you shouldn't be talking to a stranger, little girl?" said Karl.

"What about you? *You're* talking to a stranger," spit-fired the little girl in an automatic retort. "*Well?* Aren't you?"

"Good point. But I'm a bit older than you."

The little girl seemed to ponder this revelation for a few seconds before suddenly bringing the road-kill bear towards Karl's face. He could smell dog piss and dampness from its mangy fur.

"But you're not as old as me," said the bear, its bizarre toe-like lips unmoving.

"Oh, a go-between? You've got more tricks than Richard Nixon, little girl," said Karl, feeling like a proper dick, standing in the middle of the street talking to a stuffed bear.

"I'm not Little Girl. My name is Bear," said the bear, getting annoyingly closer to Karl's wary face.

"I see . . . well, I'm looking for a certain type of place that wouldn't be known by you, Bear."

"Is it Brenda's?" asked Bear.

"Pardon?"

"Brenda's. You know, the place where all the strange men go to at night?"

"Homeless shelter, you mean?"

"Are you heebiefuckingjeebie out of your head, Mister? The strange men go there to have sex. It's a whorehouse. Is that what you're looking for?"

Karl's tongue almost fell from his mouth. "No . . . no, but I'll keep that in mind, the next time I'm feeling strange." About to move on, he suddenly decided that perhaps Little-Not-So-Angelic could, after all, know the location of Ramblers.

"Ever hear of a bar called Ramblers?"

"Sure. Who hasn't? Everybody knows Ramblers. It's in Clifton Square."

"Clifton Square? You wouldn't happen to know the directions by any chance?"

"Sure."

Karl waited, but other than sure, no other word emerged. He tried again. "Can *you* direct *me* to Clifton Square?"

Bear nodded. "It'll cost."

"What else is new?" said Karl, digging into his pocket, producing some coins, before handing them to an outstretched paw and hand.

"*This* is Clifton Square," said Bear. "That's Ramblers over there, beside the bakery."

"Beside the . . ." Karl glanced across the street at the indicated building. Ramblers resembled an old church, badly converted into another old church. "No wonder I couldn't find it."

"You really shouldn't be going to that place, Mister," advised the little girl. "They're always fighting in there, and beating people up."

"Thanks. I'll try and remember that."

Outside Ramblers, Karl stepped over a rib-protruding, sleeping dog being used as a doorstop. The dog stirred and emitted a low growl before slumbering again. He wondered if the dog was an omen, if perhaps the little girl was right?

A skinny young man – mid-teens – stopped him as he was about to enter.

"Sorry, pops. Strictly members only during the afternoon. Come back on Sunday night. That's when the other old age pensioners play bingo and knit jumpers."

"That's my boot wedged in the door. Either it continues its journey through the door or goes up your arse. The choice is yours, *sonny.*"

Sonny stared into Karl's eyes before quickly looking away, mumbling, "I'm . . . I'm going to inform management on you."

"I suspected as much."

From the jukebox close to the bar, Boxcar Willie's gentle voice, singing "Gypsy Lady and the Hobo", greeted Karl.

For Karl, the first sign of trouble in the bar was just that – a sign: No Fighting With *Full* Bottles. Smash The TV And You Are Barred *For Life*. We *Do Not* Pay Your Hospital Bills. Beneath the official sign, some local wit had scrawled in blue marker: *Nor funeral arrangements.*

The place was done up like something from the cowboy shows *Bonanza* or *The High Chaparral*, with sawdusted floors, batwing salon doors and even a family of unhealthy-looking rusted spittoons under each table. Boxcar Willie faded out, replaced by the haunting achy-ness of Patsy Cline's "I Fall To Pieces".

As if to prove the authenticity of the bar's theme, a deliberate, old-wild-west hush suddenly stalked the room as Karl faked a leisurely saunter up to the counter – a saunter John Wayne would have been proud of. But despite being a converted church, Karl didn't think this particular congregation was inclined toward any religious persuasion – it was more like a lynch mob in badly faked designer denim.

Parking his arse at the end of the counter, he made a motion with his hand to the barman. "When you get a chance, partner."

The barman fixed Karl with a brow-rippling scowl, before returning his eyes to the television.

"Any chance of a drink?" persisted Karl.

The barman did not answer, but a voice from behind spoke.

"I believe you were told it's members only in the afternoon."

Karl swivelled in the chair. A keg-barrel chest of a man smiled, a golden Celtic cross dangling from his generous muscular neck. His body wasted no space, all of it packed in under his skin like muscular rivets. To Karl, he looked like a wrestler about to go to town – a town called Karl.

"I'm looking to become a member," said Karl.

"Memberships all booked up," replied Mister Wrestler. "What's your business here?"

"You the sheriff?"

"Sheriff's out at the ranch," smiled Mister Wrestler. "I'm the deputy."

"What's a man got to do to get a drink in this place?"

"You might find it difficult getting served."

"Even for a wanna-be member?"

Smiling even broader, Mister Wrestler said, "What would you like?"

"For starters, a bottle of Harp would be nice. Chilled, if possible. I'll even buy you one, because you've shown such kindness to a tenderfoot riding the open trail," said Karl, returning the smile.

"Joe? A bottle of Harp – chilled for the cowboy."

Joe dipped a massive arm into an ice case and produced the beer before handing it to Mister Wrestler, totally ignoring Karl's outstretched hand.

Instantly, the bottle disappeared into Mister Wrestler's ham-like fist. "Here," said Mister Wrestler to Karl, twisting off the cap as if snapping the neck of a small animal. "Enjoy and leave."

"I must warn you that I'm a very slow drinker."

"You look like a fast learner. Drink it fast."

Karl took a long sip of the beer. It was refreshing, hitting the back of his throat in just the right place. "That was good," he said, placing the half-finished beer on the counter.

"What exactly is it you want here?" asked Mister Wrestler.

"I'm looking for a man," said Karl, removing a business card from his pocket, reaching it out towards Mister Wrestler. "Brendan Burns."

Mister Wrestler refused to take the card. "Put it back in your pocket. This isn't the place to come looking for *anybody*. Now, finish your drink and saddle up. You've overstayed your visit."

Karl placed the card on the counter alongside the unfinished beer.

"I take it that means you'll not help?"

"Take it whatever way you want, but take yourself and leave – right now."

"What about the job you promised?" said Karl.

"What job?"

"Why, the blowjob, of course."

Mister Wrestler's skin suddenly tightened. Karl could see veins as thick as shoelaces tunnelling along the skin.

"How do you know when a dying man is about to make his exit from this world?" asked Mister Wrestler, his face suddenly resembling that of a hangman who has just discovered the perfect knot.

Karl looked immediately troubled. "I've got a foul, sinking suspicion of where this is headed, but amuse me, anyway."

That's when all the lights went out in Karl's head.

Karl groaned. His ribs hurt like hell, hands badly torn. He spat a blob of blood from his mouth. He was sure some of his teeth had migrated. Something burned in his throat, tasting like vomit. Each time he attempted to move, a surging pain went up along his spine, ringing a bell inside his head. *Ding Fucking Dong!* He was in an alleyway of some sort, flat on his back and wedged between overturned bins, their putrid contents spewed on top of him. An enormous dent in one of the bin lids gave him an indication of what he possibly had been hit *with* – as well as the ham sandwich from Mister Wrestler's hammy hand, of course.

"I *thought* I heard you moving. I've never seen a man take a beating like that before and live. That was very rare," claimed a voice, directly above Karl's head. It was Mister Wrestler, calmly smoking a cigarette, the other hand behind his back. "What is the rarest thing you can think of, cowboy?"

Karl tried grinning, but it was too painful. His intestines felt like they were quickly unravelling. "A used condom from the Pope? Your wife cuming?"

"A dying man being given the chance to live. I'm offering that to you. Do you want it?" said Mister Wrestler, bringing his other hand suddenly into play.

His attention now riveted to the bulbous gun in the non-smoking hand of Mister Wrestler, Karl whispered, "I'm . . . I'm not leaving – not until I talk to Brendan Burns."

"You are and you aren't. We could have used someone like you, years ago," said Mister Wrestler, shaking his head, as if with admiration for the tenacity of the tenderfoot. "A pity you have more balls than brains, though. All that testosterone can be bad for your health, if you don't mix it with some good old common sense." Mister Wrestler went down on one knee, placing the gun to Karl's left eye. "Do you know anything about hollow point bullets? No? Well, allow me to educate you. When the bullet hits you, the splits along its filed grooves divide into fourths, each piece going in a separate direction. That's why it leaves a hole the size of a grape in your stomach and a gap the size of a watermelon in your back." Mister Wrestler cocked the gun. "Now, are you smart or just ballsy?"

Karl spat another blob of blood from his mouth. "I'm not fucking leaving until I meet Brendan Burns, you bastard."

"Wrong answer."

The lights went out again and Karl was suddenly in a freefall of dark nothingness.

You really are heebiefuckingjeebie out of your skull, Mister, said Bear.

Chapter Thirty-Nine

*"Madness need not be at all breakdown.
It may also be break-through."*
R.D. Laing, *The Politics of Experience*

"At your age, you really need to be catching yourself on, Mister Kane," said Nurse Williams disapprovingly, all the while watching a young nurse finishing with stitches to the top of Karl's head. "Trying to prove how macho you are? Is that what this is all about?"

Easing up from the hospital chair, Karl attempted a grin but grimaced instead before walking gingerly towards Nurse Williams. His face was partially bandaged, arms and hands covered in fat, skin-coloured plasters. "I know I look like a dog's dinner, Nurse, but you want to see the other guy – looks like the place the dinner came out of."

Karl's face was a bloody scrambled mess. His collarbone jutted out of his neck at a strange angle, and all the swelling and bruising had distorted his face almost beyond recognition. Congealed blood and gravel formed a seal over the wide gash that could have been an eyebrow. His left eye was swollen shut; split lips jagged and caked with black blood. Underneath all the red and black and blue pain, his skin was white as a ghost.

"I really wish you would allow me to contact your family. You really are in a bad way – even with the painkillers you've just taken."

"It's nothing that a large Hennessy and a hot bath won't sort. Thanks for patching me up once again, Nurse. Very much appreciated. You ever need anything, let me know."

He handed her a business card.

It was over an hour later when Karl sank slowly into a bath of hot water and thick bubbles, balancing a large Hennessy. Naomi looked on from the door, her arms folded defensively.

"*Ahhhhhhhhh*. This is heaven. Almost worth the ticket to that boxing match."

"When are you going to tell me where you went or who did this?"

"Somewhere I probably should never have been, and by someone I certainly should never have seen." He sipped the brandy before continuing. "I thought I would find a man who could help me find Katie. All I found was more trouble, and discovered how totally useless a wanker I really am."

Naomi walked to the bath, dipping into a half-kneel position. "Getting killed isn't going to help Katie, Karl. The police are doing –"

"The police are doing sweet fuck all! They've given up the chase. They think she's dead."

Naomi blinked, as if slapped. "Don't talk like that."

"No? How should I talk? Polite bullshit or elegant lies? They know who has Katie. They're too corrupt to do anything about it. Don't you see? They claimed to have found nothing in any of Hannah's properties. They're all in on it. This is their payback time." Karl quickly emptied the brandy down his throat and held out the empty glass. "Fill it to the brim this time. I need something to take this lovely pain away."

Naomi stood and took the glass. "Are you sure you really need another –"

"For fuck sake, will you quit nagging, Naomi! If I wanted a nag, I'd buy a horse instead of betting on them."

"Don't you dare swear at me, Karl Kane!"

"Just give me back the glass and I'll fill the damn thing myself!" said Karl, snapping the glass out of Naomi's hand while stepping quickly out of the bath. Two seconds later, he went slipping on the wet floor, landing heavily on the tail of his spine, the back of his already wounded head doing a recoil off the floor.

"Fuck! *Arghhhhh* . . ."

"Karl!" screamed Naomi, dropping immediately beside him, her face going sick. "Are you okay? Karl, answer me."

"Just get me a drink, damn it! I need a drink! I'm fucking useless without a drink, you annoying woman!"

She pulled him into her, tightly, her strength defeating his weakened shell. He trembled. She tightened her grip, and suddenly the room was filled with the tide of his breathing and the quiet breathing of her heart.

"It's okay. It's okay," she soothed, combing back his hair with her fingers, her lips kissing his wounded face, gently. "Everything will be okay."

"I've failed her, Naomi. I've failed my beautiful wee Katie. Don't you understand? The cops are right. She's dead."

Chapter Forty

"How kind the visit that ye pay,
Like strangers on a rainy day."
Christopher Smart, "On a Bed of Guernsey Lilies"

Late afternoon, and everything around Karl in the bedroom looked dull; dull and not too clearly defined. Not enough contrast. The dim light from the window, though, was enough to expose the wreck of his face in the mirror hanging above the dresser. For an instant, the sight of another person in the room, even his own battered reflection, comforted him. He tried separating the intense pain from its reality through existential processes, telling himself that pain only existed in the mind, not the body.

Grimacing again through clenched teeth, he finally had to admit defeat: he was hurting like hell.

He had drifted through slivers of dreams about Katie last night; dreams of a half dozen events between father and daughter, in a room somewhere far away. He could still see her image branded beneath his eyelids each time he closed them. She had a face like an angel, without makeup, and without the angry lines young people had nowadays or the wrinkles from frowning. Everything about her was soft and smooth. She smiled at him, saying something to him as he was preparing to leave. But it never registered, like a vision you lose grasp of when you wake. What had she said? *I'm okay, Dad.* Was that it? *Rest yourself. You'll find me.*

For hours after, her face was all he could see. Then her face disappeared, replaced with missing little girls with darkness and suffering in their eyes.

"Karl? Are you sleeping?" asked Naomi, softly.

"Huh?"

"There's a very tall, well-dressed man downstairs in the office wanting to see you. He wouldn't give his name, only that it's very important. He says he's FBI. Obviously, just a smart-arse, plainclothes cop who's come about the assault. I told him I doubt very much that you could see him today. Perhaps tomorrow. But he was very insistent. Says it's extremely important. I can tell him to come back some other time, if you want?"

"How long have I been sleeping?"

"Roughly ten hours."

"Ten bloody hours! Why didn't you waken me before this?" he moaned, easing his body off the edge of the bed. "I should be out there, looking for Katie. Tell the cop I'll be down shortly. He might have some information for me."

Naomi turned to leave.

"Naomi?"

"Yes?"

"Sorry . . . all that nastiness . . ."

"I wouldn't have you any other way."

"What would I do without you?"

"I'm sure you'd think of something, eventually. You always do."

Less than a minute later, Karl stepped into the shower, the first hot sprays hitting him with the propulsive ferocity of porcupine quills. It felt good. It made him feel alive. What he would give for a shave, but the thought of negotiating the maze of cuts and bruises on his face held little appeal.

Five minutes later, he exited, dried and dressed, popping a duo of painkillers into his mouth before making his way slowly downstairs to the office.

"Show the man in, Naomi, please," said Karl, sitting down, grimacing slightly.

A few seconds later, an extremely tall, well-built man entered. His hair was jet-black, greying slightly at the temples. He had a rugged handsomeness and tunnelling eyes as dark as figs. A deep river of a scar ran down his face, curving upstream on his chin, all the way to the edge of his mouth, as if his face had been carved in two. To Karl, the man had an unnerving mien, something tangible yet elusively impenetrable. He looked like a man not to be fucked with, filled with the self-assurance of an untouchable. Yet despite all this, all life looked deflated from him, like a flag without air.

"That looks pretty grim," said the man.

"That's an oxymoron if ever I heard one," replied Karl. "Cut myself shaving, just a wee bit too close."

"I can see that. Had a few close shaves in my time also."

"Won't you sit down?" offered Karl.

For such a large man, there was a tight economy of movement as he pulled out a chair opposite and sat.

"You said you're from the FBI?" continued Karl.

"Fucking Big Irishman," said the man, smiling a tight smile. "Sorry about that, but I didn't want to scare you."

"Scare me? How?"

"I believe this is yours?" he replied, removing a tiny card from his pocket before placing it on the table.

Karl picked it up. His business card.

"Guilty," acknowledged Karl. "But I'm sure you didn't come all the way here just to return a business card, Mister . . . ?

"Burns. Brendan Burns."

Suddenly, Karl's heart began hammering like washers on a tin roof.

CHAPTER FORTY-ONE

"A pity beyond all telling
Is hid in the heart of love."
W.B. Yeats, *The Pity of Love*

"First, allow me to apologise for Cormac's over-protectiveness, three days ago," said Brendan Burns. "He means well."

"Cormac? You mean Mister Wrestler with the dum-dum bullets and sledgehammer hands? If that was his interpretation of meaning well, I'd hate to see him meaning ill to any unfortunate soul entering the Ponderosa."

"I suppose you're going to press charges against him?"

"Is that why you're here, to return my business card and plead for your over-zealous friend not being arrested for attempted murder?"

"That, and to ask why exactly you were enquiring about me?"

Karl hesitated for a couple of seconds. "I need your help."

"What kind of help?"

"To find my daughter."

A puzzled look appeared on Burns's face. "Your daughter? I don't understand."

"She was abducted, over a week ago. I suspect she is being held prisoner in Crumlin Road Jail."

"Crumlin Road . . . I remember you now. You were on the news after that big search in the Crum a few days ago. That was your daughter? I'm really sorry to hear that, but how would I be able to help?"

"The cops claimed to have searched every inch of the prison in a three-day extensive search. They even reopened all of the old covered-in escape tunnels, just to make sure."

"From what you've said, there's very little they didn't do. What help would I be?"

"You more than anyone are an expert when it comes to the structure of the jail. You have an extensive experience of working underground, so to speak. You know every nook and cranny in there – and I mean *every*. It's well known that you were the master tunnelling engineer in there. Someone told me you were behind every escape tunnel ever dug, in Crumlin Road Jail."

"Don't believe everything you hear, Mister Kane – especially from your cop friends."

"It's a fact, and a plea. If anyone knows the secrets of that nightmarish place, I believe it's you, Mister Burns."

"You've done your homework, it would seem. But let me shock you with a little bit of information. I've done my homework, as well. You're the brother-in-law of Mark Wilson. Correct?"

Karl hesitated before replying. "*Was*. Past tense."

"Well, Wilson and I have a lot of *past* between us – a hell of a lot. I don't think he would look too kindly on you asking for my help."

"You mean the fact that you shot him in the face, scarring him for life, almost killing him?"

A ghost of a smile appeared on Burns's face. "Looks like you were pretty thorough in your homework after all."

"Let me be up front with you, Mister Burns. I don't care what little war you and my ex-brother-in-law fought years ago, your ideals, or your political beliefs. In all honesty, I would go to the devil himself if I knew his address, to help find my daughter. Perhaps that doesn't mean a lot to you, but it means everything to me. Now, will you help me or not?"

Brendan Burns seemed to be staring at Karl as if weighing him up. It was a few seconds before he spoke. "How well did you know Wilson's right-hand man, a psychopath by the name of Duncan Bulldog McKenzie?"

Immediately blood rushed from Karl's head. He felt dizzy.

"Why . . . why do you ask?" said Karl, finally getting his tongue to move.

"You're aware he was shot dead a few months ago?"

Karl nodded. His neck felt weak.

Burns's face darkened. His lips drew back in a snarl, almost canine. "I celebrated for almost a week when I heard it. Does that shock you?"

Karl remained silent.

"I had a little girl, like your Katie, Mister Kane," continued Burns. "Patricia was her name. Eight years of age. Lovely little thing. One day she was there, then the next she was gone, for ever."

"I'm sorry to –"

"I was on the run. Wilson and his crew came to arrest me. They'd been tipped off by one of their many lowlife informers in the area. They came to my house, guns blazing, caring not an iota for anyone in my home. I was shot four times. My wife, Claire, three. They shot Patricia once. Just the once, Mister Kane. My wife and I both survived, but one bullet was enough to kill Patricia. Figure that out if you can."

"I . . ." Karl could find no words, his face suddenly turning grim.

"It was McKenzie. He fired the fatal shot. I will never forget the smirk on his face."

"There's . . . there's nothing I can say, Brendan; nothing at all that will help take away your pain. I should have dug a little deeper before blundering into your place looking for you. I can understand Cormac's reaction now. He's a true friend."

Nodding, Brendan Burns said, "At least now you know why I tried to kill Wilson. My only regret was not being the one who shot McKenzie. I would give anything to shake the hand of the man who killed Bulldog, thank him from the bottom of my heart."

Karl's face reddened. "Now, at least, I understand why you don't want to help me, Brendan. I'm too close to Wilson for you. I probably wouldn't want to help either if I were you."

"Goodbye, Mister Kane," said Brendan Burns, standing, before leaving as quickly as he had arrived.

It was almost a minute later when Naomi looked in at Karl.

"You okay?"

"Fine."

"I'm not going to ask you."

"You don't have to. The way your body is shaped like a question mark says it all. He was a man from a long time ago, a man who – justifiably – can't help looking back in anger instead of forward with hope."

"Is . . . is there anything I can do?"

Forcing a smile, Karl patted his knee. "Just sit beside me for a few minutes. Help me not to become that man."

CHAPTER FORTY-TWO

"For hope grew round me, like the twining vine,
And fruits, and foliage, not my own, seemed mine."
Samuel Taylor Coleridge, "Dejection: an Ode"

I t was the very next day, lunchtime, when Karl received a very unexpected phone call.

"Karl? Phone call, line two," said Naomi.

"Who?"

"Wouldn't give his name. Says it's important."

"Hello?" asked Karl, quickly placing the phone against his ear.

"There's a very good chance that this will get messy – *very* messy. Are you prepared for that?" asked Brendan Burns, at the other end.

"I'm prepared for anything. I just want Katie back."

"Okay, but don't say you weren't warned."

"What made you change your mind?" asked Karl, sheer relief washing over him.

Seconds of hesitancy stretched at the other end before Brendan said, "With some reluctance, I spoke to Claire last night. She said that if it were Patricia out there, held by some monster, she would want someone to help her."

"Please . . . please thank Claire for me, Brendan. I appreciate how she may have influenced your thinking. I know how hard this must have been – for you both."

"You understand that it's going to be difficult finding a way into the Crum without attracting any attention? The Antrim Road part is watched by the local police station. We'll have to find a way in the back. It's going to be very tricky."

"I already have the way. A good friend."

"Can this so-called *good friend* be trusted?"

"*I* trust him."

"Okay, but he doesn't need to know anything about me. Agreed?"

"Agreed."

"There's one other thing which needs saying, no matter how callous it sounds."

"What's that?" asked Karl.

"*If* Katie is in there, she may no longer be alive."

Silence suddenly filled the line.

"You understand that?" persisted Brendan.

"Where will we meet?" asked Karl, sidestepping the ominous question.

"Park your car on the bottom of the Antrim Road, close to Carlisle Circus. There's a little café called T 4 2, not too far from the Ulster Bank, on the corner. I'll see you inside the café at eight, tomorrow night. Don't be early and don't be late."

"Brendan?"

"Yes?"

"Thank you."

"Keep the thanks in cold storage. I haven't done anything yet."

"You've given me hope again. I'll never forget that, regardless of the outcome."

CHAPTER FORTY-THREE

"Down, down to hell; and say I sent thee thither."
William Shakespeare, *Henry VI*

Despite being the middle of summer, a weird, autumnal darkness had suddenly taken over Belfast's night sky as the trio proceeded up the Crumlin Road toward their intended target. The night's skin was a mixture of copper and dark purples, like some huge Rorschach inkblot. Karl thought the copper resembled a dead man's eyes.

"Strange sky," said Willie, as if reading Karl's thoughts.

Karl nodded in acknowledgement, but did not speak.

Brendan said nothing either, his mind seemingly preoccupied with things other than shifting weather. His broad back carried a battered, navy-blue rucksack.

The night's darkness, to Karl, had a sickly thickness to it, like black porridge spilling over the side of a bowl. It made him feel shuddery, as if trapped in some Gothic painting left unfinished by a dying hand. The diseased and derelict buildings on either side of the Crumlin Road weren't helping the feeling.

"Looks like rain," continued Willie, sounding slightly anxious. "Hasn't rained in almost six weeks, but tonight looks like we're in for a good soaking. I suppose it'll keep nosey-parkers indoors."

No response from Karl or Brendan.

"What's in the rucksack, big fella?" continued Willie, indicating with a nod towards Brendan.

"Provisions," Brendan icily responded.

"Remember what I said, Willie?" said Karl. "No questions."

Before Willie could answer, the heavens suddenly erupted, forcing the threesome to quicken their pace.

Less than five minutes later, they stood hidden in the shadows of the intimidating Victorian jail, rain pooling on the roof of a decrepit watchman's hut, coming off in waterfall fashion on to their uncovered heads.

"We're here, lads," whispered Willie, and suddenly all three craned their necks upwards, as if sketching the massive building with their eyes.

On 31 March 1996, the Governor of Belfast's Crumlin Road Jail walked out of the fortified prison, the heavy air-lock gates slamming directly behind him, shutting for their final time. That sound ended a 150-year history of incarceration, conflict and executions. For most people in Belfast – and throughout the country – Crumlin Road Jail was a ghastly monument to man's inhumanity to man. An estimated 25,000 people were imprisoned there during its turbulent history, whether as a result of internment or on remand as political prisoners.

The first official use of the jail began in March 1846 when 106 prisoners – men, women and children – were force-marched from Carrickfergus Jail. The youngest person to be hung in the prison was a boy of ten, Patrick Magee, imprisoned for the horrendous crime of stealing a shirt. Famous inmates have included the Irish president Éamon de Valera and Ian Paisley, another potential Irish president.

For almost five minutes, the trio stood, eerily silent in contemplation, as if at the gates of Hades itself, waiting for some godless ordination.

An elderly woman across the street at number eighteen watched the scene from a bedroom window of her home. Her denture-less face caved inwards as she mumbled something to herself before eventually slithering out of view.

"Nosey old bag," hissed Willie. "Bloody nothing better to do than to poke her nose into other people's business. I hate people like her."

"This jail looks like something from Charles Dickens," said Karl.

"Not a place for the fainthearted, I can tell you," volunteered Willie. "This old bastard was built in 1846, and believe it or not, was one of the most advanced prisons of its day. Seventeen prisoners were executed inside its walls. They say their ghosts can be heard, crying at night looking for freedom. Inside there are four wings, each four stories high. There are six hundred and forty cells."

"You seem to know a great deal about the place, if you don't mind me saying?" commented Brendan.

"I did nine months in this hellhole, years ago," boasted Willie. "I know its history, inside out."

"Nine months? That must have been terrible," responded Brendan.

"You can say that again. Not a place for the weak-kneed. Now, if you'll excuse me, I've got work to do."

"If someone had ever told me that one day I'd be breaking into the Crum . . ." said Brendan to Karl, while watching Willie work his magic on the medieval lock studded into the jail's side gate.

Karl said nothing, his eyes nervously glancing up and down the eerily deserted street, watching for patrolling police cars.

The rain began thundering down so heavily, visibility was becoming almost impossible.

"I can hardy see the damn lock," complained Willie, working the needle-thin tool into the lock's cavity, filthy rainwater bombarding his hands. "Can't we just use a torchlight, for a minute?"

"No. The cops would be like moths to it," said Brendan. "If they come, we won't have to worry about breaking in. They'll give us a personal invite."

"Just take your time, Willie," encouraged Karl, finally breaking his own silence. "You've worked under more stressful conditions than this."

"Tell me about it. I remember the time I was asked by a client to do this wee break-in job, right beside a police station. Ha! Those were the days when –"

"We can reminisce once we get inside," said Brendan impatiently.

"Keep your knickers on," retorted Willie. "I don't know what your role is, big fella, and I don't want to know. But without me, we aren't going anywhere. Understand?"

"Everyone here is important," cut in Karl, quickly trying to defuse the rapidly deteriorating situation. "But I need both of you to stay focused . . . please . . . for Katie's sake."

There was an embarrassing silence before Willie's contrite voice said, "You're right, Karl. We're like school kids at a pissing contest. Sorry."

"Just stay focused," reiterated Karl.

"Got it!" exclaimed Willie, triumphantly. "Got the bastard."

"Good man, Willie. Good man," encouraged Karl, immediate relief sweeping over his face.

Seconds later, the three men stepped inside, quickly closing the door behind them.

Silence greeted them. A peculiar, almost sickly silence. Neglected, one-time security lights had burned out so the only light on the narrow path between the yard and the far wings came from street lamps at the back of the prison, silhouetting the threesome like grey ghosts against the bars of the gate. Lattices of razor wire curled above the ramparts.

Karl could hear his heart thump thump thumping in his ears, as if underwater in some murky lake. *Time to strap on your balls, Karl me bucko*, thought Karl, suddenly feeling apprehensive.

"Not a soul," said Willie.

"The place is no longer guarded as such, because there's nothing left to steal. All the wings have been gutted, supposedly to make room for a five-star hotel. Only one wing remains intact," responded Brendan.

"Which one would that be?" asked Willie.

"That would be A Wing. That's the one the cops conducted their three-day search on. A Wing is where they kept republican prisoners, I believe," supplied Brendan. "If I'm not mistaken, loyalists prisoners were housed in C Wing. And the notorious Basement was the place they housed the rats."

"They housed rats?" asked Karl.

"The worse. The most treacherous. The two-legged kind."

"You've got that right," agreed Willie. "I had a couple of good friends put into C Wing because of the rats in the Basement. You still haven't told me how you know all this."

"Let's move, Willie," said Karl, trying to prevent Willie from digging further with his questioning. "We're wasting precious time."

"Okay. This way," instructed Willie, heading for the open yard, followed closely behind by Karl and Brendan. "That large door ahead should lead to the Circle. The wings all stem from there. Once inside, A Wing should be directly ahead, if my memory serves me well."

The modern door leading into the Circle held little resistance for Willie. Three minutes later, it opened. "We'll take the stairs over beside the –"

"Hold on a second, Willie," said Karl. "This is as far as you go."

"What?" Willie looked perplexed. "What the hell are you talking about?"

"Things are probably going to get very hairy from here on in. You've already taken too many chances helping us. Besides, we need you to stay outside with this walkie-talkie," said Karl, offering the device to Willie. "We need to know if anyone approaches the place. It's vitally important that we get a warning."

"You're not serious? How the hell are you two going to find your way about in there without me? Eh? Answer me that, Bamber Gascoigne?"

"*I* can answer that, Willie," supplied Brendan.

"*You?* How the hell would you know?" said Willie disdainfully.

"I was a . . . guest here, for almost twelve years."

Willie's left eyebrow curved into a hairy question mark. "You? Twelve years? You're pulling my leg. He *is* pulling my leg, Karl. Right?"

"No . . . no, Willie. Brendan's telling the truth."

Shaking his head with disbelief, Willie mumbled, "And there's me blabbering about doing nine months. I feel a right old fool."

"Don't," cut in Brendan. "Nine weeks, nine months, nine years – it's all the same when time has been stolen from you."

"I suppose you don't wish to tell me what you were in for?"

"Willie, I told you, no questions," said Karl quickly, seeing Brendan's face tighten. "Now, just do as I ask. Take the walkie-talkie, and –"

"Shoplifting," said Brendan.

"Shoplifting . . . and they gave you twelve years?" said Willie suspiciously. "Must've been a pretty expensive bit of shoplifting?"

"I lifted it twenty feet in the air."

"What?"

"Explosives."

"Oh."

"Oh indeed," cut in Karl. "Now, will you watch our backs or not?"

Nodding, Willie took the walkie-talkie before walking toward the front gate, whispering under his breath, "Twelve years . . ."

Inside, Karl and Brendan were greeted with almost pitch black. Dim papillary lights, each the size of a baby's toe, lined the walls, giving an eerie bluish hue to the darkness.

"Grim place," said Karl, feeling his stomach do its familiar trapdoor movement.

"What did you expect?"

"I don't know what I was expecting."

"Always expect the unexpected. It'll help keep you healthy," said Brendan, removing a torchlight from his rucksack before handing it to Karl. "I've got a couple of flares also, but we'll keep them in case of an emergency."

"Where do we start?" asked Karl.

"That's the easy part. Straight to the end of the wing and into the one-time canteen, on the left. Come on."

The chalky beam from the torchlight guided them, causing their shadows to dance and stretch before them.

Inside the canteen, a family of broken windows granted some jaundiced light, enough for the torchlight to be extinguished. Below the main cooking area, enormous potholes suddenly came into view.

"It's a virtual warren," said Karl in amazement. "The cops must have used jackhammers." A moment of guilt suddenly hit Karl. Wilson *had* done a thorough job, as he had claimed.

"They're the entrances of my old tunnels," said Brendan, a hint of pride in his voice. "Eight, to be exact."

"All the tunnelling was done here?"

"Most. There were twelve tunnels in all. Four more to check," said Brendan, heading for the ablutions.

The shower area resembled a war scene. Toilets and showers smashed;

plumbing mangled into metal knots. Cisterns were leaking, causing massive puddles of filthy water to spill into the cavities littering the ground. Streaks of orange rust trailed down from faucets opening to the drains, their colour developing through waste and edging towards the darkened holes.

"This is what's known in prison jargon as a sledgehammer and fine-tooth comb of a search. The cops did a thorough job," continued Brendan, surveying the devastation. "Have to give them full credit for that."

"Not a stone's been left unturned," acknowledged Karl, his stomach coiling into a cold fist of defeat. "They've checked everything in –"

Suddenly, Willie's static voice began crackling over the air.

"Karl?"

"Yes, Willie?"

"There's someone approaching the jail. Hold tight . . ."

"Fuck!" said Karl in desperation.

"Take it easy," encouraged Brendan. "There are a couple of ways out."

"*Out?* Who's looking *out?* My daughter is *in* here somewhere. Think I'm leaving without her?"

"Look, Karl, sometimes you have to walk away, so that you can –"

"Don't give me any of your wartime philosophy bullshit! You go the fuck wherever you want! I'm staying here – even if it means digging up every dirty piece of soil in this –"

"Karl? You there?" crackled Willie's whispery voice. *"Karl?"*

"Yes . . . yes, Willie. I'm here," said Karl.

"All clear, Karl. It was only someone out for a late night walk. How are things back there?"

"Everything . . . everything is fine, Willie. You're doing a great job. Keep alert."

"You've got it. See you soon . . . or, over and out, as they say in the movies."

The walkie-talkie went dead.

"I told you there were twelve tunnels," said Brendan. "So far, these make eleven."

Karl's heart began moving up a beat.

"There's one more?"

"I hope it's still there."

"Where?" said Karl, trying desperately to remain calm. "Are we far from it?"

"There is a unique passageway leading from the jail to the courthouse directly across the street. The screws used it as a security precaution to ferry prisoners to the courthouse."

"And you dug a tunnel there, right under the Crumlin Road?" asked Karl, incredulously.

"The screws' lack of intelligence and imagination made them arrogant. They never thought I had the audacity to tunnel right under their noses – or the so-called judge's arse," smiled Brendan. "Come on. It's a good ten minutes walk to get there."

It was fifteen – not ten – minutes later when Karl and Brendan entered the security passageway, known locally as The Tunnel.

Proceeding with caution, they could see bits of the old walling crumbling as they passed.

"This place is ready for collapsing," said Karl, shining the torchlight on the walls.

"Now you know why they call it crumbling jail," said Brendan, a wry smile on his face. "Don't fart or sneeze, whatever you do."

"So claustrophobic," said Karl, feeling the leprous walls moving in on him. The stench of damp decay was everywhere.

"Broad and high enough for three screws and two prisoners," said Brendan, by way of explanation.

"Has it always been this dark and clammy in here?" Katie's terrified face flashed into his mind. He quickly erased it. Now was not the time. Somehow he had to remain detached.

"See all those heating pipes attached to the walls?" asked Brendan. "Try and imagine them at full throttle, the sweat running down your back. More like an oppressive jungle. The only good thing about it was that the screws got roasted as well. They hated the tunnel assignment. All that dust and insufferable heat."

Even in the dim light, Karl could see Brendan grinning at the memory of it all as he continued speaking.

"After a while, the screws did their utmost to avoid the passageway assignment, rarely ever bothering to count the prisoners on the way back to the prison."

"I take it you were one of those prisoners they didn't bother to count?"

"I worked this passageway for almost two years. Sometimes I would go disguised as another prisoner. Sometimes an extra wage package was needed to buy a screw into turning a blind eye. It got so embarrassing that sometimes I was the one taking the other prisoners across!"

"There's something on this," said Karl, studying the disease-riddled wall. "Long reddish streaks."

"They look like blood smears," replied Brendan, studying where the torchlight's beam rested.

"I bet these flakes of paint and cement are the same as the ones trapped beneath Martina's fingernails. This has to be the place." A posse of dark, hairy spiders suddenly skittered across Karl's hands, giving him the heebie-jeebies. "Shit!"

"What?"

"Spiders. The place is crawling with them – literally. I hate spiders." A sudden flashback of a wee boy hiding in an ironing cupboard from a monster lit up in the darkness of Karl's mind.

"This is their kingdom, Karl. Never forget that. We're only guests. Besides, I used many webs to cover most of my digging in here during –"

"*Shhhh!*" hissed Karl, gripping Brendan's shoulder. "Listen. Can you hear something?"

Tilting his head, Brendan cocked his ear. "Sounds like the wind. But that's impossible. This place allows no natural sound."

"Not the wind. Something . . . *alive* . . ." The sound was sinister, evil in an almost subconscious way, like claws on a chalkboard. Its rhythmic clicking sent a momentary shiver down Karl's back, and not for the first time doubt began gnawing his thoughts.

Katie's face reappeared. He blinked it quickly away.

"Don't let it bother you, Karl. This old place can creep the strongest heart out. Anyway, *there's* the metal door leading to the courthouse," stated Brendan, pointing down the tunnel. "Come on."

The mystery sound was still troubling Karl as Brendan removed the rucksack from his shoulders.

"The gate is totally covered in rust. It'll never open," said Karl, shocked at the state of the Victorian metal gate. "How on earth is Willie going to pick the lock on that thing?"

Rummaging through the bag, Brendan suddenly produced a collection of items, some wrapped in greaseproof paper.

"Despite his expertise, Willie couldn't pick this lock, Karl. This calls for something unconventional. Something a bit more . . . flexible."

"What's that stuff you're bending?" asked Karl, staring at the brick-orange piece of rubbery substance being manipulated by Brendan's hand.

"Semtex. A plastic explosive. Very malleable and twice as powerful as TNT."

"*What?*" Karl's stomach suddenly began tightening into knots. "Are you out of your mind? You're not seriously going to use that stuff?"

"You have some other magical alternative, like abracadabra? This door hasn't been opened in years. Do you really think that a key or pick will open it? That's why the cops ignored it."

"But . . . isn't it dangerous, in such a confined space? If there's a tunnel at the back of this door, surely it'll . . ." Karl's voice trailed off.

"Collapse on anyone in there? It's not a tunnel behind those doors, but the annex area of the courthouse." Brendan shook his head. "Besides, I only need a minuscule amount, just enough to take the door down. I came prepared for this eventuality, Karl. I've calculated the risks and the chances, over and over in my head. I warned you that things would get messy."

"I didn't realise explosives would have to be brought into it."

"If we use the front of the jail to gain entry into the courthouse, the cops stationed on the Antrim Road will spot us. It would be impossible to go unnoticed. Unless, of course, you owned the place like Bob Hannah. No doubt he was able to come and go as he pleased without arousing suspicion."

"I . . ."

"Tell you what," said Brendan impatiently. "Say the word and the Semtex goes back in the bag. But I'm telling you now, there is no *other* way of that door being opened."

Karl licked dried lips. His mouth felt like cotton. "No . . . no, let's do it. Just be careful . . . please."

"We'll head back down the tunnel. I've set this timer for two minutes. It'll give us plenty of time," said Brendan, picking up his rucksack.

"Won't they hear this, outside?"

"Don't worry about that. This small amount of explosives will be well muffled by the thickness of the walls."

Karl turned, quickly walking back down The Tunnel, torchlight in his hands, expecting the whole place to collapse all around him.

"How far is safe?" asked Karl, suddenly walking faster.

"How long is a piece of string?" responded Brendan. "Just keep walking until I tell you."

"I really hope you know what you're doing . . ."

"Hope has nothing to do with it."

Hope is all I have, thought Karl.

"Okay. This is far enough," stated Brendan, halting ten seconds later. "Get tight against the wall and block your ears."

Popping his fingers into his ears, Karl waited, dreading what the sensation would be like. Each passing second seemed like an hour.

Suddenly, a muffled sound rattled along the ground, shaking Karl, sending particles of the wall crumbling down upon his head. His spine seemed to move slightly out of kilter.

"It's over," said Brendan, dusting himself down. "Are you okay?"

Opening his eyes, Karl tried blinking away the dust. Everything was weirdly silent, like snow falling on a lake. Grey darkness was everywhere as dust began settling, exposing a curtain of dull light where the old door had once been.

"That . . . that was madness. It was the craziest thing I've ever done," said Karl, shaking his head with disbelief.

"I gauged the back-draft of the explosion. There was nothing to worry about," assured Brendan.

"Nothing to worry about? Tell that to the torchlight," said Karl, holding up the cracked and now useless item.

"Shit! We needed that damn light. That's the first time I ever saw that happen."

"Just to be on the safe side, let me call Willie. See if he heard the explosion up on the street."

"You're wasting your time," said Brendan, handing Karl a walkie-talkie. "Willie – or anyone else, for that matter – wouldn't have heard the explosion. It was too muffled."

"Willie? Can you hear me, Willie," said Karl, speaking into the walkie-talkie. "Come in, Willie."

Nothing; only radio static filling the air.

"Willie? Can you hear me?"

"Willie can no longer hear you, Karl," replied the calm voice of Robert Hannah, crackling from the walkie-talkie. "He's gone to meet his maker."

CHAPTER FORTY-FOUR

"And in the icy silence of the tomb . . ."
John Keats, "This Living Hand"

"Hannah . . . ?" said Karl, hesitantly.

No answer, only static laughter.

"*Hannah!*" hissed Karl. "What . . . what have you done . . . what have you done with Willie, you bastard?"

"Done? Done is the operative word, dear Karl. All your fault, I hasten to add. You brought Silly Willie here, and he cursed your name to high heaven while I slit his throat from ear to ear. Squealed like a pig while crying for his wife. Isabel, I think her name was. Hard to make out with all that lovely warm blood gurgling in his large mouth."

"You fucking bastard!" Karl's grip tightened on the walkie-talkie. "When I get my hands on –"

"You'll have the opportunity soon. I'm so close to you, Karl, I can see the sweat on your brow, the terror in your face. Want me to reach out and touch you?"

A shiver ran immediately up Karl's spine. He glanced quickly from left to right, but before he could say another word, Brendan snatched the walkie-talkie from his hand.

"Enough! We've got work to do."

"Willie's dead," mumbled Karl, visibly shaken.

"I heard that much," replied Brendan, nodding solemnly. "I'm sorry, but we've got to keep moving. The anteroom is directly beneath us. Come on, but be careful where you walk. With no torchlight, it's going to be treacherous."

Karl followed, zombie-like, his head filling with accusations and guilt. He could see Isabel's angry face as he relayed the news of Willie's murder to her. She'd hate him for dragging her husband into this.

"Snap out of it!" snapped Brendan, suddenly shaking Karl by the shoulders. "You're becoming a liability. Wallow later in self-pity. You haven't earned the ticket for a guilt trip. Understand?"

"Yes."

Less than five minutes later, the duo stood at the entrance of the impressive anteroom.

"Is it locked?" asked Karl, watching Brendan running his hands over the door's metal skin.

"Sealed tight. I can blow it off its hinges, but it'll be so dark in there, it'll be almost impossible to see anything. I'm going to have to use one of the two flares. I wanted to keep them both, in case of an emergency."

"What's that black shadow sticking out from the wall, over there?"

"Huh?" muttered Brendan, turning to see what Karl was pointing at.

"Over beside that wall with the water pipes."

"I hope it's what I think it is," replied Brendan.

"What is it?"

Bending beside the outpost, Brendan quickly removed a cigarette lighter from his pocket before firing it up, the flame long as a welding torch. "An emergency generator," he replied, pulling at the door.

The generator's door opened without protest.

"Is it working?"

"It's been greased lately," replied Brendan, pushing his finger against a green button made of glass. "Someone's been making use of it. More than likely Hannah."

The generator began sporadically humming for a few seconds before shuddering to a deadly silence.

"Can you fix it?" asked Karl, concern in his voice.

"I'm trying," said Brendan, pushing the button once again. *"C'mon! Work!"*

The sporadic humming recommenced, slowly building into a continuation before shuddering violently.

Karl held his breath.

Suddenly, a deafening clicking sound began emitting from the generator, and the thinnest of lights magically appeared from beneath the anteroom.

"It's working! The lights are on in the anteroom. Get over in that corner – hurry," instructed Brendan, producing a tiny piece of Semtex from the rucksack, before attaching it to a timer.

Seconds later, he was running to join Karl.

"Heads down!"

The explosion was duller than the first one, but Karl's ears popped horribly.

"I could never get used to this sort of shit," mumbled Karl, nerves frayed.

"No one ever gets use to it," stated Brendan.

Both men waited, watching the dust do a tornado dance. Two minutes later, it downgraded to a harmless swirling before revealing a gaping hole where the door had once stood guard.

"Stay here," commanded Brendan. "We don't know what's in –"

"Just try and stop me," hissed Karl, pushing past Brendan. "Just try . . ."

Seconds later, both men stepped inside, with Karl immediately taking in the entire scene.

The shock flared his eyes.

The floor had been torn up with tiny mounds of dirt coning the surface. Empty take-away cartons were strewn everywhere; discarded milk bottles filling a far corner, their contents thick with curdled cobalt-coloured sourness. The milky sourness was being suffocated by a mustier undercurrent of excrement and eye-stinging piss. Shabby clothes carpeted the ground in a tapestry of eerie colours.

Discovering a small stick, Brendan bent down and began fishing the collage of debris, as if looking for clues. Hooking an item, he stood and scrutinised it, spreading it out like the wings of a dead bird. It was a bra, simple in design and filthy with grime.

Karl wanted to look more carefully at the clothing, but he dreaded what it would tell him.

Brendan seemed on the verge of asking something, but said nothing after glancing at Karl's concerned face.

Continuing his search, Brendan picked up a plastic milk carton, sniffing the contents before finally scrutinising the plastic skin. "Good," he said, breaking Karl's thoughts.

"Good? What the hell do you mean, good?"

"All this stuff. Someone's been here . . . could still *be* here. The sell-by date of this milk is still fine."

Karl felt his heart move up a notch. Everything Brendan said had the ring of possibility about it.

"We need to separate, save time," continued Brendan, pointing directly at one of two rooms stationed at the back of the anteroom. "You search the far room over there. I'll take the other one. If you find anything – no matter how insignificant it seems – holler. Understand?"

Karl nodded before entering the designated room, trying desperately to remain positive in such a negative milieu of horror. The room's ground had been torn up also, exposing sediment layers. The stench of excrement was becoming stronger, burglarising his senses.

A shovel resting against the wall like a drunken guard sent a shudder up his spine. A question immediately entered his head, but he quickly erased it, not wanting its answer.

Taking the shovel, he gently skimmed the top layer of dirt before pushing under, hitting concrete and old bricks.

"Bastard," he mumbled, trance-like, each time he struck the hardened surface, his digging becoming more desperate. Tiny sparks were dancing from the impact. He imagined the ground was Hannah's smirking face. "Bastard! Bastard! Bastard!"

"Karl!" shouted Brendan, breaking the trance. *"Karl!"*

"Y . . . yes?"

"In here . . . hurry!"

Moving quickly, Karl found Brendan scrutinising something that he'd unearthed with the stick.

"What is it?" asked Karl, breathless.

"I . . . there's a possibility . . ."

Just the top third of the face was visible, hid behind a mask of stones and dirt. Eyes, shrink-wrapped in darkness, were peering through clotted strands of filthy ropey hair, staring into space with bewilderment and terror. Withered arm bones stretched, as if reaching for something. The bony chest had been crushed into the fluted rib cage. The withered skin was red, flecked with dried blood. Most disturbing was her sex, swollen and split like an over-ripe fruit.

"No . . . oh God no . . ." Karl could feel the edges of his sanity on the move, spiralling out of control. Beyond all he had witnessed before in his life, this was the most terrifying. The claustrophobic walls were moving in. He couldn't breathe. Vomit spewed from his mouth.

"Easy . . . easy, Karl. Take deep breaths . . . easy," coaxed Brendan, gripping, preventing Karl from buckling.

"I . . . I don't want to look. I've seen enough," said Karl, fighting back tears while wiping the sourness from his mouth.

"You've got to. We need to know if it's –"

"I said *no!* Not now . . . just . . . just give me time . . ."

"Okay, okay. No problem. Let's edge back out –"

"What was that sound?" asked Karl, his damp eyes wide and crazed. "You heard it, didn't you?"

"I'll take that shovel from you, Karl," said Brendan, staring into Karl's eyes. "Just go outside and –"

"*Listen!*"

It sounded like a cat meowing in a cardboard box. A raspy mew. Hollow. Distant. Somehow intentionally creepy.

"It's probably tunnel noises, Karl . . . nothing else."

"It's coming from back there, down at the end of the room," insisted Karl, quickly pushing past Brendan, almost knocking him to the ground. "Hello? Who's there? Can you hear me?"

Nothing. Nerves and adrenaline playing fucking mind games.

He tried once more.

"Hello! Can you hear –?"

"*Help . . .*"

"Shit. You're right, Karl. The old toilets! That's where it's coming from."

Kicking in the door, almost taking it off its hinges, Karl hurriedly entered the toilet area.

"Where are . . . ?" His voice trailed off. Tight against the far wall, a naked shape patched in muck and excrement was positioned in the foetus position. It looked like an old sack of coal, with only the whiteness of terrified eyes giving any indication of being human.

"Please . . . please don't hurt me," whispered a rusted voice.

"Katie . . . ? *Katie!*" howled Karl, an anguished sound of disbelief and joy as he bent, scooping Katie in his arms.

"Dad . . . ?"

"My Katie. My beautiful Princess," he whispered tenderly, kissing her face, kissing away muck and shit, combing her hair back with his fingers.

"Oh, Dad! Is it . . . is it really you?" Tears were streaming down her mucky face. "Is it . . . really you, Dad?"

"You better believe it's me, Princess!" Tears began stinging his eyes while he quickly removed his coat, placing it gently over Katie's shoulders.

"You haven't called me Princess since I was seven."

"Five, but let's not quibble over a couple of years," said Karl, smiling, crying. "Can you stand? We've got to get out of here, sweetie."

"I . . . feel weak. I've been vomiting a lot . . ."

"It's okay, it's okay . . . just stand still. I'm calling an ambulance and the police," stated Karl, fumbling in his pocket for his mobile, before quickly hitting 999. "Hello? *Hello!* What the hell's wrong with this damn thing?"

"You'll not get a signal down here, Karl," said Brendan, placing Katie's left arm on his shoulder. "Come on. Let's get out of here as quickly as –"

Without warning, the lights went dead, and a heavy darkness immediately filled the room.

Katie began trembling.

"It's him! He's coming for me!" shouted Katie. "He always comes in the dark. Don't let him touch me again, Dad. Don't let him –"

"Shhh. Easy, love. I promise he'll never touch you again."

"Promise?"

Karl's knuckles tightened into bone-whiteness. "Promise."

"Stay here, both of you," instructed Brendan, producing a gun from his rucksack.

"What are you going to do?" asked Karl.

"I don't know until I do it. Stay here until I give the all-clear."

Karl could hear Brendan shuffling carefully out of the room. A few seconds later, the horrible silence returned.

"What will that man do if he finds the monster, Dad?"

"Brendan? I don't know, love," replied Karl, pulling Katie closer.

"I hope he kills the monster. Makes him suffer . . ." replied Katie, in a voice that sent shivers down Karl's spine.

Chapter Forty-Five

"If thou hast no name to be known by, let us call thee devil."
William Shakespeare, *Othello*

B rendan slid along the wall, moving slowly yet steadily, his mind chartering the journey he had made into the anteroom, all the while retracing his steps back out. He kept the gun at waist level, pointing at a slight angle, wishing he had brought the sawn-off shotgun with its indiscriminate blasting power, able to transform a human head into ash. The sawn-off might be socially unacceptable and awkward to use, but it was single-minded in purpose and always got the job done.

You've just described yourself perfectly, thought Brendan, moving further into the darkness.

A sound to his left made him halt. Listening, he dropped immediately on hunkers, lessening his body's target area. A grim smile appeared on his face. *Big might be better, but in this situation, smaller is smarter.*

Controlling his breathing, he gently thumbed back the hammer on the revolver. A mechanical pulse travelled through the gun's heavy steel frame: a pulse that journeyed through his body before settling in his brain like a bullet. It had been a long time since he had experienced that pulse. It was beautiful and timely. Much needed.

Crawling on elbows and knees, he inched forward painstakingly slowly, the unmerciful concrete ground cutting through clothing, sandpapering his skin into a bloody mess. He felt the clingy dampness of new blood travelling down his arms and legs, and instinctively clenched his teeth to create a pain barrier.

This is nothing. You've endured worse. Just make sure you find this bastard before he finds you.

Something whooshed close to his right ear, stopping him dead in his tracks. It sounded like a hundred angry wasps caught in a bottle.

What the hell was *that? Move!*

Rolling twice, he fired two shots in succession – *bam! bam!* – before standing, running for the far wall.

Don't panic. Assume nothing except what is taking place at the present moment.

Another whooshing sound popped his ears just as his body touched the wall. He was suddenly frightened and incredibly angry; angry for allowing himself to be trapped this clumsily.

Something moved in the darkness, ahead. He dropped to one knee, the adrenaline rushing through his body inducing an instinctual call for self-preservation. Seconds later, something hit the wall, inches above his head.

Bam! Brendan fired, the muzzle flash momentarily revealing a distorted shadow. He was sure it was Hannah. Had he hit him, wounded the bastard, hopefully killed him?

"*Arghhhhhhhhhh!*" screamed Brendan, feeling his body propelling backwards as another whooshing sound made impact, hitting him perfectly.

CHAPTER FORTY-SIX

"The last act is bloody, however charming the rest
of the play may be."
Blaise Pascal, *Pensées*

"What . . . what was all that shooting, Dad?" whispered Katie, gripping her father tighter.

"I . . . I don't know, sweetie."

"Do you think . . . do you think Brendan shot him, killed him?"

Karl couldn't answer. Darkness was pouring into his brain, making it difficult to think. Something told him Brendan was dead.

"I heard something, Dad."

"What? What, sweetie?"

"Something. Something out there. Listen . . ."

Karl listened, holding his breath. He cursed his heart, its thumping making it impossible to hear.

"I need you to rest on the ground, sweetie. Just for a minute or two."

"What? No! You're not leaving me!" screamed Katie, clinging tighter to Karl.

"Shhhhhh, sweetie. I'm not leaving you. I swear to you. But you've got to trust me. Do as I say. Quickly. We don't have much time."

"I'm scared, Dad."

"I know, sweetie, but hang in there. Have faith in your old man. Okay?"

Wiping away tears and muck, Kate nodded.

"Good girl," said Karl, easing Katie to the ground. "Just stay still and –"

A noise, a sneaky, not-wanting-to-be-heard noise moved in the darkness.

"Dad . . ."

"*Shhhhhh* . . ."

In the godless gloaming, a shape was approaching, its many-angled blackness almost impossible to discern.

A horrible sensation began stabbing into Karl's gut, travelling all the way to his bowels. Clammy sweat began hugging his face.

Closer, you bastard. That's right. Just a little bit closer and you'll –

"Karl . . . ? I'm hit . . . pretty bad . . ." moaned Brendan, collapsing.

"Brendan . . . !" shouted Karl, quickly bending over the fallen body. "What happened? I heard shots being fired and . . . you're bleeding . . . what the hell's that?"

From Brendan's upper body, an arrow's metal shaft angled outwards, protruding horribly.

"I . . . I saw him, Karl. The bastard is stark bollock naked and covered in what looks like blood and war paint. He was mere feet away from me." Brendan grimaced, sweating terribly. "He . . . he looked like the devil . . . the bastard's . . . wearing night vision goggles and –"

"Night vision? Fuck."

"– and armed to the rotten teeth with some sort of crossbow and a quiver full of lethal arrows. This one in my shoulder has to have had an expandable impact head. Feels like a steel fist, opening and closing." Brendan grimaced again.

"I can't pull that out. Too dangerous. Somehow, we've got to get you out of here, before you bleed to death."

"No! No . . . we . . . we don't have time for that nonsense," exclaimed Brendan, gritting his teeth. "Besides, it takes more than an arrow from William bloody Tell to put me out of business. Just help me up. I've got a plan B."

"Plan B?" said Karl, quickly removing his shirt, shredding it into bandage strips.

"That's right. And before you say it, hopefully it'll be better than plan A," replied Brendan, reaching out his hand before being eased up slowly from the ground.

"Let me place these strips against the wound, Brendan. They should help stem the flow of blood for a while."

"I think I hit him."

"What?"

"Not one hundred per cent, but there's a possibility I shot him, in the leg."

"That's something, anyway. Pity it wasn't his head."

"Dad? What's going to happen?" asked Katie, concern in her voice.

Karl glanced at Brendan.

"Your father and I are going to have to go and find this monster, before he finds us, Katie."

"No! Dad, tell him. You promised you wouldn't leave."

"No one's leaving you, love. Isn't that right, Brendan?"

"It's going to be difficult enough without worrying about –"

"Isn't that *right*, Brendan?"

"Okay," sighed Brendan, resigned. "Let's get moving. Just keep in mind that he can see us at all times – though he'll probably be wary, knowing we're not defenceless."

"Katie, sweetie. You'll have to walk directly behind me, love. Okay?"

"Yes . . . don't walk too fast or too far ahead . . ."

"I'll be right beside you. Don't worry."

Moving slowly, the trio exited the room, hedging themselves against the walls, Karl leading.

"I'm going forward a few feet ahead," whispered Brendan.

"Don't be a fool," hissed Karl. "He'll pick you off like a sitting duck."

"We're the ones walking like a bloody duck patrol straight into his sights. He'll pick each of us off, if we don't spread out. Let's make the bastard a little nervous, let him earn his blood."

"With those night vision goggles, he'll be watching our every move."

"He doesn't know how many guns we have, even with his goggles on. Here. Take this," said Brendan, handing the gun to Karl. "You know how to use it?"

Karl gripped the weapon in his hand. Despite the gun's heavy cargo of dead weight, there was a feeling of naturalness, a familiar intercourse with the grip. Uncannily, the gun seemed designed to fit his hand. Either that, or his hand was designed to fit the gun.

"Why are you giving me this?"

"I'm going to be a decoy. He'll go after the wounded animal first, try and finish it."

"You're in no state, Brendan, and you're starting to bleed badly again. Let me do whatever you have in mind."

"What I have in mind, only I can do. You protect your daughter. That's your priority. I've a little surprise in store for William Tell, and it isn't a damn apple. When you hear my command, just fire at anything moving. Understand?"

"No, I don't understand, but I'll do it anyway."

"Good," said Brendan, disappearing into the darkness.

"What's happening, Dad? Has Brendan left us?"

"Everything is fine, sweetie, but from here it's vitally important that we remain quiet. Okay? Katie? Katie!"

Without warning, Katie suddenly lost consciousness.

Chapter Forty-Seven

"A thick, black cloud swirled before my eyes, and my mind told me that in this cloud, unseen as yet, but about to spring out upon my appalled senses, lurked all that was vaguely horrible, all that was monstrous and inconceivably wicked in the universe."
Arthur Conan Doyle, *The Adventure of the Devil's Foot*

Brendan eased slowly down The Tunnel, his right arm dangling uselessly. Blood was flowing more freely from the gaping wound, making him light-headed. He wondered just how much time he had before losing consciousness? Tellingly, there was no pain. He suspected what that meant.

Suddenly, he heard something not too far in front. Unfortunately, it wasn't sudden enough. *You stupid bastard,* he thought, but before he could think again something hit his right leg. *"Arrrrrgggggghhhhhhhhhhhh!"*

Brendan felt new blood running down his leg, warming the skin. His left hand came up instinctively, pressing down against the wound. He felt relieved when he saw the red spray on the wall behind him, knowing it meant that there was an exit wound and that the arrow had gone right through.

Instinctively dropping to one knee, he pushed flat against the wall, breathing heavily. Seconds later another arrow smashed into a brick above his head.

"Missed, you bastard!" shouted Brendan, laughing like some crazed creature. "You're frightened of men, aren't you? That's why your hands are trembling. No longer fighting little girls, you sick bast –"

An arrow whizzed past Brendan's eyebrow, barely missing the eye. It stunned him into silence, but only for a few seconds.

"C'mon, Hannah! You can do better than that. Surely even a paedophile like you can –?"

"Surely I can," hissed Hannah, suddenly standing triumphantly over Brendan, scalpel in hand, pressing it tight against his neck. "You first, and then lovely Katie. I want Kane to witness everything before he dies. Blame him for your misfortune. He brought all this to – *arrggggggggggg-gggggghhhhhhhh!*"

"Now, Karl! *Nowwwwwww!*" shouted Brendan, holding the flaming flare in his hand, blinding Hannah. Suddenly, the entire tunnel was abruptly lit up like fireworks night. A naked Hannah was screaming, frantically clawing at the night goggles, as if acid had been thrown into his face.

Karl came rushing down the tunnel, gun pointing, stopping directly beside the screaming Hannah.

"Shoot him, Karl!" shouted Brendan. "Now, while you have the chance. Shoot the bastard!"

Karl's hand began shaking terribly as he held the gun to Hannah's head, pulling back the hammer.

Hannah continued clawing at his eyes, screaming.

Karl fired once, bringing the screaming to an end.

"It's over . . ." said Karl, lowering the gun, pushing a stunned and shaking Hannah down on to the ground beside Brendan.

"It'll never be over," said Brendan, his voice almost a whisper. "Don't you understand, Karl? Hannah has too much power and influence. He'll never see a day in prison. He'll walk free and simply wait for the right time to continue his madness. There is no cure for creatures like him. Don't you understand?"

"I don't have an answer for that."

"I do!" shouted Brendan, snapping the gun out of Karl's hands, pointing it at Hannah. "I'm not letting him roam the streets, Karl, murdering and torturing young girls. It's over for him. Take Katie and get out of here."

"Don't do it, Brendan," pleaded Karl. "You'll regret it for the rest of your life."

"You don't have much time, Karl," said Brendan, removing a small package from the discarded rucksack on the floor. "It's got a pressure plate release. It's primed to go off as soon as I remove my fingers from it."

"What . . . what the hell are you going to do with that?"

"I need you to get Katie the hell out of here! I'm ready to lose consciousness. As soon as I do, this whole area is going to kingdom come."

"Please . . . please, Brendan. Don't do this. You have a great wife who loves you dearly. Don't do this to her."

"Claire died badly, Karl," said Brendan, his voice suddenly soft and solemn. "Shortly after Patricia's funeral, and still suffering from the gunshot wounds, Claire went home and filled a bath with water before climbing in and slitting both her wrists."

"Oh God, Brendan . . . I . . . I'm so sorry . . ."

"Now, I need you to go. *Now!* Take Katie. She'll never have to worry about Hannah again."

"I . . ."

"Go, damn you!"

Offering his hand to Brendan, Karl said, "When we first met, you said you would love to shake the hand of the man who killed Bulldog."

A ghost of a smile appeared on Brendan's face, a spark of revelation in his eyes.

"Goodbye, Brendan."

"Goodbye, Karl."

For almost one minute, the sound of Karl moving down the tunnel echoed all around Brendan Burns. Then came silence.

Weakening, Brendan felt his hands trembling. "Not yet. A few more minutes!" Gritting his teeth, he willed the hands to steady.

"Who . . . who *are* you?" asked Hannah, sitting opposite, motionless, eyes glaring.

"Who?" said Brendan, grimacing a smile, pointing the gun at

Hannah's face. "I'm the one who's here to take away your purpose. I'm the end of your world."

Passing the Circle before heading in the direction of the door at the end of the corridor, Karl ran clumsily with Katie scooped tightly in his arms. Breathing was quickly becoming laboured, and his legs felt ready to collapse while running on empty.

Come on. Almost there. Despite trying to think positive, he couldn't help but wonder how long the adrenaline coursing through his body would last, before he would eventually collapse in a heap? His heart was going mad. Air was impossible to taste.

Less than twenty seconds later, he reached the door, kicking it open, the cool night air lovingly hitting his sweating face. Directly ahead, the door leading back out towards the side entrance of the prison waited for him. He blinked sweat from his eyes.

You can do it. Not too far, now. Almost . . .

Suddenly, lights were blazing in the courtyard and surrounding area. Blue. Red. Orange. They looked like spotlights dipped in dull rainbows.

"What the . . . ?" *An ambulance! Oh my God . . .* "Help! Help! Over here! *Helpppppppp!*"

The ambulance crew – two men and a woman – stared back in amazement. Two police cars were pulling up alongside the ambulance.

"Help! My daughter needs medical help! Quickly!"

Swiftly producing a stretcher from the back of the ambulance, two of the crew came rushing towards Karl. Three police officers quickly emerged from the cars and rushed forward also.

"It's okay, sir. Everything will be okay. We've got her," said one of the ambulance crew.

"How . . . how did you know to come? I called, but couldn't get a signal," asked Karl, following quickly behind as the crew reached the back of the ambulance.

"We never received any call concerning your daughter, sir. It was about this man," said the ambulance man, pointing at a figure stretched out inside the ambulance. "He was attacked, and left for dead with his throat cut."

Karl felt faint seeing Willie stretched out, unmoving.

"Do you know this man, sir?" asked one of the police officers, suddenly standing beside Karl.

"His name is Willie . . . William Morgan, a good friend of mine."

"You're going to have to make a statement, sir, down at the station. We need to know what happened here."

"My name is Karl Kane. Call Inspector Mark Wilson. He'll explain everything to you, I'm sure. Right now, I'm accompanying my daughter and friend to the hospital. Understand?"

"Well, I suppose we –"

The ground suddenly shook.

"What the hell was that?" asked one of the police officers. "Felt like a miniature earthquake."

Karl looked back towards the prison, distraught, before climbing into the back of the ambulance.

"Will he make it?" asked Karl, staring at Willie's motionless body.

"Who knows?" said the crew member, his face noncommittal. "It'll be touch and go if he lives, but if he does, he'll owe his life to Mrs Blackburn."

"Mrs Blackburn?"

"Yes. The old lady at number eighteen," replied the man, pointing at the old lady standing at her door across the street. "She saw him being attacked and called 999."

Karl stared across the street. The old lady – the one whom Willie had referred to as a nosey old bag – stood, arms folded, watching the scene and gathering crowd.

Seconds later, the ambulance began pulling away, into the night.

EPILOGUE

Lynne and Naomi sat in the apartment barely talking, while Karl busied himself producing coffee. A tangible iciness permeated the room.

"How is Katie holding up, Lynne?" asked Naomi awkwardly, concern on her face. "Karl said she was having difficulty sleeping."

Long seconds passed before Lynne finally answered. "I was with her last night, and she was in a deep sleep, but that was due to her being heavily sedated. She will have to undergo months of extensive psychological tests for the effects of post-traumatic stress."

"What a terrible nightmare she's gone through."

"Thank God it's over."

"God had nothing to do with it, Lynne," stated Karl, coming from the kitchen area. "Brendan Burns brought it to an end."

"Of course. I only meant –"

"Sorry for sounding so harsh, Lynne. I know what you meant. But God must have been sleeping when all this was going on, as well as all the other murders."

"Let's just be grateful for how it all ended," soothed Naomi, diplomatically.

"I just got off the phone to the hospital. They've downgraded Willie's condition from critical to serious. Doctors say he'll make a full recovery," said Karl, glancing from Naomi to Lynne.

"What a relief to hear," responded Lynne.

Nodding in agreement, Naomi said, "Oh, before I forget, Tom called earlier enquiring about Katie. He said the police have released the name of that young girl murdered by Hannah in the tunnel. Judy McCambridge. Another runaway, apparently."

"That bastard Hannah is in hell now," said Lynne, her face suddenly changing. "A pity he died so quickly in the explosion."

Karl said nothing, his thoughts centring on a man called Brendan Burns, the architect of the explosion. According to newspaper reports, little vestiges were found of either Burns's or Hannah's bodies, such was the force of the bomb blast in such a confined space, making it virtually impossible for the police to say for certain if one or two bodies had been discovered. The media itself was equally uncertain, debating if Brendan Burns was a hero or a villain. Despite their ambiguity, most of the media begrudgingly admitted Burns had played a major part in Katie's rescue. In contrast, Mark Wilson soon let it be known to Karl – via Lynne – that he thought Burns was nothing more than a terrorist and murderer, and that Karl had deliberately picked Burns, hoping to rub salt into the wounds in Wilson's face.

"I've got to go shortly," said Karl, finally breaking his own thoughts.

"Where?" asked Naomi. "Can't you take a break for a while?"

"I've . . . I've got to go see Dad. With all this madness, I never got the chance to see him last week." Suddenly, the sound of a car horn screamed from outside.

"That'll be my taxi. I must be going also," stated Lynne, standing, nodding to Karl while totally ignoring Naomi. "Give Cornelius my regards, Karl. Tell him his favourite daughter-in-law sends all her love."

A few seconds later, Karl and Naomi were left alone to the sound of the taxi driving away into the distance.

"*Brrrrrrrrr,*" said Naomi, forcing a smile. "Did you feel that chill, or was it purely my imagination?"

"I wouldn't worry about it, my dear. They don't call Lynne Electrolux for nothing. Actually, she wasn't as bad as I dreaded she'd be. You want to see her when she *really* dislikes a person," said Karl, smiling, kissing Naomi before walking down the stairs and out into the unseasonably cool Belfast air.

Entering the nursing home, Karl's senses immediately collided with stomach-churning smells of urine, excrement and boiled unimaginative food. But it was another encompassing smell making guilt rise to the surface of Karl's mind: loneliness.

At the reception, he was asked to wait for a moment. Doctor Moore – his father's physician – wished to speak to him.

It was just over a minute later when Moore appeared, ushering Karl into a tiny office. The normally cheerful Moore looked quite solemn.

"First things first. How's Katie coping after that horrendous ordeal?"

"She's doing well, considering. Thank you for asking, Doctor."

Moore nodded, before continuing. "It's concerning your father's tests, Karl. They arrived this morning. I'm afraid it's not good news," said Moore, opening a top drawer before producing a folder.

Something began gnawing Karl's stomach, like tiny mice in a shoebox. "What . . . what kind of tests?"

"There's no easy way to say this, Karl, but Cornelius has been diagnosed with Alzheimer's disease."

"Alzheimer's . . ." The word came out slower than he had meant. "How? I . . . mean, how long has he had it?"

"The brain scan revealed significant shrinkage of the brain, possibly over the last year."

"A year? But I was told from the start that it was a mild form of dementia, resulting in the occasional lapse of memory. How the hell could Alzheimer's not have been diagnosed?"

"When Alzheimer's begins to destroy brain cells, Karl, no outward symptoms are evident immediately. After a while, small memory lapses appear and grow more serious. The afflicted individual may forget the names of familiar people or places, the words to express what they want to say or the location of everyday objects. As the disease becomes more serious, behaviour problems develop."

"What sort of behaviour problems?"

"Memory loss and cognitive deficits, advancing to major personality changes and eventual loss of control over bodily functions. Your father wasn't showing most of these symptoms until lately. That was when I ordered the brain scan and other tests."

"I know he's been having memory lapses, but I never realised he had no control over bodily functions."

"He's been urinating and soiling himself more frequently."

"My dad's been urinating and soiling himself? Why the hell wasn't I informed?" asked Karl, trying desperately not to lose his temper.

"It only started the last few days. I made the final decision not to inform you because of what you were going through with Katie's abduction. Was I wrong not to inform you?" asked Moore, holding Karl's gaze.

"No . . . I . . . suppose not. I should have been here last week anyway."

"Under the circumstances, Karl, you know that would have been impossible. So stop blaming yourself."

"I just . . . I just wish I'd have known sooner, I suppose."

"Cornelius is becoming more aggressive towards staff. That's understandable, as it is all due to frustration. But there have been other incidents, ones that can't go unchecked indefinitely."

The gnawing in Karl's stomach increased. More mice were piling into the shoebox.

"Incidents? What kind of incidents?"

"He's . . . he's been masturbating openly at the windows to visitors and staff."

"For fuck sake." The mice began turning into rats.

"One female member of staff had to be relocated because Cornelius kept referring to her as his wife, demanding to have intercourse with her, among other things."

Karl released a long sigh. "If it wasn't so serious, it would be comical. I don't know whether to laugh or wet myself. I suppose if I wet myself, you could inform the staff that lack of control over bodily functions runs in the family."

Moore smiled politely. "I wish I could give you better news, Karl. You've gone through hell the last few weeks. I hated the thought of burdening you with this."

Something about Moore's words brought an immediate balm to the situation.

"What is the outlook, Doctor?" asked Karl, finally resigned. "I need to know so that I can prepare for whatever is coming down the line."

"There are three stages in Alzheimer's progression. Early, mid and late. People vary in the length of time spent in each stage, and in which stage the signs and symptoms appear. Because the stages overlap, it is difficult to definitely place a person in a particular stage. However, the progression is always toward a worsening of symptoms. Cornelius is showing classic late stage symptoms, I'm sorry to say."

"Isn't there any cure, something, some sort of wonder drug?"

"At the minute, Alzheimer's is a progressive fatal illness. That's not to say that medical science isn't trying to develop a cure, as we speak."

"Are . . . are you saying he's going to die soon?"

"Well . . . just letting you know to be prepared in case something sudden happens. I wish I had a different, more upbeat report, Karl."

Stunned, Karl stood, offering Moore his hand.

"Thank you, Doctor. I know Dad would be more than appreciative of what you and the staff have done for him. He always praised . . . I mean . . . he always *praises* you," said Karl, almost immediately correcting the past tense of his sentence.

"If there is anything I can do, anything at all, do not hesitate to call me," replied Moore, shaking Karl's hand.

"Just one thing. Dad hasn't had access to TV or news over the last few days, has he?"

"No. I gave strict orders to staff not to discuss Katie's abduction. In all honesty, Karl, your father probably wouldn't even know, had he been watching or listening to the news."

Cornelius was sitting, staring out the window, when Karl entered the room without knocking. His father was a tall, desiccated husk of a man, whose only flesh was prominent on the neck in small fleshy accordions of skin.

"Is it medicine time, sir?" asked Cornelius, glancing from the window, looking directly at Karl.

To Karl, his father's eyes appeared glazed over, as if in a trance. He seemed to have shrunk physically from the last time he had set eyes upon him, well over two weeks ago.

Oh God, Dad . . . "It's . . . it's me, Dad. Karl. Your son," said Karl, bending, kissing the top of Cornelius's full head of hair.

"Son . . . ?"

"I brought you some bars of Bournville chocolate, along with some bottles of Lucozade."

"Son . . . ?"

"Yes, Dad. Karl. Remember?"

"Karl . . . I remember a Karl . . . it's hard remembering . . ."

"I . . . know, Dad. It isn't easy. Don't . . . don't be worrying about it."

"He was . . . he was a good boy."

Karl felt a lump in his throat. He needed a drink of water.

From a plastic beaker stationed atop a table, he poured some water into a plastic cup for himself, before twisting the cap off the Lucozade and pouring some of it into his father's cup.

"Here you go, Dad. Wish it could be a Jameson for you," smiled Karl, thinking of his father's love of the stuff.

Cornelius took the drink from Karl's hand and immediately began sipping the Lucozade's dark orange liquid, smacking his lips at each mouthful.

"Karl . . ."

"Yes, Dad?"

"Karl . . ." repeated Cornelius. "He . . . he was a good boy . . ."

"And you're a good father, Dad. The best in the world," said Karl, feeling something uncontrollable welling up inside.

Suddenly, Cornelius gripped Karl's hand, pulling him downwards, closer, whispering, "Don't . . . don't let me . . . live like this, Karl. Promise me."

"What?" Karl tried pushing away, but his father's grip was incredibly strong.

"I still have brains. I can still laugh and cry. I still have feelings! But soon, they'll be gone . . . don't let me live like a vegetable in the dark . . . please . . . tell me you'll do the right thing . . . when the time is right . . ." Cornelius's eyes were suddenly bright and clear, the fog lifting and dispelling.

Karl wrapped his arms around his father, gripping him tightly, remembering the time a million years ago, of a young boy crying, fearful of the dark and the monster with a knife hiding in the ironing cupboard.

There is no monster, son, assured his father, hugging him tenderly. *He's gone for ever. I'll never let him touch you again.*

Promise?

I promise . . .

"I . . . I won't let any harm come to you, Dad."

"Promise?"

The air outside was beginning to cool when Karl entered the almost deserted grounds of the care home. Residents and staff were filtering towards the canteen, and the smell of fried food hung heavily in the air.

A bird of some sort – possibly a raven – balanced itself precariously on a skinny branch from a nearby tree, a few feet from where Karl sat. It seemed to be studying him.

Karl waited until quietness settled all around him before removing a handkerchief from his jacket pocket, blowing his nose loudly. Dabbing the tears in his eyes, he whispered, "I promise."